The Life O'Reilly

A Novel

by

BRIAN COHEN

iUniverse, Inc.
New York   Bloomington

iUniverse books may be ordered through booksellers or by contacting:

iUniverse
1663 Liberty Drive
Bloomington, IN 47403
www.iuniverse.com
1-800-Authors (1-800-288-4677)

Because of the dynamic nature of the Internet, any Web addresses or links contained in this book may have changed since publication and may no longer be valid. The views expressed in this work are solely those of the author and do not necessarily reflect the views of the publisher, and the publisher hereby disclaims any responsibility for them.

ISBN: 978-1-4401-5025-8 (sc)
ISBN: 978-1-4401-5026-5 (ebook)
ISBN: 978-1-4401-5027-2 (dj)

Library of Congress Control Number: 2009931615

Printed in the United States of America

iUniverse rev. date: 8/17/2009

For my wife, Dayna,

and my daughters, Reese and Drew–

the greatest gifts I will ever receive

Chapter 1

Summer of 2005

"There has to be a better way," I muttered, as I replaced the phone receiver on its cradle. I'd arrived at the office long before seven and had been embroiled in activity since the moment I'd hunkered down into my black leather swivel chair. I'd taken part in an early conference call with adversaries and also had papers that needed to be filed in Dallas by four o'clock (five o'clock New York time), and, by the time I'd turned around, the digital clock on my desk cautioned that it was eleven-twenty. That didn't provide much time before the partners' meeting, which was at noon at the Harvard Club.

Generally, the meetings were pretty much bullshit, though this one was expected to be important. After covering the usual topics like associate productivity and financial matters, the hot issue was our new policy on pro bono work. Williams Gardner & Schmidt was always among the leaders in *The American Lawyer's* list of highest profits-per-partner, but its reputation in pro bono was downright disgraceful. Williams Gardner didn't overtly discourage pro bono, but it didn't exactly encourage it either, which ultimately sealed

1

the cause's fate at the firm. Bottom line—associates were terrified to spend time on anything other than billable clients, and partners totally lacked the incentive to initiate pro bono work themselves, acutely aware that every minute of the day influenced their quarterly draw.

Until, of course, the public relations component became a factor.

The meeting took place in the club's most grandiose space; large Palladian windows revealed the New York cityscape, a gold chandelier hung from the lofty ceiling. Like the rest of the club, the room was old world (and, if you ask me, stuffy as hell), with oak-paneled walls and Venetian sconces. For a blue-collar boy, who had worked his way through Binghamton University and Brooklyn Law, this was a whole other world— an elitist world that, even after twelve-plus years with the firm (that should have been accounted for in dog years), still didn't feel quite right.

To foster an open discussion, the tables were arranged in the form of a large square with twenty lawyers on each side. Waiters fully garbed in black tuxedos with penguin-tailed jackets carefully served tossed salads, house-cured gravlax, and the main courses, orders which had been taken upon arrival. Cocktail waitresses darted to and from the bar, as the elder members of the firm had no qualms about getting sauced during lunch. Junior partners were uncomfortable with the concept, and, with stacks of work screaming for attention, we knew our limitations and stuck to soft drinks or bottled water.

At twelve forty-five, the meeting was called to order. The firm's managing partner, Wilfred J. T. Schmidt III, cleared his throat directly into the microphone set in front of him, commanding silence. Will had thick gray hair, parted neatly to the side; it was well-groomed and matched his mustache, which was affixed to a square face that projected arrogance. He held his head high and with an air of authority that, despite certain time-imposed wrinkles, spoke of ageless strength. Will sat in the middle of the north side of the makeshift square. His cohorts, cloaked in similar three-piece suits and paisley bowties, acted the part, though there was no mistaking who was in charge. After the meeting, they would retreat to the smoking room to enjoy the finest-grown tobacco, either in a pipe or a cigar, but not before donning ridiculous-looking ascots and velvet smoking jackets.

A recording secretary took attendance and kept the minutes.

Will followed the usual agenda and, in turn, introduced the chairperson of each of the firm's committees, starting with finance and going on through recruiting and technology. After a series of brief status reports, Will removed his thick, tortoiseshell-rimmed glasses, set them on the table, and turned to the important topic of the day.

"Thank you, folks. I am delighted with what I have heard today. We remain one of Wall Street's elite and most profitable law firms, which is a testament to not only the fine reputation we have earned and enjoyed over the course of our history, but to the fact that we have not rested on our laurels. Indeed, we continue to perform at the highest level and deliver the best results for both our longstanding clients as well as our new ones. We should all be proud."

"Here, here!" several partners proclaimed, raising glasses in toast and replacing them for a round of applause. Will waited for silence.

"As you know, more and more of our competitors have invigorated their commitment to the community at large … through what is known as pro bono work, if you will. For reasons unbeknownst to me, we have not made the same commitment," said Will, rolling his eyes and coaxing raucous laughter from his contemporaries and wry, placating smiles from the rest, "and, as a consequence, we have been chastised by the press as insensitive, money-hungry, selfish mongrels.

Once again, I have no idea why ..." he said, receiving a similar, yet more subdued reaction.

"But the fact of the matter is, ladies and gentlemen, this firm has always adapted to changes in the environment." The members of the small female and minority contingents gritted their teeth and bit their lips, discreetly sharing looks of disapproval with each other. "If we are going to continue to embody the touchstones of leadership and success in our field, then we must also set an example in the community. Accordingly, for all of the foregoing reasons, and based on the feedback I have received from many of you over the course of the last few months, I hereby propose the formation of a new firm committee to be known as the Pro Bono Committee."

Will paused to take a swig of scotch.

"In this regard, I have already spoken with Ruth Davidson, who has agreed to serve as chair," said Will, gesticulating toward Ruth, red of hair and pale of skin and dressed in a black pantsuit. She feigned a Mona Lisa smile. "Ruth will coordinate assignments among the attorneys and act as the firm's liaison to NYC Legal Services, a nonprofit organization here in town which, from what I am told, is the oldest provider of free legal services in the city.

"Furthermore, for this to work effectively, we must institute a formal policy, mandating that each attorney, including partners, counsel, and associates, devote three percent of his or her billable hours to such endeavors. So, if our associates are hitting their mandatory twenty-five-hundred-per-year minimum, an additional seventy-five shouldn't amount to a hill of beans. And, of course, if they don't like it, they can always go in-house and never be heard from again," said Will, provoking a mix of snorts and cackles throughout the room.

"I suspect that some of you may do so already, but, nevertheless, I would like to suggest that we all dedicate ourselves to getting involved in more ... charitable activities.

By that, I mean get involved in, sit on the board of, or even help run—if you find the time—some type of community or charitable organization. It will be a positive reflection on the firm and may help eviscerate this … shall I say … *notoriety* that has become affixed to our fine name that we and our predecessors, including my father, may he rest in peace, labored so long and hard to build. And for those who do spend time on such endeavors, that time should most certainly be credited toward the three percent threshold.

"This has effectively become a cost of doing business, ladies and gentlemen, and we must make it a priority," said Will as he glanced at the recording secretary. He waved his pointer finger, warning that what he was about to say was to be kept off the record.

"But, always keep in mind one cardinal rule," said Will, pausing to accentuate the magnitude of his impending caveat. "This cannot … will not … and *must not* conflict with or contravene the interests of our clients. They come first. When in doubt, and in times of crisis, your loyalty is to them, not to some vagabond on the street you're attempting to procure Social Security benefits for, or whatever it is we're going to be doing." Will glanced at the recording secretary again with a nod, and they were back on the record. "And against that backdrop, ladies and gentlemen, I hereby put it to a vote. All in favor of adopting the new pro bono policy I have officially proposed here today say 'aye' and raise your hands." All hands went up to the charge of "aye." "All opposed, say 'nay' and raise your hands." The second choice was met with complete silence until Will raised his hand again and shouted "Nay!" engendering pockets of nervous laughter throughout the room. "No, no, no, of course, I'm just teasing. Let the record reflect that I voted in favor."

A few laughs lingered.

"Splendid! It shall be effective immediately. A memorandum will be sent to all attorneys advising of the new program. Of course, for those overzealous folks among us, you can certainly feel free to start now and apply your time retroactively." Will took another swig of scotch.

"Oh, there is one more item in this regard that I'd like to discuss. Of course, we'll be issuing a press release and all that jazz about this new program of ours, and adding a fancy page about this to our Web site, but I feel that, to really get off to a flying start and make an indelible impression, we need ... an *exemplar*, if you will ... someone who will be a positive reflection on our firm and who, shall I say, will make us look good and handle our first case with integrity. And to play that role, I cannot think of anyone more capable or well-suited than our partner ... the recently inducted Chairman of the Trial Lawyers Section of the New York State Bar Association ... Nicholas O'Reilly."

All eyes fixed themselves on me. I nearly coughed up my sip of cola when I was startled by the unexpected sound of my own name. I quickly snatched my napkin from my lap and wiped my mouth clean. The gravitational pull of Will's intense glare drew my eyes directly to his. Will was a staunch supporter who had championed my early ascension to partnership. In other words, he had me by the balls. He knew it, and I knew it.

"Nick, my boy, you don't have any problem with that ... do you?" he asked, his tone set to call for one—and only one—answer: the one I gave.

"No, sir, absolutely not—it would be my pleasure. It sounds like a great idea and potentially a very rewarding experience, Will. I promise I'll make both you and the firm proud."

"Good. That's my boy. I understand the case is some type of family law matter, but I have all the confidence in the world in you, Nick, and I'm sure my partners share my sentiments," he said, coaxing another round of applause. When everyone quieted down, Will suggested that I contact Ruth Davidson about my assignment. I looked across the room, found Ruth, and nodded.

"Well, I think this is the perfect time for us to break," said Will. "I thank you all."

When I returned to the office, I already had a voice mail message from Ruth advising me to stop by and touch base about the project. After I returned some calls and met with a few associates, a couple of hours had gone by and I finally had a free moment to spare.

The firm's lavish office décor held up to its billing as the "Four Seasons of law firms." Aside from the faces of those who occupied them, each floor was indistinguishable. The walls were elegant, with patterned wallpaper, decorative sconces, and valuable artwork. Full-time housekeeping tended to the kitchens twenty-four-seven, regularly stocking fresh fruit, snacks, and the finest (and, more importantly, strongest) blends of gourmet coffee. The award-winning library was full and exhaustive, operated by a highly paid, veteran law librarian brought over from Columbia Law School. The firm even had its own cafeteria, which served the same variety of foods you'd find on the "outside." And, while the quality was comparable, the prices were substantially cheaper, offering yet another incentive to stay put.

Ruth's office was located two floors below mine, among her colleagues in trusts and estates and tax. I walked past two rows of offices (or cellblocks, as I thought of them) hearing only the whispers of secretaries and the pitter-patter of computer keys. Lawyers' offices were flush to the outside, the core filled with secretaries and their workstations. Paralegals were doubled up and closeted in stuffy interiors. We were usually in lockdown, meaning doors were always closed. Finally, I reached the grand spiral staircase that threaded the firm's ten floors. I took my time walking the staircase, which was carpeted in a deep maroon. By then, what was gradually becoming a consistent mid-afternoon fatigue had set in.

(At the time, I attributed this fatigue to many long years of being overworked.) I clenched the massive gold railing on the outer edge as I descended. On the way, I passed a handful of colleagues; some ignored me while others offered obligatory, tight-lipped nods.

I found Ruth reclining in her plush leather chair, legs crossed and feet resting on the edge of her polished desk, conversing on the phone in earnest with a client. I straddled the threshold of the entrance, resting against the doorframe. Diplomas from Duke and Penn Law were prominently displayed amid classic, gold-framed oil paintings. In due time, Ruth glanced up and acknowledged me with a one-second gesture. After putting the client on hold, she lowered her feet to the floor, propped herself up, and exhaled long and hard, as if she hadn't had a minute to breathe.

"Nick, I'm going to be tied up the rest of the day, and I'll also be out tomorrow and Friday, but I left you the file over there," she said, head-motioning toward the rear of her office. I ambled over to the glass coffee table. The file was labeled *Dawn Nelson*. A yellow Post-it affixed to the outside read: For Nick O'Reilly. "Why don't you take it home with you this weekend, read it over, and, if you want, we can talk about it on Monday."

"Sure. What's it about?"

"Well, let's just say it's a far cry from securities fraud," she said, very businesslike. I smiled.

"Oh, and that reminds me—I heard about your big win last week. Congrats." Ruth was referring to a case against an important client, a large insurance conglomerate, that I had got dismissed on the eve of trial. It was the kind of matter that was considered a grand slam for the firm: an opportunity to bill long and hard and get credit for a major victory without subjecting the client to the risk of having a jury decide its fate.

"Thanks—I appreciate it."

I then wished Ruth a nice weekend, but she had already resumed her conversation so the pleasantry went unreciprocated. I returned to my office, retrieved messages from my secretary, Janice Thompson, and carefully placed the Nelson file on my coffee table.

I'd been assigned countless new cases over the course of my career. But Dawn Nelson's case was different.

It changed my life forever.

Chapter 2

The breathtaking view may as well have been an exclusive every time I stepped out onto the balcony of my fifteenth-floor apartment that overlooked my front yard—Central Park South. Covered in a white, terry bathrobe, I had just showered and given myself a hot, clean shave after a twenty-minute run on the treadmill. I extended my arms above my head and spread them down like the wings of a peacock, a long shudder reverberating through me. After a labored deep breath, I set my hands on the brick, chest-high wall and stared out and admired the park.

From where I stood, the massive green oasis looked like a big square head of broccoli, the kind they bring you in a Manhattan steakhouse, with gaping holes here and there. It was peaceful to relax and have my morning coffee and temper the post-workout surge of endorphin that coursed through my body while the morning air of summer warmed me and the sunrise gradually gathered above. The only sounds were the wind whistling through the trees and the occasional chirp of a nearby bird. Traffic was thin way down below at street level, so echoing honks from cabbies were few and far between, and it was too early for the clapping of hooves that belonged to horses, laboring tirelessly as they escorted tourists, nestled in carriages with plush, red seats. I escaped here as often as possible to take refuge from the disharmonies of the competitive world I inhabited and alter the frenetic tempo of my fast-paced lifestyle.

The Saturday edition of *The New York Times* had yet to be delivered, and, other than a stack of old ones in the bathroom, I didn't have any magazines, so I grabbed the file on my pro bono project. I hoped that this new matter would be a welcome interlude among a full plate of securities and antitrust cases. The memo at the top of the file was from Tom Dooley, the Managing Director of NYC Legal Services, summarizing the basic facts of the case and providing general background information about the parties.

My new client was Dawn Nelson, twenty-six, wife of Jimmy and mother of Jordan, who was a few months shy of three. The memo began with some background information on Dawn's childhood. Her wife-beating father, Lance Mulcahy, had been a dirty narcotics cop. He was taken down by Internal Affairs and later executed on the street. Her mother, Toni, had led a promiscuous lifestyle that had branded her the neighborhood tramp. Shortly after Lance's murder, Toni moved to Arizona with one of her boyfriends, leaving Dawn to live in the Kensington section of Brooklyn with an aunt and uncle. After finishing high school, Dawn pursued a career as a pharmacist, studying at the Brooklyn campus of Long Island University while working at a drug store part-time as a pharmacy technician.

Dawn met Jimmy Nelson at a party thrown by a mutual acquaintance from the neighborhood. Consistent with his public persona, Jimmy was fragile, soft spoken, and sweet. A stockbroker for a shady "boiler room" operation called W.B. Richmen & Company, Jimmy presented himself as a successful entrepreneur, rising from the doldrums of supermarket grocery bagger to Wall Street jet-setter; he was going places and wanted Dawn to join him on the ride to the

top, which she found exhilarating. He poured his heart out
to her about his thorny childhood—abuse from his father,
his purported strong relationship with his mother, and then,
to close the deal, his mother's tragic demise in a hit-and-run
accident. After a relatively brief courtship, Jimmy was eager
to get married, move Dawn in to his house, and cast her as
the love of his life and the mother of his children, insisting
she abandon her career to have their baby. Dawn enjoyed her
work and didn't want to get pregnant right away, but Jimmy
ultimately prevailed, stripping Dawn of her independence and
monopolizing her life to the point of checking store receipts
to account for her time.

It was then that Jimmy's emotional cruelty began. He
repeatedly insulted Dawn's appearance and even belittled her
during sex, claiming dissatisfaction and threatening to stop
and watch porn instead. Often paranoid that she was going
out with other men, Jimmy escalated the tension between
himself and Dawn after she spent time away from him with
friends. He even destroyed certain outfits she loved, claiming
they made her look slutty. But it wasn't until Jimmy finally got
physical with her and then threatened harm to Jordan that
Dawn plotted her escape—with her son.

I then came to photographs of Dawn taken the day after
she had been beaten by Jimmy, her battered face all black
and blue. These pictures were accompanied by wallet-sized
pictures of Jordan, the kind taken at a shopping mall kiosk. The
child, set against a pale aqua backdrop, looked melancholy.

I sat pensively and fought off the potential distraction
of two pigeons pecking at each other atop the ledge of my
neighbor's balcony as I gaped at the pictures of Dawn and
Jordan. One bird flew away, heading in the direction of
Central Park. The other remained behind, opting for solitude.
I wondered why, when its companion and the beauty of the
park were just a few flaps away, right there for the taking.
What are you waiting for? I thought. Was the bird hurt?

Was it afraid? Perhaps a broken wing rendered it hesitant. I couldn't tell.

At this point, I stepped inside for another cup of coffee. The sliding doors opened into a dining alcove. In lieu of an impractical dinette set, I kept a beautiful baby grand piano in the alcove. Finished in traditional ebony, the piano possessed a distinct tone and presence, with keys designed to respond sensitively to commands. Though I left the top closed, the flat surface displaying photos of fun times with friends, I was always fascinated by the instrument's inner-workings— the way its sound is triggered by hammers striking down on strings, its resonance dependent upon the stroke of the pianist, and how, to endure lengthy periods of pressure and strain, the strings are crafted of steel, tight and rigid, and manufactured with minimal variation in width. Whether I'm playing something melodious or a more brooding piece, for me, playing the piano is always a form of catharsis, expressing any kind of mood I'm in with facility and passion.

A contemporary built-in bookcase was half-filled with mostly novels and old textbooks. I had filled the empty shelves with family pictures, like the ones of my parents from their wedding, and another of them at their twenty-fifth anniversary party, shots from each of my graduations (me in the middle, in cap and gown, and three big smiles in each), and me and Dad in the bleachers at Shea Stadium for Game Six of the 1986 World Series. In the living room were a honey brown leather three-seater sofa with matching love seat and, although it went with absolutely nothing in the room, my father's La-Z-Boy. The wall of windows generously exposed the park. In the corner sat a lovely (but fake) tree set deep in a fanciful brown pot, a gift from Mom that replaced a real one she'd bought when I first moved in. When the original died of malnourishment, Mom felt it was more practical to replace it with a fake; she later added a couple of others, knowing I would never go out and buy them myself.

The kitchen, done in a mix of cherrywood cabinetry and black granite, had been renovated by the prior owner. A small window faced east, and the sunlight that shone through bathed the countertops in clear illumination. An opening in the wall framed the living room and created a breakfast bar, with three stools on the other side.

After fixing my coffee with milk and artificial sweetener, I stepped outside, set my mug on the table, and sat down. I turned to my right and noticed the pigeon was gone. *Finally wised up*, I thought. I looked out toward the park, but the bird was nowhere in sight. *Could it have tried but fallen?* I hesitantly got up and looked down below. I saw nothing, and hoped for the best.

I continued rummaging through the file and returned to where I'd left off in the memo.

Angry and bitter, Dawn was eager to fight to keep Jimmy out of their lives forever. She lacked the means to hire an attorney, so NYCLS stepped in to advocate on her behalf. Since time was of the essence, the agency assisted Dawn in immediately filing a family offense petition for the purpose of obtaining a temporary order of protection for herself and Jordan. Family court Judge Samuel T. Barkley had been assigned upon filing and, within a few hours, after an informal hearing conducted *ex parte* (meaning only one party—without the adversary— had appeared), Judge Barkley issued the order and granted Dawn temporary custody of Jordan pending the resolution of the matter. Judge Barkley also issued a summons, which, along with a copy of the petition, was served on Jimmy by a police officer. But the order was only valid until the next court date, which is where I came in.

The next step in the process was a formal fact-finding hearing, where both parties were to appear to determine whether the allegations of the petition were supported by a fair preponderance of the evidence. Judge Barkley would attempt to resolve the matter, but, if an accord could not be reached, a trial would be scheduled.

Against that backdrop, my responsibilities in the respective Brooklyn courts were as follows:

> **Family court**: Obtain a permanent order
> of protection for Dawn and Jordan Nelson.
> Petition, on Dawn's behalf, for sole custody
> of Jordan.
>
> **Civil court**: Commence and litigate divorce
> proceedings.
>
> **Criminal court**: Coordinate the criminal
> prosecution of James Nelson with the Kings
> County District Attorney's office.

I drew a long, deep breath; myriad thoughts raced through my mind. I sipped my coffee, stared impassively out over the park, and contemplated how to juggle this added responsibility with the rest of my work schedule. People's lives—real, emotionally troubled lives—were being placed in my hands. It was a task far more onerous than my typical cases in which millions of my clients' (or their insurance carriers') dollars were at stake.

I retrieved the photos again. As Dawn and Jordan's pained expressions fixed my gaze, I thought about how their welfare and future were my responsibility ... how it was up to me to make the world a better place for them.

Just as I'd finished reviewing the file, I took a break to call Evan Berger, my best friend and closest (and only) confidant at the firm. Unfortunately, he was stuck in the office all weekend finalizing a brief. Evan and I had started out at the firm as summer associates and, after taking a year to clerk for federal judges, we had rejoined the firm together.

Despite the fact that I'd managed to escape for a rare weekend away, I nevertheless felt guilty about calling Evan, as he toiled away in obscurity thinking about everywhere else he'd rather be. Evan's workspace was brightened with pictures of his wife Julie and their two girls, Jenny and Rebecca, and school art projects like Jenny's Jamestown diorama and Rebecca's colorful drawing of their place in Sag Harbor. The bright yellow sun shining over their happy faces, as they stood all lined up in size order and holding hands spoke volumes and, deep down, always struck a nerve with me.

I really wanted that too.

I dialed Evan's direct line and, after two rings, he answered.

"Hey, it's me," I said.

"Hey, there he is ... the lucky winner."

"Winner? God, I'd hate to know what *loser* feels like," I said, my tongue heavy with sarcasm. "Winner of what?"

"The Will Schmidt pro bono sweepstakes."

"Now I know."

"C'mon, dude, you're Will's boy—he picks you for *all* the good stuff."

"Yeah, extra work, bag carrier, shoe shiner." Evan laughed.

"Well, look on the bright side, bro—at least you'll get to help someone who really needs it. You might actually experience real justice and feel good about yourself at the end of the day."

"*If* I can help. I have as much experience with family law as you do."

"Who said I don't know about family law? Trust me, when Julie or my mother say something, it's the law," he said in jest, as both couldn't be sweeter.

"So you're telling me that, after all these years, you don't find working day and night defending the misdeeds of Corporate America gratifying?"

16

"I find our quarterly draw gratifying," he said, pausing. "But what would *really* be gratifying is a new entertainment law firm called Berger and O'Reilly—wink wink."

"I know, I know," I said, nodding. "I'm killing you with that."

Aside from our main practice, Evan represented independent filmmakers and production companies. He had started with one client, Barry Richards, a friend from Syracuse. They'd studied film together briefly, and Barry had gone on to become a successful screenwriter/director. As Barry's career flourished, Evan's clientele expanded, spawning the birth of an entertainment subgroup at the firm, which I later joined.

For me, it all had started one night when, as a junior associate, I snuck out to catch jazz legend Donald "Pops" Jackson for a nine o'clock show at the Blue Note. In planning my escape from the office, I had set all the necessary props: desk lamp on; fresh coffee steaming in a mug; computer on with screen saver off; the brief I was working on open on my desk; briefcase conspicuously leaning against the credenza that anyone walking by would notice; clock radio on and tuned to a smooth jazz station; and, of course, the jacket I'd worn that day hanging behind my door—all of the indicia of a hardworking associate banging away solid, billable time. I remember it well because Phil Addison, a senior partner and the bane of my existence at the firm, had left relatively early for a black-tie affair, which he had told me he resented because it imposed on his work schedule.

When I arrived at the Blue Note, the bartender informed me that Pops' keyboard player was a last-minute no-show and that the gig was about to be cancelled. Pops was one of my favorite musicians, so I wasn't about to look a gift horse in the mouth.

"I can play," I suggested to the manager, a frustrated-looking, past-his-prime musician type named Charlie. He was tall and thin and outfitted in a solid black suit, white shirt, and skinny black tie—like the heavy in a Quentin Tarantino film. An unkempt salt-and-pepper mane was shoulder length and starting to recede, his face was pale and gaunt, and his eyes were dark and flat. If I had to guess, I'd say he played bass. His brows furrowed in disbelief.

"You're kidding me, right?"

"No, sir," I said with conviction. An empty stage meant thousands of dollars in refunds along with lost opportunity in the form of food and alcohol that would go unsold.

"Wait here and have a drink," he said, pointing to a barstool. "I'll see what I can do."

For about ten minutes, I sat and bullshitted with the short, round-faced bartender, a post-college jazz enthusiast whose name I never got. I listened patiently as he explained that he was working the joint for the music and the experience with an aim toward owning his own club—as if I was his father and he had to assuage my concern that all of my hard-earned tuition money had gone to waste. I had barely drunk a long-necked Budweiser past its shoulders when Charlie waved me back.

"Good luck, man—say hi to Donnie Cool," said the bartender with a smile, paying homage to one of Pops' signature tunes as he overzealously wiped a splash of beer off the counter. I stood, nervously applied a napkin to some suds that had gathered on my upper lip, and drew a deep breath. I forbade myself from trembling as I squeezed through the bevy of patrons and made my way to the back of the club.

Charlie led me into the dressing room. Pops, sunken in the deep cushions of a black leather couch with his feet up on a matching ottoman, appeared to have all the time in the world. His saxophone, only an arm's length away, rested on a metal stand. In his early fifties, he looked fit in a red blazer, black silk tee, and black slacks. His graying dark hair, closely cropped with a well-defined hairline at the forehead, connected with a neatly trimmed beard and mustache that framed his mouth. A gold pendant chain dangled from his neck.

Four other musicians from his generation sipped cocktails. The bassist and horn player were also African-American, the former tall and round in the middle, the latter short, sporting a mustache and long sideburns. The guitarist was dressed in a trim deep charcoal gray suit and black button-down; his long brown hair was thick and unwieldy and, at times, fell over his wire-framed John Lennon specs. The goateed drummer, completely bald beneath a brown fedora, dragged on a cigarette; smoke swirled upward and gathered in a thick cloud that hung in the air.

"This is the guy," Charlie said cynically. Pops looked up and smiled.

"My friend tells me you'd like to sit in."

"Yes, sir," I said as I shook his hand, which he'd graciously offered, and introduced myself.

"Pleasure's all mine, my friend. You know my music?"

I nodded and told him I was a big fan. He thanked me with an air of humility.

"So," he said, sipping a glass of water, "you really wanna' jam with us?"

"It would be an honor."

"I appreciate that," he said, nodding to a ragged notebook that lay on a nearby table. "Take a look at the set list."

After a quick rundown, I recognized all but one—maybe two—tunes, but they were toward the end, and, by that point, I'd be in a groove and could wing it. And it's not like I had to take the lead—that was the man's job; for the most part, other than a short solo or two, my role would be strictly backup in nature, filling in chords and such.

Pops asked me if I was familiar, and I looked up and nodded with confidence. He stared blankly and contemplated. He looked over at his colleagues for a second opinion, and their expressions projected support, which made his decision easy.

"All right, Nick O'Reilly, since I'm a firm believer in the power of music to unify all mankind," he said, extending his arm for a handshake, "I'm happy to welcome you to our band."

The show was a big hit. Pops was masterful, and he and his band mates were more than pleased with my performance. I wasn't about to quit my day job, but I gave Pops a business card and offered to join him if he was in town and needed backup. I also left a card with Charlie, who seemed embarrassed by the way he had initially treated me.

"Feel free to come by any time, Mr. O'Reilly—on the house."

"Take it easy," I said. "Thanks for believing."

"You're the man," said the bartender, reaching across for a high five as I turned to leave.

During the show, Charlie had taken some photos so he could hang one of Pops in the window. He'd captured a great shot of Pops and me that he thought I might enjoy. Later that week, he blew it up into an eight-by-ten, framed it, and sent it in a package to my office with a note of thanks. I immediately tucked the picture away in my briefcase to take home. I didn't want the partners to know I had outside interests.

That would have been unacceptable.

About a month or so later, I got a call from Pops' manager seeking legal advice on an intellectual property matter. Before long, he was my client, and a new practice area had blossomed into a roster of clients that included musicians and producers. By then, Evan had already been off and running, and together we built an entertainment practice with an equal balance of music and film business which, though never well-received by the partnership, was tolerated as long as it was profitable, the matters cleared conflicts, and the work didn't interfere with our primary responsibilities. Evan had been prodding me to break away with him to start our own firm, he being far more enthusiastic about it than I. Entrepreneurship was more in his blood than it was in mine (his father, Saul, owned his own textile business, which he'd started when he was in his mid-twenties).

"Hey, just think, maybe you'll get another cover out of this one," said Evan, referring to *The American Lawyer* magazine's profile of "America's Top 40 Lawyers Under 40" in which I had been featured. He knew full well how uncomfortable I was with the attention.

"Great," I said, rolling my eyes. "I'm sure that'll do wonders for my relationship with Phil."

"I know," he said with glee. "It would really piss him off, wouldn't it?"

"Right. And I'm the one who'll suffer."

After bullshitting for a few more minutes, Evan brought the conversation to a close.

"All right, man, let me go," he said. "I want to get out of here at a decent hour, and, if I'm lucky, maybe even read the girls a bedtime story."

"I hear you. I'm going to turn back to this myself."

"Sounds good, buddy," he said. "Listen, if you want, we could call it O'Reilly and Berger."

I grinned. "I might hold you to that."

"We could even call it O'Reilly and Partners, O'Reilly and Associates ... whatever—just get me out of here for crying out loud."

"I don't know. Maybe we're just different."

"The last time I checked, you live on Central Park South, right?"

"No, that's where I sleep," I said. "I live in a room right down the hall from you."

"Well, where would you *rather* live?"

"I think you know the answer to that one," I said, provoking a more staid and humorless response.

"Well then, maybe we're not so different after all," Evan said, pausing. "Nick, I don't understand—at this point, what's stopping you from leaving?"

"All right, all right, I'll give it some thought."

"I won't hold my breath," he said. "You'll never find the time."

Chapter 3

When I arrived at the office on Monday morning, I decided to get the ball rolling with my new pro bono matter. To do so, I had to call Tom Dooley.

"Hello?" answered Tom in an odd, yet gentle tone. He sounded as if he had nowhere to go, with all day to get there; in a way, I envied him. After we exchanged pleasantries, I assured Tom that I would not disappoint his organization, teeing up a diatribe extolling the virtues of public interest work that I really didn't need.

"I appreciate that, Nick, but, to tell you the truth, it's Dawn that you should worry about not disappointing. People like Dawn depend on us to help them with their legal battles in order to continue with their lives in a fruitful and productive manner. Not everyone can afford to pay for representation. Nevertheless, our clients' needs are no less important than ... I don't know, *yours*, for example. The work we do here is challenging, yet very rewarding and satisfying at the same time."

"I know, Tom. I read through Dawn's file this past weekend, and, to tell you the truth, I can't get the pictures of her and her son out of my mind. That's why I called you first thing this morning. I want to help."

"Oh, okay, good. It's that type of empathy and passion that facilitates our mission and ultimately gets the job done around here. There's no money in this kind of work, so your heart really has to be in the right place, and, as far as I can tell, Nick, it seems like yours is. And with your credentials—editor-in-chief of the *Brooklyn Law Review*, federal clerkship, partner at Williams Gardner—I'd say Dawn is in pretty good hands. I'm looking forward to working with you."

I let him know that the feeling was mutual, and we went ahead and confirmed a meeting for the following Monday. Tom advised me that both Dawn and Jordan would be attending.

"Oh, and by the way, after the first consultation, you'll be dealing with Dawn directly. We'll be here to assist you from a legal and administrative standpoint since, I assume, custody battles and orders of protection aren't exactly your bailiwick. We have staff attorneys who specialize in those areas and can give you whatever guidance you need. But beyond that, Nick, you're completely on your own."

"No problem. I'll await your phone call and speak to you soon."

"Right-o."

By the middle of the week, Tom confirmed our appointment—not that I had much time to think about it, though. As usual, I was bogged down with briefs and had to simultaneously juggle a couple of other bullshit tasks that, although unexpected, were very much routine and kept me in the office until eleven-thirty every night. Two of my adversaries had sent letters that completely misrepresented positions I had taken on certain issues during conference calls, so I had to play troubleshooter, shut down whatever I was doing at the time, and prepare responses, making a record and memorializing what had really been said. I hated that. It's like the work created itself out of nothing, showing up out of nowhere, wreaking havoc and seizing control of my life.

That weekend, I was anxious about the meeting with Dawn. I didn't know what to expect, but was nevertheless excited about the prospect of helping Dawn—someone who really needed help—and taking on a new challenge to break up the monotony of my everyday life.

I arrived at the NYCLS offices and introduced myself to the receptionist, a young college-aged girl named Lindsey; she was dressed casually, with her long blond hair tied back. At Lindsey's suggestion, I found a comfy spot on the old, shabby couch. I relaxed for a few moments before Tom, a hefty and jolly, sandals-in-the-winter hippie, with short ponytail and Jerry Garcia–like beard, emerged to greet me. He wore a light flannel shirt tucked into worn khakis; old Birkenstocks exposed hairy, bare feet.

"Howdy-do, my friend!" he cheered. Lindsey smiled in amusement, as if Tom's shtick never got old. Wasting no time, he offered me his "fifty-cent tour" of the office.

"Nick, as an institution that specializes in domestic relations issues and children's rights, whether through our cases in which we fight for custody or many of the child abuse and neglect matters we take on, at NYCLS we always have kids in the office and enjoy fostering a warm and friendly environment for them and their parents or guardians. It also adds refreshment to our law office that, believe it or not, can be somewhat stuffy despite the relaxed, collegial atmosphere and nonprofit culture. Everyone seems happier when the office is teeming with little ones."

"I'll bet."

"As a nonprofit, we survive on grants and donations and have to keep our spending down. Enriching the quality of our downtrodden clients' lives is our priority, not gourmet coffee and fancy golf outings like I'm sure *you're* used to."

I bit my lip and let the cynical remark go. After the tour, we killed time in Tom's office, a small space crammed with files that looked as if they should have been sent to storage years ago. "Take a load off." I found one of the few empty spots on the floor to place my litigation bag to free my hands. After removing three overstuffed files, I carefully lowered myself onto the fold-up chair in front of Tom's old, steel desk that could have belonged to one of my elementary school teachers. It was cluttered with pleadings and correspondences.

"Yeah, just toss those anywhere," said Tom, chortling. The walls were drab—a pale milky white—and, other than a few old news clippings and a corkboard that hung slightly askew above his computer desk, were unadorned. A three-tiered black bookcase functioned as both a library and file cabinet. A framed eight-by-ten of Tom with his arms around an Asian-American woman about his age and a young girl, who looked like they could have been his wife and daughter, was set on the windowsill.

At around one o'clock, Tom got a call from Lindsey, who let him know that Dawn and Jordan had arrived for the meeting. Tom advised her to escort them to the conference room, which he had reserved for the remainder of the afternoon. He had them wait for about fifteen minutes while we ran through the facts one last time.

We arrived at the closed conference room door, and Tom knocked twice.

"Come in," said a female voice.

"Good afternoon, folks," said Tom with a big, toothy smile as he pushed the door open. A large, wooden conference table overpowered the room; it bore deep scars in the form of kids' names, like the initials of young lovers carved into the bark of a schoolyard tree, set against an expanse of scratches that zigzagged like the design of a Jackson Pollack. There wasn't a window in the room.

"Hey, Jordan, how ya doin', buddy?" asked Tom. Clad in miniature jeans and a Knicks T-shirt bearing a bright red blotch that evidenced a Hawaiian Punch accident, Jordan, brown haired and olive complexioned, rose from the frayed navy blue carpeted floor. With eyes full of despair, he studied us and then quickly returned to the cozy solitude of the corner of the room, with crayons and a coloring book.

"Dawn, this is Nick O'Reilly. He's a partner at a big law firm in town called Williams Gardner & Schmidt, and he'll be representing you."

A momentary look of discomfort crossed Dawn's face. She stared at me for a moment before rising out of her chair and walking around the table, carefully avoiding the random assortment of toys strewn across the floor. She was nicely dressed in a black pantsuit, crisp white shirt with the collars spread over the lapels of her jacket, exposing a pearl necklace, and black low-heeled, open-toed sandals. Dawn's beauty was striking, what with her straight, shining black hair pulled back, and a face, shaped by distinctive bone structure, that was natural and touched up with very little makeup around emerald green eyes. I couldn't believe she was the same woman as the one in the horrific photos in the file.

"Hi," she said softly, straight-faced. Dawn kept her distance as she reached to shake my hand. I encroached her safe zone just enough to connect. Holding her gaze with what I hoped was an affable, disarming smile, I introduced myself. Just then, a phone mounted on the wall by the door rang twice. Tom answered it ("Yessum!"), and, after apologizing for the disruption, he excused himself and stepped out, closing the door behind him.

"And this must be Jordan," I said, grabbing his attention. I set my litigation bag on the table, went over to the corner, and squatted in a catcher's position. I asked him what he was making.

"A picture," he said shyly and subdued.

"A picture of what?"

"Of me and my mommy."

"Wow, that's really nice," I said, before a closer, more focused look revealed faces marked with frowns and tears. I asked him what was wrong.

"Daddy's mean to me and Mommy," he said, brooding. "That's why we're sad."

I shot a quick glance at Dawn, who weighed me with a critical squint. Then I returned my focus to Jordan.

"I know, buddy. But we're going to try to make sure that doesn't happen again, okay? We're going to help you and your mommy. You want to draw smiley faces, right?"

Jordan nodded, his eyes focused on the picture.

"Hey, you know what? I brought you a surprise."

"A surprise?" Jordan said with an inquisitive smile, eyebrows arched, features animated like a cartoon character. He looked up at Dawn, whose lips parted in surprise. I nodded to let him know I was serious, and a happy grin spread across his face. I strenuously rose from my crouching position; since my knees weren't what they used to be, the timing was perfect. I snapped open the gold locks on my litigation bag and pulled out a gift-wrapped box.

"Here you go, buddy," I said, handing it to Jordan. He tore off the paper unrelentingly until a Thomas the Tank Engine train was revealed. I hadn't known what to get, so I had relied on the sales girl at the store to recommend something.

"Look, Mommy! Thomas!" Jordan exclaimed, as Dawn's smile widened doubly.

"Wow, that's really nice, honey—what do you say to Mr. O'Reilly?" Dawn's voice was sweet, with a tinge of a tough-girl, Brooklyn accent. Jordan thanked me, removed the toy from the box, and hugged it as if he'd just been reunited with a long-lost friend.

"You're very welcome!"

Dawn thanked me, and, for the first time, her face creased

into a smile, exposing perfect, pearly white teeth. I thought she was beautiful. I told her it was my pleasure and that she should call me Nick. She smiled again, but this time it was different; it featured interest. I was just being myself, a nice guy without ulterior motives, and a girl found that attractive. Though I was unsure as to whether my assessment was accurate, I went with it.

"Sorry about that, folks," said Tom as he barged in. Lindsey followed closely behind, and the plan was for Lindsey to take Jordan next door for playtime. Given the sensitive nature of the topics that we were about to discuss, removing Jordan from the room was absolutely necessary. Jordan hovered near his mother. "Sweetheart, you go with Lindsey and play with Thomas, okay? I'll be right here talking with Nick and Tom in case you need me." She was very motherly ... adoring and sweet. She cupped the child's head with her hands that looked soft and well-manicured and kissed him several times. Dawn's nurturing manner provided a comfy feeling, like being in front of a homey fire, a warm blanket wrapped tightly around me. It was soothing, calming *my* nerves that were as taut as tennis racket strings. And then, considering what I knew about her background, I thought about how strong she must be. I was intrigued by her.

Lindsey took Jordan's hand and escorted him out. After she closed the door, Dawn, Tom, and I took seats at the conference table. Tom and I sat on one side; Dawn sat directly across from me. After we had gotten settled, I told Dawn that I had reviewed her file carefully and that, before we discussed strategy, I had a few questions to ask. Her voice fragile, she said that was fine.

I first asked Dawn about her living situation. She told me that she and Jordan were staying with her best friend, Milena D'Angelo. Milena lived on one side of a two-family house on Ocean Parkway; Milena's parents owned the house and, along with Milena's younger sister Sonia, occupied the other side. Dawn was without alternatives, as her only family, an aunt and uncle with whom she had lived after her mother left town, had moved to Florida a couple of years earlier. I then asked Dawn about her work as a pharmacy technician at a local drug store, Silver Rod Super Drugs on Beverly Road.

"Milena's house is within walking distance. Unfortunately, it's still near Jimmy, but I really need this job. My boss is good to me, and I feel like I have a future there, if I can ever graduate and get my license. And the people I work with are nice too. I still need to have some type of support system around me. Even though Jimmy's nearby, I feel safer than I would if I moved somewhere else where I'd have no one. You know?"

I nodded.

"I also have Frank—Frank Keenan, my father's ex-partner. After my mother left, Frank came to me and told me that he and my father had made a pact to look out for each other's kids in the event something happened to either one of them. He lived up to his oath and kept an eye on me. I never told him about how I was being treated because I was afraid of what he'd do to Jimmy. But I always got the feeling that he suspected something was wrong, the way he questioned me, always skeptical of my answers. I finally told him after that night … when I knew we had to leave. But I didn't want him to hurt Jimmy. I just wanted out."

Dawn explained the escape. One morning, after she called Jimmy at work to make sure he was there, Frank and Milena's father came over to help move them out. She had planned her escape well in advance—she had taken out a new credit card, opened a bank account, and removed important documents from their safety deposit box, like social security cards and birth certificates.

I then asked Dawn about Jimmy.

"I feel like he stalks me constantly," she said. "I can't go anywhere without looking over my shoulder. He refuses to let us go. I don't get it. Aren't we cramping his lifestyle? What does he want us for? Why won't he just let us move on? He has an out. And he doesn't have to pay child support, either. That's perfectly fine. We can wipe the slate clean."

"Dawn, that's exactly the point," I said. "You're all he's got. You're *his* support. You've been providing him with stability. He basically wants to have his cake and eat it too."

She nodded. "You should've seen the way he used to harass me, coming in at all hours of the night and expecting me to be at his beck and call, have his dinner ready when he got home from work—anything and everything. And why did I put up with it? So he could ignore me and go sit on the couch in front of the TV with a six-pack and his hand in his pants?" she vented, with righteous indignation before pausing to catch her breath. "This is my wonderful life."

We talked about the stalking, and Dawn said that, at times, she'd see Jimmy from afar, usually standing across the street from the drug store smoking cigarettes.

"Then there was the night, right after we moved out. I was walking home from work, and he snuck up from behind and grabbed me by my hair and put his hand over my mouth. It was dark and late, and of course no one saw us at first. He said if I screamed he'd kill me. He told me that there was no way I could leave him and take his family away from him. He said that I had to move back in with him and that, if I didn't, terrible things would happen to me—and Jordan. I told him to just leave me alone ... and ... I felt like he was going to hit me when we heard a couple of people coming around the corner. He quickly whispered, 'I'm not finished with you yet, you fuckin' whore,' and then let me go. That was the last time I saw him. But it's like he's always there, lurking in the shadows."

I asked Dawn if she told Frank. She nodded and explained that it was after that incident that she finally gave him the go-ahead to approach Jimmy. Although Jimmy hadn't bothered her since, there were times when she felt that he might be watching her from a distance.

I shifted the conversation to Jordan, and Dawn took it from there.

"When he was first born, Jimmy wasn't that bad, though he was definitely screwing around on me and drinking a lot. Then he started ridiculing me, at first in private, but then in front of Jordan.

"One time, toward the end, he ripped my blouse off in front of him, calling me a 'fuckin' slut' and yelling, 'Come on, you wanna' show the kid how Mommy fucks?' while he laughed the entire time. He was totally out of his mind." I maintained my composure and nodded for her to continue.

"I pleaded for him to keep it behind closed doors. Let the kid have his innocence, you know? I mean, he may be young, but you'd be surprised at how much they pick up on at that age. And then, finally, there was that one night that put it over the top."

Dawn turned to face me directly and leaned forward, clenching her hands together in a fist and resting her forearms on the table. She took a deep breath and exhaled.

"It was about two in the morning. Jordan had been fast asleep, and I was in the den, watching TV and waiting up for Jimmy. I was furious. He was very involved with work and was partying a lot. It had been going on for a while, you know, him staying out late, not telling me where he was going. It was stupid. He didn't even want to take me out or spend any quality time with me. It's like, we got married and had a child, and his lifestyle didn't change a bit. We weren't even intimate. And I'm not talking about sex. I mean, we never even cuddled on the couch and talked and just enjoyed each other. The thing is, after a while, I didn't even care. Little by little, I exposed his incompetence and lost all respect for him, which I think enraged him even more."

"Okay. What time did he get home?"

"It was sometime a little after two. *Saturday Night Live* had ended at one, and I had been flipping through the channels for about an hour when I heard the screen door creak open and slam. He stumbled over and banged loudly, yelling at me to open up. I ran over to the door to shut him up so that he wouldn't wake up Jordan," she said. "I asked him why he couldn't just use his key. 'Shut the fuck up,' he said. He was too drunk and stupid." Dawn drew a deep breath and then continued.

"After I got him inside and locked the door, I led him into the den and told him that I had had it up to here with him," she said, raising her hand to her temples, the thoughts clearly tearing away at her insides. Dawn's eyes could not hide the maelstrom of anguish in which she was entwined, but she stayed strong and articulately regurgitated the facts. Every time she looked up at me, my eyes were waiting for her.

"So I ran upstairs to the bedroom where he kept his stuff and started throwing it into a duffel bag. He followed me there, so I didn't have much of a chance. He pulled me away from the bag and threw me on the bed, telling me to 'Shut the fuck up, bitch.'" She drew another deep breath.

"I started crying and yelling at him to go away, but he started pounding on me. He hurt me real bad," she said, her fury nearly choking her. Puddles were starting to form in her eyes, but she fought hard against the tears she refused to let fall. Dawn masked her inner turmoil with a deceptive calmness, imposing an iron control on herself and trying to get through the story without distraction.

"I just curled up on the bed, hoping he would stop. Then he said, 'Just keep your mouth shut, bitch!'" But then the dams broke, releasing her tears. Tom pulled a few tissues from the box of Kleenex on the table and handed them to her. She accepted them and forced her lips to part in an appreciative smile, thanking him while wiping her eyes.

"He actually had the decency to close the door which, believe it or not, made the situation a lot more tolerable. I didn't want Jordan to hear what was happening. Before I knew it, he was on top of me yelling, 'Shut the fuck up or I'll slap you silly, bitch.' I tried to fight, but he whaled on me a couple of times to get me to stop, which of course I did," she said as she started to shudder, bristling with indignation.

"Take your time," I said, calmly. "You're doing fine."

"Then he tore my shirt off and then my panties. I was completely naked. I saw him undo his belt, and I just started praying. Once his pants were down, I started to cry and then he told me to 'shut the fuck up' again." She looked away, her face flushed with humiliation and a deep sense of shame. "Then he grabbed my hips and flipped me over on my belly. The last thing I wanted was to have another baby with him. I was planning on going on the pill. I had the doctor's appointment set up and everything. I didn't tell him that, though."

She paused for another moment, stirring uneasily in her chair.

"Then, he forced himself inside me … and at first, in a sick sort of way, I was relieved, because … let's just say I knew I wouldn't get pregnant."

Dawn yielded to the compulsive sobs that shook her as tears found their way down her cheeks. She closed her eyes, bowed her head, and covered her face with her hands. I really wanted to lend a hand, and racked my brain to find words both tactful and comforting, but I was at a loss. Tom and I sat quietly, affording her the moment until she had the strength to continue. When she looked up and dried her eyes, I noticed that Dawn's mascara had run so I reached into my pocket for a handkerchief and offered it, which she graciously accepted. Dawn forced herself to settle down and continued to speak with a quiet, but desperate, firmness.

"After that, he just kept going. While he was doing it he was slapping me and calling me his bitch. I thought it would never end. It hurt so badly," she said, clenching her jaw to kill the sob in her throat. "Then he finished and got dressed, warning me that if I told anyone, he'd kill me *and* Jordan. 'Shit, it's not as if anyone would even know you were gone, or even give a fuck for that matter,' he said. And he just left me there like that. He went downstairs for a while, drank beer, and watched TV. Eventually, he came back up and got into bed. And then he just went to sleep, like it was nothing. 'Goodnight darling,' he said, laughing himself to sleep. But I was up all night, and all I kept thinking about was how he'd said he'd kill Jordan. That was what put me over the edge. That was when I knew it was time to leave."

Just then, someone knocked on the door. After Tom gave permission to enter, Lindsey opened the door with Jordan by her side. Lindsey noticed that Dawn was crying. "Oh, I'm so sorry for interrupting … he really wanted to say hello."

"Mommy?"

"It's okay, sweetie," Dawn said with outstretched arms, inviting Jordan to sit on her lap. With his new toy in hand, Jordan scooted over. Dawn quickly wiped away a few tears and held him tightly.

"I'm crying because I love you, honey, and I'm just really happy to be here with you. Sometimes people cry when they're happy." I watched as Dawn clenched Jordan tightly, savoring every moment. She kissed him as if it were the last time she would ever see him … as if she was about to be carted off to do twenty-five to life. Observing the way Dawn interacted with Jordan, the way she doted on him, I got that warm feeling again. I felt myself smiling during all of these moments. As Dawn wiped the remaining tears from her eyes, I encouraged her to take her time. She used my handkerchief, expressed appreciation for my patience, and thanked me. A few more moments passed, and then Dawn gave Jordan a kiss. Knowing that we'd completed the sensitive nature of the discussion, Tom invited Jordan to stay and thanked Lindsey for her assistance. After Lindsey closed the door, Dawn told Jordan that she needed a few more minutes to talk and that, in the meantime, he should continue playing with Thomas. He happily obliged and cracked himself up all the way to the corner of the room.

"So what do we do now?"

I walked Dawn through the procedural aspects of the three matters as delineated in Tom's memo and shared my thoughts on the outlook. I acknowledged Dawn for all of her strengths, emphasizing that she was a good citizen with a clean record in pursuit of a professional career with only a bit of college left—not to mention that she was a kind-hearted person who loved her son dearly. For these reasons, I explained, I had no concerns that the judge would find her fit to care for Jordan. I asked if she had people who would vouch for her, and she responded with confidence that the D'Angelos and her boss would testify on her behalf. Tom agreed with my position that all of this would make the difference in family court. But for Dawn and Jordan to move forward with peace of mind, they needed Jimmy out of their lives, and I explained that the only way that could really happen was if the criminal court found him guilty and sent him to prison. I advised Dawn that the prosecution's entire case would ride on her testimony and asked if she could recount her story in court the way she had moments earlier.

"Whatever it takes," she said firmly.

"Great. I'm sure you'll do fine."

"Thank you, Nick. All I want is for us to have normal lives. I'm sick of this."

"I know. We're going to help you."

"From your mouth to God's ears—he's such a loser," said Dawn. I could just imagine how the thought of Jimmy behind bars infused her with comfort.

"Remember, though, the criminal proceeding is out of our hands. I'm not an expert in that area, but prosecuting these types of cases isn't as easy as you might think. Anything can happen, so we shouldn't give ourselves false hopes." Dawn nodded. It wasn't exactly what she wanted to hear, but I was her lawyer and had to tell it to her straight. I reached into my breast pocket, retrieved a business card, and passed it to her.

"Feel free to call me any time. If you have any questions or if you're in any kind of trouble, I'll make myself available." Dawn nodded with a wry smile. My corporate clients had no qualms about calling me at all hours of the night, and I thought she deserved equal treatment.

"With my crazy life, I'm sure I'll have to take you up on that."

"Dawn, just remember ... you're young and bright and you have a healthy child—you're going to get through this and come out way ahead."

"I hope so."

Dawn thanked me again, but not before taking advantage of an opportunity to teach Jordan proper manners. "Sweetie, what do you say to Nick for bringing you Thomas?"

"Thank you, mister," said Jordan, coaxing a laugh out of everyone and ending the afternoon on a perfect note.

"You got it, buddy."

I'd never experienced an initial conference with a client like that before. My conferences had all become garden variety and were usually conducted over dinner at one of the city's finest restaurants, with executives from Fortune 500 companies cackling about shareholder litigation over martinis, forty-dollar steaks, and expensive Cuban cigars.

As I headed back to the office, I sat on the uptown express subway thinking about Dawn and what she had said: "All I want is for us to have normal lives."

There has to be a way, I thought ... *a way to help Dawn find salvation. There has to be a way that she can have a happy life ... so she can just wake up in the morning and have the same worries as everyone else, like, will Jordan get into a good college or will he marry a nice girl. She deserves happiness,* I thought, as I conjured up a vision of Dawn resting on the porch of a home in a nice suburban neighborhood, relaxing and watching Jordan at play. In my daydream, she was happy and at peace, having triumphed and overcome terrible circumstances.

I arrived at the office at three o'clock and felt completely drained. Thoughts of Dawn and Jordan and what it was going to take to help them filled my overwrought brain, like a mammoth oak tree squeezed into the middle of an already thick and crowded forest. I wanted nothing more than to head back to my apartment, plop down on the couch, and crash. But people had been looking for me all afternoon; clients had called in, and associates needed me to sign off on documents that, like everything else, were on tight deadlines. So, back to the office it was.

After all, where would my billionaire corporate clients be without *me*?

Chapter 4

Despite feeling as if someone had sucked the life out of me, I managed to finish the rest of the day without a nap. After tending to other matters and clearing my desk of the day's priorities, with the facts still fresh in my mind, I rolled up my sleeves, loosened my tie, and anxiously dove into the Nelson matter. I started with a few of hours of background—a basic primer on family and matrimonial law followed by more focused research specific to the factual context of my case. After gaining momentum and even finding enjoyment in studying a new area of law, I worked feverishly until about three in the morning, preparing the necessary pleadings, as well as a document subpoena and deposition notice for Jimmy. Since discovery was limited to financial issues, I could seek to obtain only records and testimony concerning Jimmy's finances; wrongful acts like rape and abuse were off limits, and, even if they weren't, with a criminal trial pending, Jimmy would simply plead the Fifth. I e-mailed drafts to Tom Dooley before heading out.

Though I had no life, I always tried to at least "have a night" for myself after work: sports highlights on ESPN, Letterman, and occasionally Conan O'Brien. That night, I'd managed to get through about half of a replay of SportsCenter before fading out. After waking for my first middle-of-the-night pee, I turned off the TV, which had been showing some cheesy get-rich-quick infomercial.

After my final bathroom run, I'd fallen back into such a deep sleep that, when I awoke at twelve thirty-eight p.m. the next day to the sound of my phone ringing, after unfastening one crusted eyelid and noticing the time, I wondered why my alarm clock hadn't buzzed at eight. I didn't bother reaching for the phone, opting instead to let the answering machine—which had been blinking with two messages—pick it up.

"Uh … hi, Nick, it's Janice," she said in a broken whisper that was nervous, almost frightened. "I've called you twice already this morning. Duncan Shaw and Ted Wickersham are here. They're in the large conference room waiting for you. You were supposed to meet with them at twelve-fifteen to prepare Mr. Shaw for his deposition."

Oh shit! I'd nearly slept through my meeting with Duncan Shaw, the CEO of Advanced Technology Resources and one of my biggest clients, whom I was defending in a securities fraud class action. Ted Wickersham, whom Duncan never seemed to go anywhere important without, was the company's general counsel.

"They're very upset that you're not here … uh …"

I grabbed the phone. "Hello?" I said, groggily.

"Hi, Nick, it's Janice … uh, I'm terribly sorry, listen …"

"Nick?" said Phil Addison in a nasty tone. I was shocked and caught off guard. That woke me up real quick.

"Hi, Phil, I …"

"Nick, where the *fuck* are you?"

"Phil, I'm sorry, but I …"

"Are you out of your goddamn mind? Shaw and Wickersham are here wondering where the hell you are. You're supposed to be prepping him for his testimony, but instead, you're lying in bed doing God knows what while I have to put on a happy face and stroke this guy over sandwiches, fruit salad, and cookies. And you know damn well they have to be on a plane to Washington later this afternoon."

"I didn't get out until three last night."

"Doing what?" he asked. I paused with trepidation.

"Getting the pro bono matter started."

Phil hit the ceiling. "Wha—" he said, stopping to lower his voice to a whisper. "Didn't you hear Will? Our—paying—clients—come—*first.*" He spit the words at me. I had nothing to say. I waited while Phil caught his breath.

"I don't know what else to talk to this guy about, Nick. I feel like we've covered everything. I listened to him talk about his daughter's wedding, his Elvis Presley record collection, and Graceland—a place that I'll never visit anyway. We even talked about the weather … the fucking weather, for chrissakes, Nick," said Phil, pausing to catch his breath before continuing to vent.

"You know him better than I do, Nick. What else can we talk about?"

I suggested golf.

"Fine—golf it is. I can keep him preoccupied for about another half hour over lunch, but by then you had better fucking be here. Understand?" His voice faded a bit. "As it is, I had to postpone a conference call that I'm supposed to be on right now just to do damage control for you."

"All right, I'll be there ASAP, but just for my edification, how exactly did you cover for me?"

"I told him you had a family emergency."

Family emergency? I was almost afraid to ask, but I needed to know. Phil told them that my mother had to be rushed to the hospital out on Long Island.

"What?" Bitterness spilled over into my voice. "Who says that?"

"Nick, who the hell do you think you are? You've got a lot of fucking balls. Maybe it's the one excuse that you never use, but, as a practical matter, it's the best excuse in the book and works every time, just like it is right now. And at the end of the day, Shaw and ATR do a tremendous amount of business with the firm, both in the litigation and corporate ..."

"I know what he generates, Phil. He's my client."

"Excuse me? Uh ... he's the *firm's* client, Nick, not yours. Look, you know what? Later on this afternoon, when these guys are gone, you and I are going to sit down and have a little chat. Right now, though, I suggest you do whatever it takes to get your ass over here. I've got to get back to the conference room to bullshit about Tiger Woods."

"Davis Love III."

"What?"

"He's a big fan of Davis Love III," I said. "Stick with him. I wouldn't go the Tiger Woods route."

"Whatever," he said with contempt. "Just get your fucking ass over here, *pronto.*"

Within moments, I was in the shower. I left it cold and scrubbed hard and fast and achieved the rest of my get-ready routine in record time: close shave, hair finger-combed to the side with the aid of a light styling gel, two five-second sprays of deodorant, and a quick brush of my teeth. As for attire, I grabbed a navy blue pinstripe that had fortuitously just come back from the cleaners along with a set of assorted dress shirts. I chose a solid white with a straight collar and methodically tied a solid gray necktie, carefully pinching the fabric beneath the knot, leaving a dimple. My black cap toes still held a decent shine—a few mild scuffs, but nothing to be self-conscious about.

After greeting me in the lobby of my apartment building with a perfunctory nod, the top-hatted doorman—a tall, older gentleman wearing a reddish, Abe Lincoln–like beard and no mustache—opened one of the large double glass doors. I thanked him and stepped outside, abandoning the comfort of the air-conditioned lobby for a torrent of Manhattan summer sauna-like heat. The long, rectangular awning that extended to the curb provided shade while I powered my BlackBerry. I didn't want to greet Duncan and Ted drenched in sweat, and, since Phil's excuse bought me a couple of extra minutes, I moseyed my usual five-block route slowly, as if the sidewalks were a thin icy sheath atop a frozen pond. I headed east on Central Park South toward Fifth Avenue. Doormen were hailing cabs with the aid of loud, piercing whistles; awnings displayed tony addresses. Flourishing trees lined sidewalks that were sometimes so spotted with remains left behind by inconsiderate dog owners that I had to play hopscotch just to keep my Kenneth Coles looking presentable. Across the way, horses waited to give buggy rides to people who had lives and time to enjoy Central Park. I, on the other hand, one of the park's relatively few true neighbors, felt that my connection to it was limited to the view from my balcony—essentially tantamount to the relationship one has with his wallpaper.

I stopped into my office and said hello to Janice, a tall African-American woman in her mid-thirties. She wore a beige pantsuit, and her long black hair was pulled back. She greeted me with an unpleasant, rueful countenance, grabbed four message memos, and followed me inside.

"Nick, I'm really sorry—there was nothing I could do," she said, her voice filled with entreaty. Knowing full well that Phil had put her up to it, I assuaged her concerns. Then she began to brief me on who had called. I shook my head and raised my hand, cutting her off.

"Only if it's an absolute emergency." I advised her to hold my calls and told her I would be in Conference Room 47C over the next couple of hours. I quickly gathered a stack of materials, bolted out the door, and power walked down the hall. I paused to wipe my forehead with a handkerchief, which I replaced in my inside jacket pocket before I opened the door. The room was dominated by a long, black marble table. Framed by mahogany crown molding, the walls were covered in a camel-colored, textured wallpaper and decorated with original art. A wall of floor-to-ceiling windows exposed an incredible view of the west side.

"Gentlemen, I'm terribly sorry." My visitors politely rose out of their chairs. Phil, with his back to me, remained seated and reclined, legs crossed, hands interlocked behind his head, not moving a muscle. After all the phony smiling, he was relaxing his face. His sore, aching cheekbones probably needed ice or Bengay, the way some of the muscles in my body did after working out for the first time in ages.

After setting my materials down on the table, I greeted my clients.

"Hello, Duncan," I said, as I extended my arm for a handshake that was strong and firm. Duncan's presence was compelling. In his early fifties, he stood tall. He was athletically built and self-confident, and, when it came to his looks, was as vain as a movie star. His hair was black—not a single gray in sight—and slicked back from his forehead, tapered neatly to the collar. A wide smile showcased perfect, bleached white teeth that contrasted with an artificial lightly bronzed tan. His clothing was expensive and looked as if he spent time honing every detail: a black double-breasted suit with a faint pinstripe picked up by a white handkerchief stuffed perfectly into the front pocket, and a silk yellow tie that was perfectly knotted (dimple and all).

"Hi, Nick, good to see you—I hope all is well with your mother."

"Oh, thank God she's fine—thanks," I said. I looked away and clenched my teeth.

"Hi, Ted, it's nice to see you." Several inches shorter than his boss, Ted was heavy set and thick necked with dark, curly hair and a walrus mustache. His solid navy, two-button suit was overstuffed and looked as if it may have been let out a couple of times. He was polite, professional, and very bright, though his slumped posture and demeanor suggested disappointment. It was as if he'd realized that, after dreaming of becoming CEO and believing he had what it took to be a great one (and certainly better than Duncan), he'd reached the pinnacle of his career and would never amount to anything more than the walking shadow of a brighter star. He was the perfect sidekick for a guy like Duncan—no threat whatsoever. All of Duncan's key people seemed to fit the same profile.

"Pleasure's mine, Nick," he said, warmly. "Glad to hear everything's all right."

I replied with an impersonal, closed-mouth smile and a nod. Enough with that shit, already.

Phil lifted his left arm slightly, turned his forearm in across his midsection, and purposely shot his gold Rolex out from underneath his French cuff, checking the time.

"Well, I won't keep you gentlemen from getting down to business. I know you have a plane to catch later," said Phil as he rose from his chair. He was a puny-looking man with a full head of hair that was graying. "But it was very nice both chatting and dining with you. If there is ever anything I can do, just give me a ring."

After one final labored and agonizing smile, he passed out business cards.

"Nick, I'll talk to you later," he said, patting me on the shoulder as if we were brothers. "Safe trip, gentlemen."

Phil exited and gently closed the door behind him.

"Your partner's a nice guy, Nick," said Duncan. "A real pleasure to chat with."

"Oh, Phil? Sure, Phil's a sweetheart. He was one of my mentors before I made partner. I know what you mean. I'm a big fan myself," I said, nearly ruining what moments earlier had been a hearty appetite. Silence hung over the room for a moment before I asked Duncan and Ted if they minded if I grabbed a quick bite before we got started.

"Go right ahead, Nick, take your time. I don't think the company jet's gonna' take off without us," he said, boasting.

On a black marble buffet, an abundance of assorted half-sandwiches remained on a disposable, shell-shaped platter amid a generous spread of fruit salad, assorted pastries, and various soft drinks. Carafes of regular and decaf coffee were set beside a double-tiered stack of fancy mugs bearing the firm logo. After brief deliberation, I placed a tuna on rye and half-sour pickle on a shiny black plastic plate. I poured myself a glass of soda that effervesced with the addition of ice cubes.

"So Mom's okay, Nick?" Duncan asked.

"She'll be fine," I said, tersely. Duncan leaned forward and lowered his voice.

"Yeah, I tell you, Nick, heart attacks are never easy. I had one myself about eight years ago, you know."

Heart attack? I took a very long, deep breath and exhaled before responding.

"No, Duncan, I'm sorry, I didn't know that."

"Yeah, sure did. It scared the shit out of me, Nick. Changes your outlook on life, Nick, you know? It's only during a crisis like that when you really learn quickly about what's most important in life. Best thing that can come out of a situation like that, Nick, besides of course making a full, healthy recovery, is that you get your priorities in order. Since then, I've spent a lot more time out on the golf course, traveling … that sort of thing. I nearly killed myself building this company up from scratch, and, if I can afford to have my people help run it, then why not? What's the point of working so damn hard if you can't enjoy the fruits of your labor?"

"Tell me about it."

The meeting was productive. The deposition was about a week away, and, though I usually tried to prep witnesses as close to the day of the testimony as possible, with both of our schedules packed tight, that day was the most mutually convenient day to do it. It didn't matter, though. I had all the confidence in the world that my witness would be an all-star. In a way, I thought Duncan was *too* prepared and *too* good. He knew how to dodge every bullet as if he'd done it a hundred times before.

We called it a day at about three-thirty. After seeing them off, I stopped at the kitchen to pick up a much-needed dose of caffeine. I passed Janice on my way to my office. She was dangling two message memos that I grabbed on the fly and thanked her for as I entered my sanctum and closed the door. I tossed my stuff down on the desk and reviewed my messages.

Then the phone rang, and, since I usually made it my business to answer my own phone when I was available, I hurried to grab it.

"Hi, Nickie," said my mother. Charlotte O'Reilly had the cheerful, honeyed voice of the elementary school art teacher that she is. I asked about her, and she quickly shifted the focus to me. Sounding fatigued, I told her things were crazy, which I regretted because all she does is worry. Mom probed further, and I gave her the quick gist.

"You've always worked long hours, honey, why would it be any different now?" It wasn't the right time for that conversation, so I abruptly changed the subject and suggested the possibility of visiting soon.

"Oh, that would be wonderful," she said as my other line rang. I let it go and asked if she was getting out at all.

"Oh, sure. You know, I still have my weekly game with the girls, and we go shopping and have lunch … things like that," she said, her voice gradually trailing off. As a widow with married friends, Mom's social life was limited. As much as I couldn't imagine anyone other than Dad being in Mom's life, there were moments when I appreciated what a little companionship would do for her. I didn't want her to be alone, yet I couldn't bring myself to encourage her to date. At Mom's age, a relationship with another man wouldn't just be like two eighty-something companions living out their twilight years with nice slow walks in the park, sharing ice cream cones, matinee films, and early-bird specials. There was still potential for a youth-like romance, with love and sex, which to me would be a new beginning—a new life without Dad.

Suddenly, there came a knock at the door. Janice entered and slipped a note advising that Phil was on hold. I hated to, but told Mom I had another call.

"Okay, you go. I know you're busy," she said. "I love you, honey."

"Love you too—I'll come by soon, I promise," I said before hitting line two and transforming into my alter ego.

"Yes, Phil."

"Nick, come see me right away," he said, replacing the receiver, not waiting for an answer. In the interest of putting the issue to bed as quickly as possible, I pushed myself up out of my chair and anxiously bustled down the hall to Phil's corner office. The door was closed, and I knocked twice. At first, there was silence.

"Come in." I opened the door to find Phil leaning against the window on the south side of his office, studying what looked to be a case printed off of Westlaw online legal research.

I entered and was besieged by Phil's overgrown ego wall. Diplomas from Yale and Harvard Law, bar admission certificates, articles authored and bearing quotes, and photos with federal judges hung in black frames against beige wallpaper. A glass case mounted on the opposite wall displayed Civil War memorabilia: four rows of hatpins, badges, and miscellaneous battlefield relics, like bullets and bugle mouthpieces—a sampling of his home collection which includes guns, swords, and, rumor had it, slave tags. Antique furniture—the kind one is afraid to touch, let alone sit on—was placed for decorative purposes only in positions that discouraged visitors from making themselves comfortable (which was fine by me). A fancy rug and vast mahogany bookcase completed Phil's sanctum. The token family photo—a five-by-seven of Phil with his wife and their son and daughter taken from a distance—was simply framed and set on his desk facing outward.

Philip Charles Addison was born and raised in Manhattan, with summers spent on Martha's Vineyard. His father, Henry, a contemporary and client of Will Schmidt's father, was one of the first legendary corporate raiders. Phil's mother, Winnie Mansfield Addison, was one of the city's most prominent socialites and a fixture on the benefit circuit. Neither had been around very much for Phil and his older sister, who had relocated to northern Virginia.

After spending a harsh twelve years with Phil, I couldn't remember him discussing anything other than himself or topics on which he considered himself an expert. Everything he did, like each of his cases, was "very important"—so important that, on September 11, 2001, after the news of the attacks on the World Trade Center broke, while others were stunned and rendered immobile, Phil worked right through the disaster without missing a beat. "I have battles of my own to fight!" he'd proclaimed.

Phil took his sweet-ass time. He shook his head vehemently, as if disapproving of the judge's reasoning. He finally glanced up, acknowledged my presence, and ordered me to sit.

A staunch opponent of casual Friday ("We should still be dressing like lawyers!" he'd exclaimed in a memo to all partners on the issue of whether the firm should adopt the then-fast-growing trend), Phil sported his "lawyer's uniform"—custom navy pinstripe suit; light blue shirt, initials embroidered on the chest pocket, white collar, and French cuffs fastened with gold links; conservative red and blue tie with matching braces; and black wingtips buffed to a high sheen.

Phil continued to do his own thing for a solid six or seven

minutes. The silence between us, broken only by the turning of pages, deep breaths, and sniffles, was excruciating.

Looking mousy with beady eyes, Phil positioned himself on his enormous leather chair, his miniature body completely framed. He slowly removed his gold-rimmed reading glasses, which had been perched upon his beak, and delicately set them on the desk, in the manner of one who deals in precious stones or rare stamps. Then he sat back and placed both arms on their respective rests. He reminded me of the [not-so] Wonderful Wizard of Oz. Though, on the surface, I had to respect him for his stature at the firm, it was impossible for me to take him seriously.

"Nick, I'm not interested in going to any great lengths to discuss today's fiasco. This isn't some lovers' quarrel, nor is it some schoolyard fight that has to be sorted out in the principal's office. We're busy lawyers with way too much billable time to spend talking about this. And, in the spirit of billable time, you know damn well that the pro bono matter revolves around clients like Duncan Shaw, the lifeblood of this firm, *not* the other way around. I would submit that your conduct was unbecoming of a partner of this firm. You should know better."

"Phil, listen ..."

Phil abruptly thrust himself forward and admonished me with measured words, his eyeballs swelling and nearly bursting from their sockets. "Don't you tell me to listen," he said, cold and lashing. I found myself staring down the tip of his pale, scrawny index finger as if it were the barrel of a gun. "I don't want to discuss this any further. If I were interested in debating the merits of the situation, I would have dragged you into Will's office for a formal discussion, but, as I indicated earlier in the conversation, I believe this will preempt the need for that, so let's just see to it that it never happens again. Understood?"

I sighed heavily with agitation, clasped my hands together,

and stared. As much as, deep down, I wanted to reach across the desk and shove my fist down the little Wizard's throat, as always, I veiled my fury under the guise of indifference.

"Sure."

I worked past midnight every night for the rest of the week, completely buried in paper. Thousands of documents produced in the ATR litigation lined the perimeter of my office, stacked unevenly, forming the shape of the New York City skyline.

I had barely slept, and not just because I was working so hard. As soon as my head hit the pillow, I would toss and turn thinking about Dawn and Jordan. Their lives were hell, and, unlike in a typical civil lawsuit, every minute that ticked by was crucial. The case had to proceed expeditiously.

At about eight forty-five on Thursday night, I was in the middle of reviewing documents produced by the auditors in the ATR litigation with my associate on the case, Tim Baxter. We expected a late night, and, since I was getting hungry, it seemed as good a time as any to break for dinner.

I stepped outside. Thick haze and humidity larded the air. The moon emerged from a blockade of thick, gray clouds, its natural glow obviated by the city's overpowering self-illumination. After a short walk, I arrived at the Carnegie Deli on Seventh Avenue. I seated myself at a table off the wall, flanked by autographed headshots of local celebrities. A waitress noticed me and scooted over to take my order. Not a day under sixty, she was frumpy, dressed in a uniform of black pants and vest. A pair of granny glasses from the sixties dangled from a chain around her neck.

"What's it gonna' be, fella?" she asked, quickly scanning her other tables. I ordered a corned beef on rye, a side of well-done French fries, and a Dr. Brown's black cherry. I'd offered to bring something back for Tim, and placed his order—pastrami on a roll—to go.

I sat for about a half an hour picking at my sandwich and trying to relax over the sports section of *The New York Post*. I was stressed about Dawn and Jordan ... about how I couldn't possibly move fast enough for them. Then I thought about how, as unappealing as my life was, Dawn was probably getting ready to leave work and dreading her walk home because of what Jimmy might do to her. I hoped she had someone to walk with.

On Friday morning, Tom finally e-mailed the draft pleadings back to me, and I spent an hour making final edits for filing and service. The petition filed in family court was also transferred to the criminal court. Charges had been filed against Jimmy and he had been arrested at home. Assistant District Attorney Steve Leventhal from the Brooklyn DA's office argued vigorously in support of having Jimmy remanded to Riker's Island pending trial. The allegations were substantial, but Jimmy's record was clean, and the judge set bail at fifty thousand. Having the money socked away, Jimmy easily posted and was a free man.

Shortly after the papers were served, a young lawyer named Mike Carroll, who had recently started his own practice after putting in several years at the Manhattan DA's office, was retained to represent Jimmy. I put my feelers out, and the book on Carroll was that he was talented and hard working and would make a formidable adversary. The court appointed a law guardian to advocate on Jordan's behalf, a seasoned veteran of the matrimonial bar named Rachel Schor. Since it was her job to recommend to the court which party to the litigation should be granted custody of Jordan, it was just as important to persuade her concerning Dawn's fitness as a parent as it was to persuade the judge.

In the meantime, I had spent all weekend slaving away in the name of Corporate America. I was also in the process of negotiating a record deal for one of my music clients, and, as much as I relished that area of my practice, with everything else on my plate, it amounted to more of a burden than anything else.

What was I doing with myself? I couldn't help but think about my unsavory corporate clients, off in their weekend cottages and vacation homes, water-skiing behind yachts and diving in Grand Cayman, basking in the comfort of knowing their misconduct was easily being covered by directors and officers liability insurance, boasting about how royally they screwed their own shareholders.

Ha, ha, ha, fraud, schmaud!

And then I thought about Dawn and drifted off on my office couch for a while until the phone rang.

It was Dawn.

And it didn't sound good.

Chapter 5

"Hi, Nick, it's Dawn Nelson," she said, her here-we-go-again tone sounding tired and frustrated. I listened as Dawn's tremulous, tear-smothered voice told me that Jimmy had showed up at Jordan's daycare center. Dawn's forewarning to the babysitters notwithstanding, Jimmy managed to surreptitiously creep up to the fence that hemmed in the outdoor play area. Apparently, he wooed Jordan over with a lollipop, tucked it into the side pocket of his jeans shorts, and told him to save it for "when Mommy isn't looking." Milena had taken Jordan home that day, and, when Jordan asked her to remove the wrapper, knowing it wasn't the type they kept in the house for him, she had asked him where it had come from. "My daddy gave it to me. He loves me ... we're going to be a family again!"

Above and beyond the typical wear and tear of a long exhausting day, I felt weary and feverish, as if I was coming down with some kind of virus. My hourly application of cold compresses amounted to an exercise in futility, and I really needed to lie down. But I also wanted to be there for Dawn, so I asked if I could call her from home in about twenty minutes, and she said that was fine.

I slowly inserted my arms into the sleeves of my jacket, my

muscles screaming from the strain. I was about to step out of my office when Phil emerged unexpectedly.

"Leaving early, Nick?" he asked, checking the time on his watch. He shook his head slowly, as he said, "*Tsk, tsk, tsk … I know, it's been a long day.*"

His sarcasm grated on me.

"It *has* been a long day," I said, with effort.

"I see, I see—if you weren't in the heat of discovery on ATR, with a multitude of depositions to prepare for, I would assume you weren't all that busy, Nick," he said, as he strolled the perimeter of my office, hands in pockets and head arched high, before stopping at the bookcase to examine my personal library (which he'd done several times over the past twelve years). I straddled the doorway, my briefcase feeling extra heavy and weighing me down on my left side, and watched painfully as Phil took his time to fuck with me, slowly inspecting book after book after book. He picked up a volume.

"Actually, I'm extremely busy, as always."

"Life must be tough for you, Nick," he said, drawing the words out extra slowly. "Being *young* and *single* and making as much *money* as you do. We've been really unfair to you here, Nick, I know." He replaced the book on the shelf and took one last glance before finally making his way back toward the door.

Everything I have, I've earned—you didn't hand me shit, I wanted to say. The more senior and "independent" I became in terms of running my own practice, the more Phil's desire for control over me seemed to intensify. It was as if, deep down, he felt I owed him something for making me a partner. My Faustian pact with the firm wasn't enough.

"I'm just a little under the weather today, Phil," I said listlessly. Phil sneered and shook his head disapprovingly.

"You know, they just don't make junior lawyers the way they used to," he said with a lively twinkle in his eye that enraged me even more. I sighed. My chest rose and fell beneath heavy, labored breathing.

"I'd rather talk about this tomorrow ... in private," I said, knowing the office remained crowded. No one at the firm had lives, and so the stories about who was banging who were trite; on the other hand, a brawl between me and Phil—now *that* would be legendary.

Phil rolled his eyes and then caught the stare of an interested associate down the hall.

"You're right, Nick, maybe we should talk about this tomorrow. You ought to get going—I hear tonight's a good TV night."

"Have a good evening," I said, turning and ambling toward the elevator.

"Hey, Nick," said Phil when I was halfway down the hall. I stopped in midstride, twisted around on my heel and cast an exhausted, impatient look, making no attempt whatsoever to conceal the loathing in my eyes. Felix Contreras, a big-boned, mean-looking Cuban fellow from the copy center, who was working the late shift, was nearby making his rounds.

"Shouldn't you be out on Long Island? You know ... *caring for mother?*" he said, flinging back his head and roaring with laughter. There were a million things I wanted to say, but I restrained myself. Felix saw what was brewing and hung around just in case.

I fantasized for a moment about what I so badly wanted to do to Phil. I'd throw a quick jab to the stomach, knocking the wind out of him and forcing him to hunch over. Then, I'd undercut a hard right to the face, cracking his cheekbone. And if that didn't knock him down, I'd kick him square in the face, finishing him off, good and proper. But before walking away, I'd let him know that the beating was on behalf of every subordinate he'd ever abused over the course of his career.

I had played out that fantasy in my mind countless times.

Instead of carrying it out, I bit my lip and drew a deep breath.

"Better hurry, Nick," said Phil, glancing at his watch. "I think a new episode of—what do they call that?—*Survivor!*—is about to start." I ignored him and continued on my way as Phil's laughter lingered.

I caught an elevator fairly quickly, stepped inside, and pushed the *L* button like mad until the wrought-iron double doors came together. A soft instrumental version of Louis Armstrong's "What a Wonderful World" began to play.

At the firm, hostility ran deep and tempers routinely flared.

There were stories of many sad lives at the firm.

And mine was no exception.

On my brisk walk home, I agonized over what I should say to Dawn. I hated the idea of playing the stuffy lawyer, boring her with procedure and evidence. *She needs someone to talk to ... to be there for her*, I thought as I entered the lobby of my building. I wished the nighttime doorman, Ralph—the one I knew the best—a good night as I passed him and headed to the elevator.

I entered my apartment into the small foyer, tiled with a mixture of beige and brown tones. A round, contemporary lighting fixture made of frosted glass hung close to the ceiling. I tossed my keys onto the stainless-steel console table that was currently bombarded by an overflow of unopened mail. Beneath the table, a week's worth of newspapers were stacked high like an IHOP special. The tiled flooring flowed into hardwood oak floors that were bare and shined to a gloss.

After dropping my briefcase and removing my shoes, I meandered to the bedroom and switched on the bright track lighting, which I quickly dimmed to a faint minimum. I sat myself down on the queen bed and relaxed my feet on the softness of the brown carpet that picked up the tones of the basic, contemporary dark-wood furniture, all of which matched as I had bought it as a set. I finally stood, tossed my watch onto the dresser, and undressed, leaving my suit strewn across the plain beige comforter.

I looked up into the round mirror, suspended low like a rising sun, which offered a glimpse of my silhouette. The rest of the mirror pictured the window behind me—I could see that it had started to rain.

I walked into the kitchen and poured myself some orange juice, then I sat down on the couch and set my glass atop a black rubber coaster on the dark-wood coffee table. I took in a deep breath, pursed my lips, and exhaled loudly. I dialed, and Dawn answered. Tentatively, I said hello over the distressing racket of rain attacking the windows.

"Hi, Nick," she said faintly, choking back tears, her mind no doubt burning with the horrid specter of not so much what had happened earlier, but of what could happen in the future. I let her know that it was okay to cry.

"Thank you so much for calling," she said in a whisper. "You must be exhausted."

"No, actually, I'm wide awake," I said, feigning vitality. An eerie silence loomed for a moment, and I then advised that Jimmy's actions were a violation of the protective order. On the other end, I heard a deep breath that sounded heavy with dissatisfaction.

"Nick, I can't live like this anymore," she said in a low, tormented voice, swallowing a sob that rose in her throat.

"I know. I want to contact the DA's office." She balked at the suggestion.

"Nick, if I keep going after him, he's just going to get more enraged, and then God knows what he'll do," she said with a bitter edge of cynicism.

"Dawn, I can't allow Jimmy to violate court orders like this. Let me at least talk to Tom and see what our options are." She didn't respond. I assured her that everything would be fine.

"I hope so."

"We have to look for the best in every situation, including ones like today."

"Nick, I've been doing that my whole life. How do you think I've made it this far? I have hope that something good is going to come out of all of this," she said, sounding desperate, "... that my life will amount to something."

"It already has. You've got a great kid."

She paused for a moment before responding. "I know."

"Speaking of Jordan, how *is* the little guy?"

"He's okay, I guess. Thanks again for giving him the toy train. That was so nice of you. It's all he plays with—he loves it."

"I'm glad," I said, smiling.

"Jimmy never did anything for him like that."

"Really?" I said softly with a hint of sadness.

"Nope."

Dawn then shared a couple of funny stories, and even told me about Jordan's favorite foods, how he liked to wear them all over himself. By the way she spoke, I sensed that her features had become more animated; I pictured joy shining in her eyes. She also told me about Milena and her family and how her parents would do anything for her. Milena had met Dawn in first grade and, fully aware of what Dawn's situation was at home, the D'Angelos were happy to have Dawn over as much as she wanted. As kids, the girls did normal things like trading stickers and playing with dolls. Friday nights were for sleepovers, and, on Saturdays, after a hearty breakfast worked up by Milena's mom, they'd spend the afternoon at gymnastics.

"My mother was only too happy to give me money for things like that. They kept me out of the house and were probably worth every penny to her."

Later on, they did typical girlfriend things like go to the movies "alone" (they sat by themselves, but were chaperoned by one or both of Milena's parents, who sat somewhere else in the theater). In high school, they went to parties and an occasional concert; but riding the F-train into Manhattan and strolling Madison and Fifth Avenues, visiting boutiques, and trying on clothes was what they had enjoyed the most.

After she talked for a while, Dawn settled down, and we continued to enjoy nice conversation. I felt as if we had a good rapport—so far, anyway. It was getting late, and I was starting to fade, so, at the right moment, I wound the conversation down. I told Dawn that I needed to speak to Tom and confer with him before I made any decisions. "And then, at some point," I said, wondering how in the world I'd clear my schedule, "we'll meet and discuss it."

"I'd like that," she said, cheerily.

Unsure as to how to respond, I paused for a moment, and then, keeping my tone matter-of fact, replied, "And, again, if you need me for anything, I'm only a phone call away."

"Sounds good," she said. We wished each other goodnight.

Chapter 6

After quickly preparing a letter to Mike Carroll first thing in the morning memorializing the event at Jordan's daycare, I turned back to ATR. I had been in deep thought, reviewing a set of key documents that had been produced in the litigation in preparation for Duncan's deposition the following day when Janice buzzed me.

"What's up?" I asked, throwing my voice toward the speakerphone.

"Nick, Duncan Shaw is at reception—he said he's here to see you."

Oh, shit, not again, I thought. Janice assured me that nothing had been scheduled and asked if she should escort him to my office. Normally I would go to reception and greet him myself, but, this time, I just wasn't in the mood.

"If you don't mind, Janice, I'd really appreciate it." Moments later, Duncan knocked three times and entered, looking slick and urbanely attired, as always.

"Duncan!" I exclaimed, bright-eyed and smiley-faced, feigning excitement.

"Hello, Nick. Sorry to barge in unexpected like this. I had a meeting around the corner and had something I wanted to talk about real quick, so I thought I'd stop by. I hope it's not a bad time," he said. Janice waited by the door.

"No, no, that's quite all right. Can we get you some coffee, something to drink?" I offered.

"That's okay, I won't even be a minute," he said. I thanked Janice, and she closed the door. I didn't like sitting behind my desk when meeting with clients, preferring more of a relax-and-chat atmosphere, so I offered Duncan a seat on the couch in my "living area"—a black leather couch and love seat adjoined by an end table.

Although I didn't like surprises, there were a couple of other last minute issues that I wanted to discuss with Duncan that I hadn't covered in our meeting, particularly about the company's accountants. Having been in the throes of reviewing his documents with the issues fresh in my mind, I jumped right into it. After I asked a very simple question, which lent itself to a yes-or-no answer (which was all I wanted), Duncan launched into a discourse that offered more than I cared to hear. Most of my corporate clients had at least three traits in common: high-and-mighty attitude, invincibility complex, and—worst of all—a bad case of diarrhea of the mouth. They just didn't know when to shut up.

Duncan whispered in a tone that was deliberately low and secretive. The meeting made me feel as if we were two mob bosses seated at a private table in the corner of a restaurant, dividing up territory.

"They knew what was going on the whole time, Nick. I mean, for crying out loud, they were one of the biggest marketers of our products! The money they made from the audit was *peanuts* compared to what they made on the back end. Auditing was a loss leader for them, Nick, there was no money in that. The *consulting* side ... now *that* was the coin of the realm."

"Sure," I said, nodding. As ATR's lead counsel, I knew the accounting was shady.

"I tell you, Nick, we could've switched accountants any time we wanted. But with these guys, there was no reason to. I mean, shit, we were beating the Street's numbers every quarter, Nick. And our bankers, too—they underwrote our IPO and handled a couple of other deals for us. But the quid pro quo was the coverage on the research side. They pumped us up all the time—strong buy here, strong buy there. I mean, it was nuts, Nick. The stock skyrocketed, and guys like me and my board and our CFO—you know, guys with boatloads of stock and options—we made a fucking fortune."

I felt nauseous.

"I don't know how it all got out, Nick—you know, the shit about the financials that *Fortune* got wind of—but, when we had to announce that restatement, the ride was over. I mean, the stock going kaput like that? Seventy percent, for chrissakes! It's a good thing we cleared out beforehand. We all socked away millions, Nick, and most of it's in our wives' and kids' names in offshore accounts. Totally untouchable. So, we looked bad for a while ... big fucking deal. Bottom line, Nick—it's all about bucks."

I bit my lip.

"Well, Duncan, I'm sure everything will work out for you guys," I said, hoping he'd stop right there.

"For the most part. I mean, we've had to make some changes, Nick. We can't report the way we used to, and we've had to make some cuts ... close a couple of offices and fire a bunch of people, but whatever ... that's just the name of the game."

I felt as if I needed a shower.

Just like that, he dismissed the fact that hundreds, if not thousands, of lives had been changed by the snap of his finger. That struck an already frayed nerve, and, as disgusted with the meeting as I had been, at that point, it was time to pull the plug. I asked Duncan if there was anything else he wanted to cover.

"Ah, I almost forgot, Nick. As a token of my appreciation for all of your hard work on the litigation, I wanted to offer you and your colleagues my skybox at Shea Stadium for the Mets-Braves game. It's all yours, Nick, and it'll be fully stocked with plenty of food and liquor and such," he said, as he retrieved an envelope from the inside pocket of his blazer and handed it to me.

"Oh, thank you, Duncan, that's very generous of you," I said. I checked the date on the tickets and then took a quick look at my calendar. I noticed that I had a brief due the following day. "Actually, Duncan, my workload's looking pretty heavy that week, I don't know if ..."

"Say no more, Nick. I want you to have them anyway. I'm sure you'll find a way to make it. Maybe you can rearrange your schedule or something. It's the only good game I've got left, and I really want you to have it, so no need to go any further."

I expressed my gratitude and assured Duncan that the tickets would go to good use.

"I know, son—just enjoy and keep up the good work," he said, patting me on the knee. "We're very fond of you and the firm." I hated to say it, but I had no choice—I had to take one for the "team."

"Well, the feeling's mutual, Duncan." After advising Duncan to meet me at the office at nine the following morning for the deposition, I saw him to the elevator and wished him well. Then I went to the bathroom to douse my face with cold water. Before I returned to my office, I stopped at the kitchen to fix a cup of coffee.

When I returned to my office, I found a free moment to call Tom Dooley and relay my conversation with Dawn; he suggested I forward the information on to the DA's office and wished me luck. Then I called Dawn to confirm the plan. But no one answered, so I left a message on Milena's answering machine.

The morning session of Duncan's deposition was fairly uneventful. The plaintiffs' lawyers spent most of the time covering background material and laying a foundation for the key issues, which I expected them to hit after the lunch break. Duncan and Ted went out for lunch, and I went back to my office to check e-mail and voice mail messages. Dawn returned my call, first apologizing for not getting back to me the night before as she had worked until closing (at ten o'clock). Reluctantly, she was willing to proceed upon our advice to contact the DA's office.

I immediately called the prosecutor on the case, Steve Leventhal.

"So she wants to press charges?" he asked.

"Absolutely. Add it to the list."

"That's fine, but I'll need a sworn statement from someone other than a two-and-a-half-year-old," he advised. My gut told me that the only witnesses were Jimmy and Jordan.

"I'll follow up with Dawn, but I don't think anyone at the daycare center saw it."

"How about street eyewitnesses?"

"Not likely."

"Well, if all you've got is Jordan, then there's nothing left to talk about," he said. I was speechless. "Nick, you there?"

"Yeah, Steve, I hear you. I'll be in touch."

As expected, the afternoon session was far more contentious than the morning. The plaintiffs had landed a few punches, and things got a little testy when they questioned Duncan about their allegations that he had instructed Cindy Holland, his former assistant and mistress, to destroy internal memos sent by upper-level accounting personnel concerning the company's improper overstatement of revenues. Though the memos had been shown to him at the deposition, Duncan denied ever seeing them, let alone having any knowledge of their existence. At other critical moments, either his recollection conveniently failed him or he blamed everything on the auditors. As I sat and listened, I could only wonder what in the world I was doing sitting next to him ... on *his* side of the table.

That evening, I returned to my office and let it all sink in. I sat back in my chair and took a breather. When I came out of my daze and sat back up in front of my desk, I glanced over at the envelope containing Duncan's tickets. As much as I loved the Mets and would find it difficult to pass up an opportunity to catch a game, there was something about the skybox that irked me—it was a symbol of both Duncan's greed and his indifference to ordinary people who worked for him and invested in his company. The skybox reminded me of all the folks like Duncan—people who were too big for their britches and who were above sitting in the stands with everyone else.

That gave me an idea.

The mailroom was located on the bottom of the firm's ten floors, along with other back-office functions, including bookkeeping, technology, and the copy center. I knocked on the steel door and a voice on the other side gave me permission to enter. George, Luis, and Darryl, whose ages ranged from mid-twenties to late thirties, were keeping themselves busy, processing faxes, preparing packages for delivery, and sorting mail for distribution. Each wore a colored button-down and a loud tie, with jeans or khakis, and sneakers. They were on their feet all day, and the firm had no problem relaxing the dress code for these workers. Not that it really mattered, though. They pretty much kept to themselves and interacted mostly with secretaries who came to them to drop off or pick up.

The room was relatively small for three people and all their equipment. Thin commercial-grade carpet, in desperate need of replacement, used to be a chocolate brown, its color having faded over many years. White walls were adorned with office-related information and memos, like the phone directory and firm holiday schedule. A corkboard set in front of a desk was used mostly to pin up photos of kids and significant others. An old portable stereo was tuned to an R&B station, its volume kept low, a stack of assorted CDs set on top. A college textbook was spread open mid-chapter, a well-used spiral notebook beside it.

"Hey, guys," I said as I entered. Each of them greeted me warmly.

"So, Nick, you up for playing ball with us this summer, or what?" asked George, short and thin and still battling acne into his twenties. He wore glasses, the frames thick and black, and a large diamond stud in his left earlobe that shined bright in the light. But neither was enough to detract attention. His kept his dirty blond crew cut tilted downward, as if protecting himself from insensitive stares.

The guys used to play for our basketball team in the lawyers' league until it became strictly professionals only. Large law firms were competitive at everything, even the intramural sports leagues, and, when it got to the point where it was more mailroom versus mailroom, the league adopted the rule. I had played fairly regularly up until a couple of years ago. After developing a good rapport with the guys, they invited me to meet them on weekends for games in their local parks in Brooklyn and the Bronx.

"I don't think so," I said. "My knees don't feel the way they used to."

"That's too bad," said Luis, with a slight shake of the head. His hair, black and spiked, framed a round face. He looked a little out of shape for full court, but apparently that didn't stop him.

"Guys, I'm sorry to interrupt, but can you lower the music for a second? I want to talk to you about something."

"Sure, Nick, what's up?" said Darryl, a tall African-American still built like a big-time power forward. He pushed a large red button, powering off the stereo. They stopped what they were doing, turned, and gave me their full, undivided attention.

"Are you guys interested in going to a Mets-Braves game?" I anticipated an enthusiastic response, as Mets-Braves was always a hot ticket, no matter how bad the Mets were at the time. In unison, they glanced at each other, nodded, shrugged their shoulders, and pursed their lips, as if to say, sure, why not.

"Absolutely," said Darryl, the de facto leader, being the oldest and longest tenured at the firm.

"That's great … because I've got a skybox."

"Get out of town," said Luis, his smile widening in approval.

"That sounds great, Nick," said George. "Thanks a lot."

"No problem, I got it from a client. The game's in two weeks. I don't think I'm going to be able to go, but I want you guys to enjoy it. Invite everyone in the copy center and feel free to bring your kids. I'm sure they'll enjoy it."

"What about our honeys?" said Luis.

"Forget them, man!" said Darryl, scolding.

"No, no, that's okay, they can come too. But there can't be more than fifteen people in the box, so make sure you keep it at that." They all agreed to respect my limitations and thanked me profusely.

"My pleasure," I said, before remembering the best part. "Oh, and one other thing. The box will be fully stocked with food and beer." Now, they *really* seemed excited. They each thanked me again on my way out.

I headed back up to my office.

For a moment there, I felt pretty good about myself.

Chapter 7

The following morning, I arrived at the office and was greeted by a copy of a third-party subpoena the plaintiffs had served in the ATR litigation. They wanted to put Cindy Holland in the hot seat and question her concerning her alleged document destruction at Duncan's behest. Duncan and Cindy had been together for over two years, during which time Duncan had put her up, at the company's expense, in a luxury high-rise condo on the east side. Cindy knew way more than she should have—even more than some of Duncan's top executives knew, and certainly more than the board of directors, who were either in the dark or turned a blind eye to pretty much everything. Duncan had broken it off with Cindy and terminated her employment after his wife found out about their affair and threatened to take him to the cleaners. Despite a generous severance package, Cindy remained bitter, making her a potentially dangerous witness, so, to prevent her from testifying, I had to seek judicial intervention and make a motion to quash the subpoena.

With a court-ordered deadline for the close of fact discovery approaching, before drafting any papers, I sent a letter to the judge, with a copy to plaintiffs' counsel, advising our intentions. As anticipated, the judge set us on an expedited briefing schedule: we had seven days to move, the plaintiffs had seven days to oppose, and we had two days to reply.

Going in, I expected an uphill battle. The discovery rules are liberal and allow a party to request the production of anything "reasonably calculated to lead to the discovery of admissible evidence." In this case, since the plaintiffs had both confidential sources as well as documentary evidence to substantiate their allegations, the chances of the judge quashing the subpoena were slim to none. But we had to give it a shot, so I assigned Tim the task of drafting the papers, which had to be turned around within a couple of days to give me ample time for review.

I spent the rest of the day beneath a mountain of paper. By the time I turned around, it was eight-thirty, and I felt as if I was just getting started. The aroma of freshly brewed coffee seeped into the halls and found its way into my office. Associates swapped menus and placed dinner orders to gear up for a long evening, like stock cars fueling up for the final laps. Although the firm was still very busy at that hour, since it nevertheless felt quieter with the secretaries and support staff gone for the evening, I liked to keep my door open.

I took a quick walk to the kitchen to grab coffee and returned to find a fax concerning the Nelson matter on my chair. It was a letter from Mike Carroll responding to my discovery requests. He claimed his client had no money, that there was nothing other than the Nelsons' joint bank account, and that Jimmy was prepared to testify to that and only that. He also stated that the few documents he had would be forthcoming in the next day or so. From what I knew about Jimmy's business and hard-partying lifestyle, I was far from convinced. I didn't doubt Carroll's integrity, but I was sure that Jimmy had plenty to hide. I immediately sought referrals for top investigators and forensic accountants to sniff out and uncover my hunches.

After tossing Carroll's letter into my inbox, I turned back to ATR. I was studying a document and sipping my coffee when I noticed Phil stroll by and peek his little head into my office. After all these years, he was still conducting his "bed checks." Pulling that shit with associates was bad enough, but I was a partner and should have been exempt.

"Well, this is unusual," said Phil.

Impatient, I felt my face crease in annoyance. My voice hoarse, I responded, "What's unusual?"

"You know, you working late."

"I beg your pardon?"

"Well, you usually leave early, don't you?"

It was as if all of my years of getting in at the crack of dawn and working long past midnight had never even happened.

"No, I don't actually."

"So ... will I see you here this weekend?"

"Nope."

"Ahah, I see ... taking work home with you?"

"Nope."

Phil laughed.

"We must not be keeping you busy enough, Nick."

"I keep myself busy, Phil," I said, sternly. "I make my own schedule, with my own clients. I've been a partner here for over four years now, remember?"

"Uh, Nick ... they're the *firm's* clients, and you're never on your own." I nodded along, feigning acknowledgment.

"Well, then you have yourself a pleasant evening, Nick."

"Thank you."

"Open or closed, Nick?"

"Closed," I said, as Phil left slowly, closing the door behind him.

As I'd conditioned myself over the course of several long years with the firm, I channeled my frustration away to someplace deep in my unconscious to allow me to focus strictly on my work product. I pressed on and worked until after midnight.

The next day, I had to follow up with Dawn to relay my discussion with Steve Leventhal about the Jimmy-and-Jordan incident. I called her on her cell phone, and she answered with a ring of enthusiasm. I told her why I was calling.

"I'm actually in the city right now, not far from you," she said, sounding a bit distant. "I'm about to go to a doctor's appointment."

I asked Dawn about how she was feeling and, after assuring me that everything was fine, she asked me to meet her for coffee.

I knew I could have accomplished the same thing over the phone; I could have told Dawn that I had meetings scheduled and was unable to step out, but I felt as if I desperately needed to see daylight and breathe a bit of fresh air, and, since Tim wasn't going to get me a draft of the motion to quash the Cindy Holland subpoena until the following day, I figured I'd take advantage of an opportunity to step out. I told Dawn it sounded good and asked her where and what time. She suggested a Starbucks near her doctor's office and told me she'd call in a couple of hours.

At least if Phil saw me leaving, I could have legitimately told him I was meeting with a client.

To pass the time, I turned back to my ATR documents. But, just as I was about to get started, someone knocked on the door. I glanced up as Evan poked his head in.

"Hey, buddy," said Evan as he entered and closed the door in one deft motion. He stood tall, fit comfortably into sharp, fashionable suits, and could easily pass for a high-powered Hollywood talent agent. He had brown eyes flecked with hazel, an angular jaw, and thick, black hair carefully parted sideways with grays around the temples that would only add distinction down the road. Evan carried himself with an air of self-confidence, but was the furthest from cocky.

"Hey, what's up?"

"Same old, same old," he said, taking a seat in one of the two matching desk chairs across from me.

"How does Jenny like camp?"

"Loves it," he said, smiling with satisfaction. "Kid's having the time of her life."

"Awesome—when's visiting day?"

"This weekend," he said as his face turned glum. "But I just found out from Phil that I have to oversee a brief that's due on Monday."

I shook my head in disgust.

"So bang it out."

"I can't—I've got other shit on my plate."

"Can't you get an associate started?" I asked. He shook his head.

"Everyone's buried."

"So, what ... you're just not going?"

"I'm winging it," he said. "Hopefully I'll get it far enough along that I can afford to be out for a day."

"Did you tell Phil?" I asked. Evan nodded.

"And what did he say?"

"'Oh, you don't have to go to that. Your wife can go,'" he recounted, rolling his eyes with contempt. Coming from Phil, I wasn't surprised, but was nonetheless appalled. Evan loathed being a subordinate more than anyone I knew. He hated waking up every morning and living his life on other people's terms.

"It's nice, isn't it, how they make family-related decisions for us around here?" I said. Evan shook his head in disgust.

"Ask not what you did for me five minutes ago ... but what you can do for me now," he said, slowly, for effect. I smiled in appreciation and then asked how Julie was taking it. A frown set into his features.

"It ain't pretty."

"She's not used to this by now?"

"Do you ever get used to it?"

I felt bad for Evan. On one level, I had gotten used to this bullshit. But I didn't have a wife and kids, so I couldn't completely relate, as much as I wanted to.

"You can't miss Jenny's weekend," I said. "Tell Phil I'll handle the brief—*seriously*."

"No, no, no," he said. "You've got enough on your plate as it is."

"Whatever—what's another project?" I said. "It's not like I have people at home waiting for me."

Evan began to slowly shake his head. His mouth opened as if he were about to say, But why does that matter? You have a life, too. Then he paused and gathered his thoughts, as if something had been building up.

"The last thing you need is another project," he said, pausing, his expression and tone marked with concern. "I've been meaning to tell you this, but you don't look so hot, bro. Take a vacation … get away and rest."

"Don't worry about me, I'm fine—I'll get it done," I said, unconvincingly. Evan's face clouded with guilt.

"I don't know," he said, slowly shaking his head. I started to get a little testy.

"Relax, I'm fine … *really*."

Evan thought to himself for a moment and then said that he would consider taking me up on it. "No, you *will* take me up on it," I insisted. "Don't worry about it."

He finally relented, nodding. "That would be great, buddy. I appreciate it."

We spent the next few minutes talking about our passion, the entertainment practice. One of my clients, an alternative rock band, had just hit the top of the Billboard charts, and their label opened up negotiations for a new contract. On the film side, Evan had been retained by a hot new writer whose first screenplay was drawing the attention of several "A-list" directors. Things were happening, and our discussion left Evan in better spirits.

"All right, man, let me get cracking," Evan said as he rose from his chair and reached across the desk for a hard, sideways hand slap that ended with clenched fists. He looked me in the eyes and studied my face for a moment, as if to reinforce his concerns. As he approached the door on his way out, I told him to send over whatever I would need for the brief. He twisted his head around just enough to make eye contact.

"I will, thanks," he said, turning toward the door but then back again. "Oh, by the way, speaking of new projects, how's that pro bono case coming?"

"It's interesting," I said, my tone lowered. "Got another minute?"

Evan nodded. I waved him back in, and, after he returned to his chair, I gave him a quick rendition of the basic facts of the case, with extra time dedicated to Dawn and Jordan.

"I don't know, man," I said, casually, "there's something about her … it's like I can't seem to get her out of my mind."

"Whoa, wait a second," he said, making the time-out sign like a referee. Digging his elbow into the armrest of his chair, Evan cradled his chin with his hand and closed his eyes. He left me for a moment of deep reflection, as if thinking back to something he once learned and digging it out of the archives as it unexpectedly became relevant again. He then opened his eyes and folded his hands in his lap.

"You said this is a domestic relations matter?" he said, eyes squinted with hope that I'd answer in the negative. I nodded, and he quickly responded in a troubled voice.

"Dude, this woman's your client—you know the limits in these types of cases," he admonished.

I nodded. "So, what's your point?" I said, shrugging it off.

He proceeded to scrutinize me. "Has anything happened?"

"What?!" I said, my eyes squinted, brows furrowed. "What the hell are you talking about? *No!*" I said in a what-are-you-crazy? tone, my forehead creased. He asked me if I had taken her out, and I paused.

"No, Your Honor, I haven't." We exchanged a subtle look of amusement. "But I'm meeting her for coffee in a little while." His chuckle rose to a nervous laugh.

"To talk about what?" he asked with a cynical smirk, like a police detective who didn't trust his suspect.

I responded with a bit of condescension. "Uh ... her case?"

"He-yeah, right, and what else?" Evan stared at me with waiting silence, waving his hand in a circular motion as if he expected more.

I shrugged and casually responded, "I have no idea," in a way that suggested I was amenable to the subject matter of our meeting going beyond business.

Evan leaned forward and lowered his voice. "You sure that's a good idea?" he asked, his tone coolly disapproving. I shifted my position from reclining to upright, getting serious.

"Look, I'm not sure of anything anymore," I said, with a bit of a lost-soul quality, "but putting that to the side ... what, when you meet with clients, you never get sidetracked with nonbusiness-related conversation? What are you getting all bent out of shape about?"

Evan nodded, acknowledging the merits of my point; he was about to interject and, without a doubt, draw a distinction between the situations, when I cut him off.

"All right, I know what you're alluding to," I said, nodding, "and I appreciate your concern, but I would never step out of bounds, okay?"

He stared at me with an affronted frown, distrusting.

Now, I was starting to get pissed. "Why are you looking

at me like I'm some kind of womanizer? You know I'm not like that."

"Yes, I know you're not like that. But I also know you're looking to meet someone, and I'm sensing that you might dig this chick. I'm worried that it might cloud your judgment, that's all."

I shook my head in dismissal. "It won't, I promise."

"You sure?" he said, easing up a bit.

"Yes, I'm sure—I'm a big boy."

"Okay," Evan said, nodding assuredly as if the issue was laid to rest. He rose and headed out.

"Remember," I said as he opened the door, "send over those papers."

"I will," he said. "Thanks again."

Before exiting, he pointed at me like Uncle Sam in an I–Want–You–For–U.S.Army poster and counseled me one last time: "Be careful."

"Taxi!" I yelled, waving my arm after spotting a cab with its open-for-business light illuminated. The cab made enemies as it darted across Fifth Avenue to reel me in. I told the driver where to and then slammed the door shut. He activated the meter and headed downtown. The driver's body odor was totally repugnant—as if he hadn't showered in weeks—so I rolled down the windows all the way on both sides for ventilation.

When I arrived, Dawn was seated at a table in a quiet corner. Our eyes met, and she greeted me with a glowing smile. Her hair was down—smooth and silky. She wore a pink, lightweight sweater set with white stretch Capri pants and matching pink sandals. As beautiful as she was, she carried herself as if she had no idea.

"Hi," she said with a smile as she rose out of her chair to greet me.

"Hi, Dawn, how are you?" I asked with my best amalgam of warmth and professionalism.

"Fine, thanks," she replied, smiling. I rested my briefcase next to my chair and asked Dawn if she wanted anything. She said black coffee would be great and went into her purse to find money, but I insisted on paying. I went off, ordered our coffees, fixed mine, and returned. At first, we sat awkwardly facing each other, carefully sipping our drinks. I broke the silence by bringing up the case—my discussion with Steve Leventhal, and Mike Carroll's letter concerning Jimmy's finances. Though looking directly at me as I spoke, Dawn responded with a bland half-smile. She looked nervous and uptight.

"Hey, everything's going to work out."

"I hope so," she said, glum. We stared across the table at each other before I asked about Jordan.

"Things have been difficult with him," she said, her eyes downcast. "He's been a total nightmare. He used to hate his father, was scared to death of him. But ever since Jimmy showed up with the lollipop, he's been acting out constantly, screaming that he wants to see his daddy. It's been one meltdown after the other. It's really upsetting."

Dawn's eyes darkened with pain; a glazed look of despair spread over her face. I felt responsible, as if I'd just unstitched a wound that was still fresh.

"It's amazing," she said. "No matter how bad a parent might be, kids will always fight for his love."

"I think a parent's love is one of life's basic needs—right up there with food, water, and shelter," I said. "For a boy, though, a father figure is critical."

Dawn asked me if I was close with my father, and I told her that he was deceased. She looked at me with pity and gave her condolences.

"No, no, that's okay," I said, smiling. Taking me by surprise, she asked about him. I appreciated her interest.

"Eddie O'Reilly. To this day, the greatest man I have ever known." Dawn nodded with a wry smile and asked me to tell her more. I talked about my family, starting with my grandparents, who had come over from Ireland and settled in Queens and, with very little, managed to get by and provide a happy home life. My parents met in high school, and, after my mother graduated from college, they got married.

I told Dawn about what my father did for a living. She continued listening intently as I described his career with Bailey's, the old chain of five-and-dime stores. He had started there as a stock boy and, over time, worked his way up to manager of one of their biggest stores. My father had a knack for merchandising; he knew how to sell and really understood what customers needed. Dad was a company guy; always carrying the company tote bag and donning the company golf shirt and cap. Dawn seemed impressed when I told her that my father's store was one of the country's top performers.

"Eventually, they promoted him to branch manager, then district manager, and ultimately to the corporate office as a consultant which, believe it or not, was the worst thing that could have happened to him."

"Why?"

"Well, as you know, they wound up closing the old five-and-dimes. The company didn't see any future in them anymore, so it shifted its focus to more youthful athletic apparel stores. By this point, my father was in his fifties, and, with the new strategy, they had no use for an old-school retailer, so they threw him out like an old, worn out pair of shoes."

"That's terrible." I nodded in appreciation and continued.

"It gets worse. Even after closing the five-and-dimes, the company was still doing poorly, so they didn't want to have to pay him and his contemporaries their accrued pension benefits. The only way to achieve that was to terminate for cause as opposed to just laying off."

Dawn looked at me with concern and asked what happened.

"They made up false allegations that my dad was leaking inside information to an industry analyst who was issuing 'sell' reports on the company."

"Oh my God, that's awful," said Dawn, her brows drawn together in a pitiful frown. "These companies will do anything just to save a few pennies." I nodded, agreeing.

"What's so ridiculous about it is that everyone else on Wall Street was slamming Bailey's too. Except, in my father's case, the company knew that one of the retail analysts reporting on the company was an old friend of his, so they pulled my father's phone records from the office and saw that certain calls had been made to the analyst from my father's phone line. But so what? My father talked to a lot of his friends from the office. Everyone does. That was all they had, mere phone calls. They couldn't even say what was said on those calls."

"Did you ask your dad?"

"Of course. They talked about baseball and their families. My father was like a Boy Scout, Dawn. He never stepped out of line nor did he ever say a bad thing about anyone in his life. Until this happened. The worst part about it was the undignified way they did it. They called in a uniformed security guard to watch him remove his personal belongings from his desk and then escort him out of the building. Now, the man that everyone in the company loved and respected would forever be branded.

"He was never the same. Just like that, everything he had worked for was taken away—everything from his pension to his dignity to his manhood. And believe me when I tell you, his dignity was much more important to him than money."

Her brows drew together in a sorrowful expression. She asked if there was anything he could have done, and I explained that he had consulted with a few attorneys, but they either weren't interested or were too costly. At that time,

I had just started working and had neither the money nor the experience to help him, so he let it go.

"Did he try going back to work?" she asked.

I nodded, brooding. "He was able to pick up a couple of temp jobs here and there through contacts in the industry, but, at his stage of the game, it was impossible to find full-time work."

"So what did he do after that?"

"Nothing. And being unemployed while my mother went to work every day made things even worse. Then one night he went to sleep and never woke up. Cardiac arrest."

"I'm so sorry," she said, with sympathy.

I responded with an appreciative nod. "You know, it wasn't until recently that I realized that it's these corporate scoundrels who ruined my father's life that I now make my living representing. I became a lawyer to make a lot of money so that I wouldn't end up in Dad's position. It's like that's all I thought about when I joined the firm. It was just the money."

"Nick, you shouldn't feel guilty about what you do."

I let her point hang and continued to vent. "I just wanted to focus on being great at whatever it was I was doing. When I joined the firm, litigation was hot, and they needed lawyers in that department, so that's where I was assigned. It could have been anything—corporate, real estate, bankruptcy, whatever. For me, it was litigation. And, after a few years of doing nothing but that, and enjoying some success, I fell into it, and that's where I stayed. I'm telling you, if my father knew who I was representing, he'd probably turn over in his grave." A humiliating and deflated feeling swept over me. I could feel my face flush.

"I'm sure your father would be very proud of you," she said. If we had been on a date, she might have reached across the table and taken my hand.

We were silent for a few moments and took time to sip

our coffees. Then I looked down beside the table and noticed a copy of Harper Lee's *To Kill a Mockingbird* jutting out of her bag. I pointed to the book and asked about it. She looked down and then back at me.

"I love it. Milena and I are in a book club—we just started it, and I can't put it down."

I asked her about the book club, and she told me that, once a month, a group of women get together at someone's home, have drinks and hors d'oeuvres, and discuss the selection.

"I've always loved reading fiction. At first I turned to it as a form of escape, you know? I'd just close my bedroom door, lie in bed, and lose myself in other people's worlds. Those are the stories I enjoy the most—the ones where you get to see the world through someone else's eyes and join them on their journey as they come of age, share in their triumphs, feel their pain. Like Scout in *Mockingbird*."

I gazed at Dawn with admiration. Then she lifted her finger, making an oh-just-a-second gesture, as if a thought had come to her that she didn't want to forget. She reached for the book, removed it from her bag, and quickly thumbed her way through, searching for a certain passage. When she finally found the spot, she smiled with satisfaction, eyebrows arched.

"Better yet," she said with excitement in her eyes, "as Atticus Finch would say, 'You never really understand a person until you consider things from his point of view, until you climb inside of his skin and walk around in it.'" She looked up from the book and smiled at me.

Dawn's resourcefulness was impressive ... the way she experienced life and faraway places through reading. This hardscrabble Brooklyn girl was well-traveled ... much more than I.

"You know, I think I read it in high school, and, frankly, I don't really remember much about it. But let's talk about it when you're finished. Maybe you'll jog my memory, and we can have a meaningful discussion." Dawn's smile widened in approval at my suggestion that we reserve time in the future for conversations not related to the case. She told me she would like that. I then noticed her gently stroking the brim of her cup; it was totally subconscious, and I thought I'd once heard something about the significance of that sort of action—that it was a good thing ... that it spoke of attraction.

"Me too," I replied. Dawn asked me about what I liked to read, and I told her that, with work, I didn't have time to read fiction, though I used to enjoy thrillers. We continued talking about books, and Dawn revealed to me that she wanted to write someday. I encouraged her to go for it, that it's never too late to start. She shrugged matter-of-factly.

"I want to resolve this mess first, get Jimmy out of our lives, and then I feel like we'll be able to move forward. Nothing good can happen until this is behind us." I nodded and assured Dawn that such a day would come. Her eyes met mine, and I noted resolve ... and something else I couldn't describe. "I trust you, Nick," she said, confident.

That was it. Dawn and Jordan's welfare were in my hands, and she had faith. I would climb the highest mountain before I'd let them down. The conversation about my father flashed back through my head, and I vowed to myself right then and there that I wouldn't let another person I cared for suffer as he had.

I brought the conversation back to a more mundane level by asking Dawn if she planned to finish pharmacy school.

"I hope so," she said, pausing. "I really love being a mother, though. In that way, I feel very fulfilled." The way Dawn garnered satisfaction and reward from motherhood warmed me. There was so much to Dawn beneath the surface ... so much that I wanted to learn about.

"Can I ask you something?"

"Sure," she said, as if I could ask her anything.

"Why Jimmy?"

Dawn took in a deep breath and exhaled, readying herself for a response.

"Milena told me not to get involved with him—that he was nothing but trouble. But he showed up at a time when I really needed someone to love me, you know? And, believe it or not, at the time, he was very, very sweet. It's so pathetic, but at first, I thought the two of us were like soul mates who had been put together to help heal each other's wounds. I wanted to take care of him, save him, and help him become the great husband and father that I'd been hoping for. I had a fantasy that we'd have this normal, happy family life ... something neither of us had growing up."

"The way you felt was perfectly normal—and having a healthy family life is more than just possible. You just need to find the right person. You shouldn't give up on your dream," I said, realizing at that moment that I was better at advising others than I was myself.

Before we knew it, an hour and a half had passed, and what remained of my coffee was ice cold. It felt like the right time to call it an evening.

"It's a nice night. Feel like taking a stroll?" she asked, with a smile that was eager.

"In your skin? Anytime," I said in jest. She picked up on the *Mockingbird* reference immediately, and amusement flickered in her eyes.

"Slow down, counselor, we just met," she said, playfully. "But you can walk me to the subway if that's okay?"

"You got it."

I left Dawn in good spirits. Truth be told, though, the harder I tried to ignore my desires, the more they persisted. I dismissed my cynical inner voice in favor of my feelings for Dawn that I allowed to surface ... in favor of the sense of fulfillment and satisfaction that our colloquy engendered— the way we connected, the way she looked at me, and the serenity of her company. These were memories that I wanted to cling to as one would a life preserver when trapped in a violent tidal wave. My heart swelled with a feeling that I never knew existed.

For the remainder of the evening, my thoughts were bent on Dawn, and I even fantasized about her being my girlfriend. I pictured us strolling through Central Park in the height of autumn, our arms clasped around each other's waists. Clear blue skies hovered above. Stone-paved walkways were partially blanketed with leaves; we were surrounded by a pretty fusion of reds and browns. The trees, their leaves fluttered by a soft breeze, thrived and provided a colorful canopy as we lowered our arms and joined hands, engaged in deep conversation. We would stop sometimes to kiss. I conjured up images of how excited we'd be to introduce one another to our friends and families. We were a couple and wanted the whole world to know it. I could see us staying in on Sundays, curled up on the couch in our pajamas, with coffee and the newspaper.

With every thought, I felt my face spread into a smile.

But Dawn was my client, so my fantasy would have to remain just that.

Chapter 8

As promised, I spent all day Saturday of that weekend covering for Evan while he was away visiting Jenny at camp. The brief was in great shape, and all Evan needed was a few hours on Sunday to finalize.

On Sunday, in an attempt to recharge my batteries, I slept in and woke up when my body decided it was good and ready. After a long, hot shower, I threw on an old comfy T-shirt, tan knee-length cargo shorts, and flip-flops. My Saturday *Times* was two inches thick (three including Sunday) and perfectly intact. I grabbed myself a bagel and a large iced coffee and picked a nice shaded spot beneath a tree in the center of Central Park. I relished my time alone, and even nodded off for about an hour.

Later in the afternoon, I called Mom to check in and confirm that we were on for dinner. I told her I hoped I'd make it out by a little after six.

"No problem, honey, don't rush. Just be careful."

After changing into jeans and a golf shirt, I left to meet my mother. I exited my building to the sight of a string of horse-drawn carriages along the perimeter of Central Park South. Tourists were lined deep and looked anxious to ride. One of the horses absorbed my attention; it looked weary from a long day, its hooves beaten like a tattered pair of sneakers. As a young couple climbed into the carriage, the horse's jockey-sized master smacked it as if to inject just enough life to earn his fee. I had to turn away, heading for my garage.

With typical Long Island traffic, it took me well over an hour to get home. I veered my black SUV off of Sunrise Highway, sloped downward, and proceeded on beneath the Long Island Rail Road tracks to the north and predominantly blue-collar side of my hometown. I continued on for about a half a mile, slowed up on the approach to Riverton Street, and turned left.

Despite a fair amount of turnover in favor of younger families, the neighborhood's predominantly Irish and Italian demographic remained the same. It was safe, and folks came and went in peace without disturbance.

I took my time traveling down the street, my elbow sticking out the open window. The sun, still going strong at that hour, beamed off the windshields of parked cars. I stared out, my eyes darting from side to side as if watching a tennis match to cover both sides. The block was lined with modest-sized homes, each with a small lawn, swimming pool too big for the backyard, and a one-car garage. Most were kept up nicely, with impeccably sheared lawns. Stone-paved walkways led to front porches, American flags hung from poles affixed diagonally to the railings; doors with shiny brass plates were flanked by mailboxes that bore the owners' names and house numbers. The block's aesthetic pleasure, however, was blemished every few houses or so by a house that was a disgrace to the neighborhood—a dark mole on a pretty face. These houses were totally dilapidated—shingles rotted, waterlogged newspapers accumulated by the entrance, and grass growing out like hedgerows. The properties were surrounded by rusted fences and guarded by wild, salivating Dobermans. Beware of Dog signs and NRA membership stickers were conspicuous from the curb.

Young kids played outside, leaving me nostalgic for memories of my friends; departing the dinner table early for stickball in the street; chalking the pavement with makeshift bases to the chagrin of Mrs. Hausman across the street, always in her purple housedress with her needlepoint; building go-carts and racing them recklessly down the block; the surge of excitement brought on by the around-the-corner ding-a-ling-a-ling of the Good Humor truck, as I scurried to plead for money ('Hurry, hurry, we're gonna' miss him, Dad!'), and then my invariable dilemma: a toasted almond bar or the classic King Cone? And finally being old enough to ride our bikes into town for pizza and video games.

Good stuff.

Thanks to Mom, the house was as beautiful as it had always been. The neutral blend of tan aluminum siding and a freshly watered bed of hunter green grass was brightened by an array of colorful flowers and small, round bushes sheared as artfully as a show dog. My old basketball hoop was just that and looked desperate for a comeback, the dark pole slightly discolored, the once-bright orange rim closer to brown and without a net.

I rolled up, pulled into the driveway, and found Mom relaxing on the porch, cross-legged on the cushioned wicker bench, absorbed in a paperback. She immediately removed her thin reading glasses, inserted a placeholder, and closed her book, carefully setting it down behind her along with her glasses. I killed the engine and stepped out of the car to the refreshing, suburban scent of summer and sweet sounds of birds chirping above. A group of ten-year-olds played two-on-two next door.

With a spring in her gait, Mom walked briskly to greet me. At sixty, she looked great. Her hair, a rich, strawberry blond, side parted and falling just below her chin, framed a natural, rosy complexion augmented by light eyeliner and a soft lipstick. About five-foot-four, she was slender and graceful. Her attire—a soft white cotton tee and light beige, cotton twill pants—was both casual and stylish. She looked comfortable in white canvas walking shoes.

"Hi, sweetheart," she said, her familiar there's-my-pride-and-joy smile spread wide. I bent slightly as she opened her arms and clenched me for an extra long hug as if I had just stepped off a plane, and she was relieved that I had arrived safe and sound. She pulled back, clasped my head with soft, manicured hands, and kissed me twice, setting me free after checking my cheek for lipstick.

I complimented Mom on how good the house looked, particularly the landscaping and floral arrangement. She took a lot of pride in it.

"Oh, thanks, honey," she said, as if, up until that moment, she had been unsure.

"Sorry, I'm late, Mom. The traffic was brutal."

"Late?" she said. "I was expecting you to call and say you were stuck in the office and weren't coming at all. You're actually bright and early."

"Yeah, well, I'm working on that."

"Good, you should … such a shame the way they work you to death over there," she said, shaking her head with a resentful frown. The stone path cut through the lawn and took us to the ground-level, sheltered porch. I opened the screen door for Mom, followed her inside, and was welcomed home by the distinctive aroma of home cooking. The scent was so good, it set my stomach demanding instant gratification.

"I guess we're eating in?"

"Yeah, why not?" she said. "I figured it's been a while since you've had a home-cooked meal, and I thought it would be nice if we spent some time here in the house."

"I agree—sounds and smells great."

I stepped into the foyer onto an old welcome mat. Despite Mom's repeated attempts to refinish the bleached hardwood floor, the accumulation of many years of scuffs and scrapes was palpable. And I had to take credit for most of them, having subjected the floor to cleats, roller-skates, and other boyhood paraphernalia, not to mention boyish enthusiasm.

Straight ahead, twin louver doors opened to a modest-sized kitchen. I went to the refrigerator and grabbed a Bud, removing the cap with two twists. Mom didn't drink beer, but always had it on hand when I came over. Bud had also been Dad's favorite.

From the kitchen, five steps led down to a small, carpeted den, with a leather couch, entertainment center, and brick fireplace. I stepped down for a quick peek at the den and took a seat and relaxed. The absence of Dad's chair, now ensconced in my apartment, was apparent, evoking an eerie, uncomfortable feeling that stirred me. A lot of man-to-man talks had gone down in that room, and there definitely had been some good ones. Like how to handle the school bully, and how I wouldn't get him to back off and respect me until I knocked him down. And the one about the man with no shoes, who felt sorry for himself until he saw a man with no feet—a story to help me keep things in perspective and appreciate what I had. But then there were certain lessons on old-school principles of hard work and loyalty that, looking back, sounded more like boilerplate rhetoric that could have been lifted from one of his old employee handbooks. They almost sounded memorized, like answers I practiced at home the night before a quiz. Though, in the end, those lessons were probably more for Dad's edification than mine, back then they impressed upon me just the same.

On the other hand, I remember the way Dad loved Mom, how committed they were to each other. I had vivid recollections of long, silent stares across the room with smiles in their eyes; impromptu gatherings in each others' arms when, at that moment, no matter what was happening, the world stopped and they were alone. I recall looking up from my piano and opening my eyes, surprised to find them dancing. And they weren't even looking over at me as though they were there to enjoy the moment because it was their son who was playing. I may as well have been an old forty-five spinning on Dad's vintage turntable.

Indeed, of all the topics Dad sat me down to talk about, his love for my mother—their marriage and dedication to each other—was the one he never preached about. Not even a single word.

Yet it turned out to be his greatest lesson.

I quickly returned to the kitchen. Mom, wrapped in a flowery apron and wearing matching hand mitts, was at work in the preparation area, which was decorated with oak cabinets and a beige-tiled backsplash. A cushioned banquette provided a plush alternative to three wooden chairs that matched a square table. Double windows overlooked a tiny backyard; a door opened to a small wood deck that held a gas barbeque and an old set of outdoor furniture.

Mom removed the hot tray of roast from the oven and set it on the granite countertop.

"Relax, honey," she said. "Dinner will be ready in just a minute."

From the kitchen, I walked through an entryway into the adjoining dining room. A rectangular, wooden table with a thick oak top was finished in a dark brown and illuminated by an old chandelier. I sat at the head of the table—one of the two places that had already been set. My mother's collection of figurines and china resided behind glass on four shelves of a brown hutch that dated back well over thirty years. I had been staring into it for a moment when Mom emerged from the kitchen with our feast: pot roast, sweet potatoes, and steamed asparagus. Then she took a seat. Before we started to eat, she looked me over long and hard.

"Do you feel okay?" she asked, her eyes sharp and assessing.

Feeling sluggish, I responded unconvincingly. "I guess so. Why?"

"What do you mean you guess so?" she responded. Using the arms of her chair to push herself up, she rose and approached me. Just as she had when I was a child, she placed her hand on my forehead and then kissed it, as if taking my temperature.

"Nickie, you don't look well," she said. "Did you lose weight?"

"I don't know ... maybe a little."

"Something's not right, honey. I want you to go to the doctor."

"Mom, I don't need to go to the doctor," I said impatiently.

"Oh no? When was the last time you went?" she asked, her tone carrying an unusual force. I paused, feigning contemplation.

"I don't remember," I said, looking up slightly.

"Who's your internist?" she asked, like an unrelenting trial lawyer in the heat of an intense cross. There was no doubt I had inherited my lawyering skills from Mom. Knowing full well what my answer was, Mom could definitely frame an argument, but only did so if and when she had to.

"I don't have one."

"I know you don't," she said. "I'll get a referral for you, and we'll make the appointment together."

"That's okay. I promise I'll make an appointment."

"Don't just promise to make an appointment—promise you'll go, and *soon*."

"All right, all right," I said, surrendering. We were silent for a moment.

"Can we talk about something else ... please?"

"Of course." We spent a few moments filling our plates.

"So, what's new, Nickie?" Mom asked.

I told her about my pro bono project—a general synopsis

of the case and a little bit about Dawn. She thought it sounded interesting and was happy that I was doing public interest work.

"And I think I kinda like her," I said, trying to slip it in there subtly. We were silent for a moment.

"Really?" she asked, excitedly.

"Uh huh," I said in a whisper, fretfully drenching a slab of meat in the blotch of ketchup on my plate. Mom looked as if she had something to say, but was taking a moment to consider the most tactful way. She scooped up a forkful of sweet potato, raised it to her mouth, and turned to me. She squinted inquisitively and asked, "Is that okay?"

I quickly shook my head. "Not until the case is resolved."

Mom gave me an oh-well-so-much-for-that look, as if she was foolish for getting her hopes up high, and said, "And we know how long *those* can take."

"What do you want from me?" I asked, wearily. Mom set her fork down and turned to me.

"I want you to be happy, honey. I want you to find some balance in your life and meet someone special," she said, holding my gaze in earnest and lowering her tone to something a little more sympathetic. "You've spent all these years alone, sacrificing your life for your career. None of it will mean anything if you don't have anyone to share it with. You're thirty-six, sweetie, and I know I'm your mother, and I'm a little biased, but for a catch like you, you're long overdue."

I nodded and then took a moment to absorb what she had said.

"Mom, I know how you feel, and I appreciate it … sincerely," I said, turning back to devouring my dinner as if I hadn't eaten in days. We stayed silent for a couple of minutes and enjoyed the meal.

"As always, you outdid yourself. Everything's delicious."

"Oh, thanks," she said, with a shake of her head and flap of her hand as if she'd whipped it up in five minutes. As much as I loved being able to eat out anywhere I wanted, I always find a home-cooked meal has a distinct taste that no restaurant can replicate.

Throughout the rest of dinner, I couldn't help venting about my work issues: Phil, the hours, my clients ... Phil (or, as Mom had dubbed him, "That Mean Little Man"). Mom was easy to talk to and always there to listen, so every now and again when I needed to get "stuff" off my chest, she was the go-to person.

"All right, enough about me and my bullshit," I said. "What's doing with you?" After running through the same-old-same-old (her job at school, her friends, the neighborhood), we fell into a discussion about Dad ... about good times, and certain quirks.

"He would have been so proud of you, honey ... how great you're doing," she said, a look of sorrow passing over her features. Mom started to get a little emotional and got up to clear the table. I rose to help, grabbed the large silver tray of leftover roast, and followed her into the kitchen.

"Oh, just leave everything, I'll take care of it," Mom insisted. "I'd rather you sit and play something for me." I said I would after I helped her clear the table.

"Okay, thanks, but just keep your fork," she said.

I liked the sound of that—it meant something sweet was next.

I walked into the living room. The half-moon sectional couch was covered in a soft ivory fabric. A glass coffee table was set atop a rug. The table featured a series of black leather-bound scrapbooks that chronicled our family history. A marble buffet against the wall displayed framed photos. Potted plants, large and small, were ubiquitous. The baby grand, made in walnut, sat adjacent to windows that faced out into the street.

I sat down and took a shot at Rachmaninov's Piano

Concerto Number Two while Mom finished up in the kitchen. After fumbling a few times, I switched over to some light jazz that, with my limited practice schedule, was a more relaxing no-brainer. Over the sound of the music and running water from the sink, Mom asked if I wanted coffee.

"High test?" I yelled above the music, not missing a note.

"If that's what you'd like, sure."

Just as I was finishing a tune, Mom brought out her famous homemade apple pie and a strawberry shortcake from my favorite local bakery and set them on the table. She made two more trips for plates and mugs and a carafe. I got up and joined her, excited as a little kid.

"Are you trying to fatten me up here, Mom?"

"Yes, actually, I am."

On Monday morning, I received a call from Mom with the name and number of a doctor in Manhattan that a friend had recommended. After confirming that he accepted my insurance, I made an appointment and called Mom back to assure her that I had done so.

I then spent a good part of the day fielding calls from some of my other clients, both corporate and entertainment. I prepared a letter to Mike Carroll proposing a handful of dates for Jimmy's deposition. Then I turned back to the ATR litigation and took a look at Tim's draft of the motion to quash the Cindy Holland subpoena. Other than a couple of typos, it looked fine. We seemed to have pretty good authority for our position. I called Tim and asked him to join me in my office.

Tim's office was right down the hall, and he arrived at my office in less than thirty seconds, legal pad and pen in hand. "Hi," he said, smiling. I knew that, beneath the feigned enthusiasm, was an overworked, sleep-deprived associate. Like the rest of us, he had too much on his plate, but somehow got the work done anyway. I told him that the brief was in great shape and ready to go. He graciously accepted the positive reinforcement, which was rarely dispensed at the firm.

"Listen, we're not going to get the plaintiffs' opposition until Monday, so go ahead and take this weekend off, okay?"

As much as I knew Tim liked me and believed that I wouldn't sell him out, I was still a partner, and he was still an associate, and he clearly felt awkward about answering that kind of question candidly. He paused, and his mouth hung open with an I-don't-know-what-to-say expression. It was summer, and I insisted that he take the time. He smiled.

"Thanks a lot, Nick," he said, rising out of his chair and heading to the door.

Later on in the day, I received a call from Will Schmidt's secretary.

"Nick, Mr. Schmidt would like to see you," she said, with a wisp of a British accent. Will's office was down the hall, and I was there in less than thirty seconds. Like Tim, I stood in the doorway, at attention. My favorite person, Phil, was also there to greet me. They wanted a status report on my pro bono matter.

"Nick, my boy, come on in," said Will.

"Hi," I said as I entered.

"Have a seat, son," said Will, as I sat down next to my good pal.

"So, tell us about your experience so far, Nick," said Will. I proceeded to tell them about the case, filling them in with a brief synopsis and certain issues that I had been faced with.

"Sounds like things are progressing nicely," said Phil, low and monotone, looking down in his lap. I agreed.

"Nick, we're going to send an e-mail memorandum around to all attorneys in the firm about this. We want everyone to know about what a great job you're doing, and, hopefully, we'll inspire a few folks to do the same," said Will.

"But not *too* many," said Phil, looking up at Will for approval. They both laughed. I forged a placating smile.

"I'm also planning on having someone from both the *Law Journal* and *The American Lawyer* come down to meet with you. This is big stuff for the firm, Nick. *Big stuff!*" said Will.

"Wait a second," I said, shaking my head with disapproval. "I'm not comfortable with that."

"What do you mean?" said Phil, sternly.

"Just what I said. This case is a domestic dispute that involves the welfare of a child. And it's also not what I'm supposed to be getting out of this."

"First of all, Nick, it's not about what *you're* supposed to be getting out of this. It's about what the *firm* is supposed to be getting out of this. And publicity ... *good* publicity ... is what we want," said Phil, snarling.

"Nick, what's the problem?" said Will, more calmly, sitting up straight, folding his arms, and setting them down, looking across the desk at me.

"I'm just not comfortable with this, Will. I don't like it," I said firmly, standing my ground. Phil was getting even more agitated, but Will shooed him off. Will had Phil to kick around, Phil had me, I guess I had my associates (though I didn't view my relationship with them that way), and even my associates had their minions who had their minions, and so on and so forth all the way down the totem pole.

"We won't allow any names to be released, Nick," said Will. "They'll be kept confidential."

"It doesn't matter. This woman is our client, Will, and, with all due respect to you both and the firm, I think it's in poor taste. She put our trust in us, and I don't think it's appropriate to be using her for publicity, nor do I think she would appreciate it."

"Oh, she reads the *Law Journal*?" said Phil condescendingly, smirking. "Where do you think this blurb is going, Nick? The

Post? We're talking to the *legal* press here. She'll never even know about it."

"Well, Tom Dooley will know about it, and I don't know that he wouldn't say anything."

"All right, all right, Nick, I won't make any arrangements yet," said Will. "But I would like you to give it some more thought, ponder our position more carefully, and perhaps reconsider."

"No problem," I said, quickly rising out of my chair, anxious to split.

"Oh, and again, nice job," said Will.

Phil didn't say a word.

I stormed back to my office, my footsteps roaring down the hallway. After slamming the door, I sat back in my chair, stared at the ceiling, and tried clearing my head, but to no avail.

I had to move Dawn's case along. The longer it lingered, the more likely this whole PR thing would take on a life of its own, so I sat and brainstormed for a while and considered what I could do to shake things up. How could I build leverage to push Jimmy's back to the wall to force the most favorable resolution for Dawn within the quickest time frame? What could I threaten? As far as jail, what we had on Jimmy was already out there, so, unless he slipped up again—but this time, with concrete evidence to back it up—that component of the matter was what it was.

Given the difficulty of prosecuting criminals, I had to assume the criminal charges couldn't stick. And I was confident that Jimmy had no interest whatsoever in gaining custody of Jordan (and even if he did, he had no chance of winning). So, actually, this case was ultimately no different than any other civil litigation and would come down to one thing: money.

Tom had given me access to his agency's online repository of legal documents and forms, so, to set the wheels in motion

I logged on and started perusing with the hope that I might generate some ideas. After a while, I came up with a strategy that I thought was surefire: I'd make an application to the court seeking *pendente lite* relief—an order awarding a needy spouse temporary maintenance and child support consistent with the parties' prior standard of living. Not only would Jimmy be required to pay until the matter was resolved, but I would also seek relief retroactive to the date Dawn filed for divorce. I ran it by Tom, and he thought it was a winner. "Time to see how deep this clown's pockets really are," he said with zeal. "I like it, Nick—go for it."

But getting Dawn to sign off would take a little prodding, as she'd made it crystal clear from the outset that she wasn't interested in Jimmy's money. When I finally got Dawn on the phone, I started off pitching the virtues of this tactic purely in terms of legal strategy, but she wouldn't hear it until I couched it in terms of how it could work to Jordan's benefit.

"Dawn, if that's how you feel, then you personally don't have to use the money—you can sock it away in a college fund," I said. She paused for a moment, pondered my suggestion, and agreed. I then advised on the necessary tasks, which included filing a motion and an accompanying memorandum of law along with an affidavit from Dawn in which she would attest to her inability to provide sufficiently for the needs of Jordan as well as the urgent need for the relief. It was a lot of work, and, with depositions in ATR to prepare for, my schedule in the immediate near future was packed tight, so I had to push Dawn's project off a bit. I glanced at my calendar and figured I needed a couple of weeks to get the work done and fit in a meeting with Dawn.

"I'm going to need you to review and sign your affidavit, so how about we meet ..." I said, pausing as I checked my calendar, "... two weeks from Thursday? Sometime after work?"

We were silent for a bit as Dawn glanced at her schedule.

She said it was fine, as Milena or her parents would babysit, and asked for the details.

"Not sure where yet, but probably around eight o'clock or so—I'll come up with a place downtown, maybe a diner or something," I said, eliminating a potential run-in with Phil. "We can grab a quick bite, and you can review and sign the papers and then fill me in on how you and Jordan are holding up. Does that work?"

"Definitely."

"All right, I'll shoot you an e-mail and confirm the place and time."

"Sounds great—thanks, Nick."

"No problem," I said. "And if you need anything in the interim, just let me know."

"Will do."

Chapter 9

With Dawn's consent to proceed out of the way, I turned back to ATR and spent the rest of the week in depositions. On Monday, we received the plaintiffs' opposition to our motion to quash the Cindy Holland subpoena, which I immediately passed off to Tim who had to turn around a short reply brief within twenty-four hours. We got it out late Tuesday night, and I then spent the next couple of days preparing for the hearing on the motion, which was scheduled for Friday morning.

I went into court feeling as if I'd exhausted my preparation; I knew my arguments and all of the relevant case law inside and out. Tim sat at the table beside me and took notes; Ted Wickersham sat in the pews and observed.

I argued that, since Cindy had nothing to do with the preparation of the alleged documents, she had no firsthand knowledge of any of the relevant issues. And, given her position with the company—a secretary to a person who was only an alleged recipient of the memos—she was not an appropriate witness. I then argued that, though the plaintiffs purported to have confidential sources regarding the authors of these memos, they had no witnesses who either saw Cindy destroying the memos or were present when Duncan instructed her to do so. Of course, I concluded with the usual catchall arguments—that the subpoena was burdensome, harassing, and amounted to nothing more than a routine fishing expedition by the plaintiffs. I had decent authority for my position, and I discussed a couple of the cases cited in our briefs.

Before the infamous corporate meltdowns of Enron, WorldCom, and the like, my arguments would have been a slam-dunk. But with new legislation enacted to reform corporate governance and prioritize accountability to shareholders, the judiciary was forced to take a more rigid stance on fraud and, when it came to issues like document destruction, viewed the allegations in a light more favorable to the plaintiffs.

Needless to say, the judge denied our motion and ordered that Cindy's deposition take place before the close of discovery.

By now, the Nelson matter had been on the backburner for over two weeks, so, to move things along, I worked all weekend preparing Dawn's application for *pendente lite* relief. On Monday night, I e-mailed Tom drafts of the three documents; he faxed back some minor comments, and, a couple of days later, I put the papers in final draft form. At that point, the papers were ready for filing, subject to Dawn's approval. I then went ahead and sent Dawn an e-mail setting up a time and place for us to meet. I asked if she could meet me at a diner in Greenwich Village the following evening at eight, and she replied that we were on.

I rode the Number 1 subway to the Christopher Street Station and, with my briefcase dangling by my side, took about a five-minute walk to the restaurant to meet Dawn. Charming turn-of-the-century brick and brownstone townhouses with arched entries and pediment-topped windows filled tree-lined blocks. Trendy restaurants, bars, coffee houses, boutiques, sex shops, and specialty book and record stores were abundant. And, from clean-cut and affluent to tattooed and pierced, everyone was welcome and accepted. The homeless made themselves comfortable too. Covered in soot and filth, they cuddled with sickly looking dogs, sat cross-legged, and held cardboard signs that pleaded their causes in magic marker. A worn but hopeful collection cup sat beside each of them.

As I turned a corner and approached the restaurant, I saw Dawn.

"Hi," she said with a smile that took the shape of a rosy flower. She looked sweet in a white tee, a red sweater draped over the shoulders, a smooth flowery skirt cut just above the knee, and heeled sandals. Her feet looked soft and well-kept, her toes descending evenly in size order like a staircase, her nails full and cut perfectly beneath a fresh gleaming gloss of red. Her hair was as dark as midnight and glistened like polished ebony. Her beauty was gentle. Dawn looked so good that it seemed as if she'd gone out of her way, as if our get-together was more a date than a meeting.

I, on the other hand, felt like shit. Though I was wearing a nice navy pinstripe suit, white oxford button-down, and sky blue tie, not only had I been covered in my lawyer's uniform all day, but I'd just spent over forty minutes walking through the humid city and packed tight like a sardine on a crowded subway. My hair was slightly disheveled, and I could feel the layer of sweat pasted on my forehead. I felt a little uncomfortable greeting her this way.

"Hi," I said, awkwardly. Given how good and put together Dawn looked, I vacillated between complimenting her and guilting myself out of it, hearkening back to my conversation with Evan, whose caveat echoed loudly ("Dude, this woman's your client. You know the limits ...."). I heeded Evan's advice and passed, but she deserved a compliment, so my decision left me feeling a little insensitive.

"Not looking too good," Dawn said as we turned and faced the restaurant. It was dark, and a sign in the window advised of a temporary closing due to a recent fire in the kitchen.

"That's too bad," I said, with a twinge of disappointment.

"Yeah," she said, peering intently through the window.

I suggested we take a walk and pick something else. We stopped at a corner as I considered our next direction; the bright light of a street lamp etched our silhouette onto the narrow cobblestone road. I was anxious to find something.

We finally stumbled on a place a couple of blocks away. A red, neon "Chow Fun" with "Restaurant" beneath it was affixed to a small window against a backdrop of velvet blackout drapes. I thought Chinese food was perfect—casual and unpretentious. The unassuming, old brick façade, though, offered no clue as to what was really inside.

"How about here?" I asked.

"Works for me."

The entrance to the restaurant opened into a narrow foyer beneath a low ceiling. The walls were covered in red velvet; the carpet was black, sprinkled with red hearts that matched the walls. The area was faintly illuminated by a series of candelabra sconces, each of which held three white, dripping candles. In the distance, noisy chatter blended with loud eighties music. We were greeted by what, at first glance, appeared to be a woman, but turned out to be a guy in drag. He stood behind a lectern; a brass reading lamped was arched over a reservation diary.

"Oh goodie, you're just in time!" he said, clapping his hands carefully to protect long, dragon-like nails. His head was covered with a curly blond wig, and his face was decorated with a thick shell of white makeup, bright pink lipstick, and long, false eyelashes. A tight black halter-top exposed a round belly and biceps that were twice the size of mine (a fire-breathing dragon on the left, barbed wire on the right).

Dawn and I looked at each other, bewildered. It was a classic think-fast moment, and I blew it big time. The host(ess) grabbed two menus and a wine list and quickly shuffled us into the dining area that neither looked nor felt like a Chinese restaurant. The décor stayed consistent, with gold-framed portraits of drag queens lining the walls; the ambiance was set dim with creative lighting fixtures. A sea of bistro tables was arranged cabaret style and packed tight, each with an unobstructed view of the stage, its velvet curtain framed with hearts. A small deejay booth stood off to the side. The restaurant was packed with mostly all-girl groups and a few male couples here and there. An illuminated disco ball hung in the center and rotated, its mirrored tiles shooting light shafts around the room.

We were seated at a corner table, a raging bachelorette party close by. A quick glance at the menu showed all continental cuisine.

"So much for Kung Pao chicken," said Dawn, smirking.

"Don't abandon hope just yet," I said, lifting my eyes for a reaction. Dawn was smiling.

We sat in silence for a few moments, peering around as reality set in. More drag queens emerged and flounced through the restaurant, tending to their tables.

An African-American waiter came over to take our order. He stood tall in stilettos, the rest of his getup including a turquoise cocktail dress, fishnet stockings, straight black wig down to the shoulders with bangs cut just above the brow, blue eye shadow, and heavy red lipstick.

"Hey, kiddies, welcome to Chow Fun. I'm Devon, and I'll be serving you tonight," he said, with a deep, manly voice and a huskiness lingering in his tone. "Do you know what you'd like for dinner?"

I didn't see "Nothing" on the menu and considered asking if it was available. "I think we might need a minute."

"Okay, but the show is about to start so make it a quickie!"

I felt nervous and uptight and awkwardly cleared my throat.

"Listen, if you don't see anything you like, we don't have to stay. There are plenty of other restaurants in the area," I said, my fingers crossed in my lap, hidden from sight. But instead of taking the bait, Dawn served it right back to me. I got the sense that she felt just as uncomfortable about walking out and making a scene as I did—neither of us wanted to seem rude.

Her response was choppy, unsure. "I think I can find something here," she said. "I don't know … what do you think?"

Great—I had two choices. Leave and make an embarrassing scene, or suck it up and spend the evening with drag queens. I responded tentatively. "I guess I could have pasta."

"Me too," she said, smiling with optimism. I looked into the crowd, found Devon, and waved him over. He took our dinner orders and then asked about drinks. Dawn and I exchanged we're-gonna-need-it nods. Since this was supposed to be a business meeting, I would have only ordered a diet soda, but the circumstances called for an exception, and I made it a gin-and-tonic.

"One gin and tonic—easy on the tonic, I take it?" said Devon, winking at Dawn. He then looked back at me, and I grimaced. "Why don't you loosen that tie and relax, honey … I promise, we don't bite." He turned back to Dawn, who ordered a glass of white wine.

"You got it, girlfriend," he said, collecting the menus. "Be right b*aaa*aack."

Silence loomed over the table as Dawn and I looked at each other and then our surroundings. Partiers loitered through the restaurant, engaging in loud, drunken conversation as if the night had begun hours ago. But as festive as the environment was, I may as well have been at a funeral.

"So," I said.

"So," she said, brushing her hair away from her face in one graceful motion.

"I take it now's not the time to go over your affidavit?"

Dawn grinned. "I don't think so."

I took Devon's advice and released the top button on my shirt, pulling my tie down about an inch or so. Moments later, he returned.

"Yoo hoo, here I am," he said, setting our drinks in front of us. "Drink up!"

I lifted my drink to make a toast, and Dawn followed. I took a quick look around and returned my eyes to her with a wry, twisted smile.

"To … life," I said, my tone and expression very here-goes-nothing, "and the different directions it takes us in."

"Cheers," said Dawn, smiling, as we clicked glasses.

We sipped our drinks for a moment before the house lights went dark. The crowd hushed. The stage curtains parted, and a troupe of four drag queens, who called themselves Sharlene, Coco, Lola, and Kitty, sashayed on stage for a lip-sync act. Powerful, multihued spotlights focused the audience's attention. Sharlene, Lola, and Kitty performed a medley of songs, while Coco chimed in with wisecracks about each of them.

During the show, our dinner was served. While Dawn picked at hers, I left mine completely untouched.

Before the grand finale, the performers stepped off stage and into the crowd with microphones in hand. *Oh, God, please don't come over here*, I thought (over and over again). A tight knot formed in my stomach. I felt ill, as if beleaguered by a virus that had been brewing, anticipating a breakthrough at any moment. In an effort to stave them off, I tried to make myself look busy: small talk with Dawn, pretending to check my BlackBerry for text messages, and sorting my penne with a fork, as if enjoying and totally immersed in it—all to no avail.

"Ladies, I think I found myself a playmate!" said Sharlene, suddenly clasping my shoulder with an iron grip. The music stopped, and the room went silent. A spotlight shone on my face. Folks with obstructed angles adjusted for a better view.

All eyes were on me.

Sharlene sat on my lap and twirled my hair. I just sat there, my arms draped heavy by my sides. A look of discomfort crossed Dawn's face, lines of worry connecting her eyes.

"What's your name, sugar?" he asked, placing the microphone close to my lips. I took a deep breath and responded in a whisper.

"Oooooh," he said, looking out at the crowd. "I like Nicks."

"You're getting some Nick tonight?" said Lola from across the room.

"I don't know, honey. I think this Nick's spoken for," said Sharlene, before turning to me and asking, "What's your girlfriend's name, sweetie?"

"She's not my girlfriend," I said uneasily, "but her name is Dawn."

"Dawn—a pretty name for a pretty girl," he said. "How *are* you, precious?"

"Good, thank you."

"So, Dawn, tell us … if you two ain't an item, then what are y'all doin' here?" he asked, offering Dawn the microphone. She paused and thought for a moment.

"It's a long story," she said, a bit nervous.

"Well, that's okay, we've got plenty of time," he said, looking to the crowd. Laughter ensued and, when it settled down, Dawn responded tentatively, "He's my lawyer."

"Hey now!" he said, surprised, turning to me. "This is your

idea of entertaining clients, counselor? Hanging out with a bunch of queens?"

"No, actually, we walked by and thought this was a Chinese restaurant," said Dawn. The audience laughed uproariously.

"Well, we average about two-point-three accidental tourists a night, so don't feel so bad," he said. I felt better already ... as if it wasn't even happening.

"As you can see, sugar, we're all-American, here, but I tell you what—we're gonna' spice things up anyhow. C'mon, counselor—take a little walk with me," he said, leaving my lap. He took my hand and, in one quick, fluid motion, pulled me up and out of my chair. A flicker of apprehension coursed through me. Butterflies fluttered in my stomach. Beads of perspiration broke through my pores, one by one. Ugh.

"How about a big hand for The Nick ... come on, ladies, make him feel at home," said Sharlene. The audience responded with thunderous, ear-splitting applause.

A chair was promptly placed at center stage, and Sharlene plopped me down on it. Coco, Lola, and Kitty sauntered on stage as the nineties hit "I'm Too Sexy" began to play. Heavy bass pumped through speakers set in the ceiling. Each performer took turns lap dancing me, kissing my head, and running "her" hands through my hair. Filled with humiliation, I looked out at Dawn, whose long face was marked with pity; she covered her mouth with her hands.

"Ea-sy access tonight, girls," said Coco, running his hand down my loosely buttoned shirt. I twitched and squirmed, as if to shake him off.

"Wait, wait, wait ... hold the music," said Sharlene. The music stopped. "I think The Nick said that he's too sexy for his shirt. Didn't you all hear that?"

Applause followed.

"I thought so," he said, the deejay continuing the song. Lola and Kitty took turns removing my jacket and tie and then unbuttoning and removing my shirt, tossing my clothing into the crowd.

I was mortified. A business meeting with a client, and there I was, topless, with drag queens groping me. I peered out at Dawn, who looked as if she was about to cry. Suddenly, she rose from her seat, as if impelled by force, and ambled to the stage.

"Ladies and gentlemen, Dawn to the rescue!" said Sharlene, the audience cheering. "Don't worry, we're taking good care of him up here, honey." Dawn didn't respond. Instead, she climbed up onto my lap and whispered "I'm sorry" into my ear.

"Wait, wait, wait, hold the music," said Sharlene. The music stopped. He looked at Dawn.

"This stand-by-your-man thing is sweet and all, honey, but it doesn't seem fair that Nick's showing us some skin while you're sitting pretty up here all covered up like Mary Poppins," he said, turning to the crowd. "Don't you agree, people?"

The crowd cheered in response.

I didn't like where this was going, especially when Coco stepped out from behind the curtain with a whipped cream dispenser. I whispered "let's go" to Dawn, gently tapping the small of her back. But just then, Dawn removed her shirt, revealing a white, silk bra. She dropped the shirt beneath our chair and put her arms around me for a warm, we're-in-this-together hug and buried her face in my shoulder. With my arm around her waist, I looked out at the crowd that rose in a standing ovation.

"Ladies and gentlemen of the jury, how do you find?" Sharlene shouted, pointing the microphone out at the crowd.

"Guilty!" they responded, nearly in unison.

"The people have spoken, counselor—you're guilty as sin!"

I actually laughed at that. Strangely, I didn't care about what was happening anymore, as if my body had been completely exhumed of every fleck of tension. My mood was suddenly buoyant, and I even reveled in the moment. As long as Dawn was with me, I felt as if I could have stayed up there all night (or at least a few more minutes, anyway). It was as if there was a shell around us and we were in our own little world.

"I think Dawn and The Nick have been good sports. Let's give these two a big hand, girls," said Sharlene. Dawn quickly replaced her shirt and, after mine was passed up to the stage, I did the same. We stepped down to a generous round of applause and returned to our table. I let out a long, hard deep breath and took a sip of my cocktail, which had turned lukewarm.

"Are you okay?"

"I am *now*," I said, like a rookie athlete finally feeling comfortable after getting into a game and taking a couple of hard hits. I felt as if I'd gone from timid to fearless, and was ready for, and could take, just about anything.

I politely waited until the show was over to ask for the check. I left behind the receipt, as there was no way in hell I was going to submit it to the firm for reimbursement. Dawn offered to pay her way. I thanked her, but insisted that it was on me. I thought that said a lot about her.

"I don't know about you, but I'm starving," I said, after stepping outside.

"Me too," she said. "How about dessert?"

"Ice cream?"

Her smile widened in approval, eyebrows arched. "Definitely."

"Cool. I know a great place … on the Upper East Side," I said. "I'm not taking any more chances down here."

"Good idea."

"Yeah, we might actually achieve the purpose of tonight's meeting," I said with a smile, which she returned.

On the ride up, Dawn called Milena from her cell to see how everything had gone with Jordan. After carrying on for a little while, he'd calmed down, snuggled up for bedtime stories, and fallen fast asleep halfway through the second book. Dawn seemed relieved, as if it had been on her mind and she could finally relax.

I took Dawn to a great old-fashioned ice cream parlor famous for gargantuan hot fudge sundaes; it was an institutional, hole-in-the-wall-type joint, still hanging on to its original black-and-white tiled décor. After seeing just how big the sundaes really were, Dawn suggested we share one, which was fine by me. The place was third-generation owned, and the waiter, a short, skinny middle-aged fellow with a salt-and-pepper fold-over, could have been family. On his own with all eight tables, he looked worn and weathered, as if he'd had enough and didn't care if we ate there or not. People came for the legendary sundaes, which sold themselves. No personality required.

After piling on what seemed like almost every topping on the menu, the waiter asked if we wanted whipped cream. Dawn and I looked at each other and couldn't help but laugh.

"Inside joke," I said to the waiter, "but not what you think."

"Whatever," he said, rolling his eyes and seeming to prefer wherever his imagination had taken him. "It's none of my business."

"I think we'll take it on the side," said Dawn, motioning with her hand.

We then went over the affidavit. I had Dawn review it carefully to make sure all of the facts, especially those concerning her present financial situation as well as Dawn and Jimmy's lifestyle during their marriage, all of which I'd pulled from the file, were still accurate. While she read, I focused my attention on the sundae. It took her ten minutes to review, and about halfway through, she looked up and started laughing.

"Are you going to save some for me?" she asked, noticing that half the bowl was empty. I smiled and set my spoon down, sitting back and distancing myself from the sundae. She smiled.

"Sorry," I said, "My appetite hasn't been this hearty in a long time."

"That's okay, I'm kidding. It's all yours."

I waited anyway. After taking a few more minutes to review the document and ask questions, to which I gave satisfactory answers, she signed it. I then notarized it and returned it to my briefcase. Dawn, wasting no more time, anxiously grabbed her spoon and dove right in.

"Mmmm, this is amazing!"

"I wouldn't steer you wrong." Dawn looked up at me with a stare, her whipped cream-covered grin spreading wider and turning to laughter—closed-mouthed as she hadn't yet swallowed her spoonful of ice cream. I appreciated the humor in my remark.

"Okay, well, not twice in one night, anyway."

We had underestimated our appetites and wound up splitting a malted afterward. It was fun, the way we devoured it all free of any self-imposed inhibitions. We post-mortemed our performance at the drag club, still astonished that such a thing could actually happen, let alone to us. We laughed about it and even at ourselves, with no punches pulled. I told Dawn I couldn't believe what she had done.

"Women walk on the beach in bikinis that show a lot more," she said, "and no one gives it a second thought."

"Well, I don't know about *no one*." Dawn smiled.

"Think about it—on any given day, you can open up a newspaper or popular magazine and see ads with women posing in bras. It's really not a big deal … and besides, other than you, no one in there was interested."

"You've got a point."

As we continued to enjoy our dessert, I asked about Jordan. Dawn gazed at me through bleary eyes. "Everything okay?" I asked.

"Not really. He beat up another kid at daycare yesterday … over a toy," she replied in a low, tormented voice, girding herself with resolve. "He'll be fine. We just need to get through this—he's been through way too much already."

"I know," I said with empathy. "Do you want to talk about it?"

"Maybe for a little while—I really just want to enjoy the rest of the night though, okay?" she pleaded, softly. "I can use it."

"No problem." Her lips spread into a closed-mouthed smile.

In keeping with Dawn's wishes, we kept our discussion about Jordan's issues brief and then took pleasure in more easy conversation: nothing case related, nothing too deep or serious … light topics, like favorite movies, music, and fun things to do in the city. It was nice for a change. Our conversation lent itself to an occasional joke by me. Dawn laughed each time as if sincerely amused, but with a dab of excitement that was above and beyond the humor itself.

Talking with Dawn felt more like catching up with an old friend … as if we'd known each other forever, had lost touch for a few years, and then picked up right where we left off.

I really enjoyed her company, and was just starting to realize what I'd been missing.

Chapter 10

The following morning, I woke up early and relaxed out on the balcony. As I sipped my coffee and gazed out at the park, I thought about Dawn—the way she held me up on stage, the sensation of our skin touching, and how, when we talked, she seemed to naturally understand and accept me for who I was. All of these thoughts aroused deep, intimate feelings. I realized how good I felt when I thought about her—how I felt like the person I wanted to be.

Thinking about Dawn and my work issues reminded me of my conversation with my mother ... about how I wasn't getting any younger and that it was time to find someone special and give my life meaning—something a lot deeper than being Phil Addison's bitch and helping the Duncan Shaws of the world evade liability.

After taking a quick run on the treadmill and getting myself ready for work, I arrived at the office at nine-fifteen. I finalized Dawn's application for *pendente lite* relief, had the papers sent out for filing with the court, and then forwarded a copy to Mike Carroll. To expedite the process, I made the application by order to show cause, which meant that Carroll would have only eight business days to respond.

As soon as the papers were out the door, I took a break

and grabbed a quick breakfast at the firm cafeteria. When I returned, Janice followed me into my office and all the way to my desk, her expression glum. In a whisper, she advised that Messrs. Schmidt and Addison wanted to see me immediately. "Is there a problem?"

"I think so," she said. "It seems pretty serious."

I took a few moments and then walked to Will's office. I knocked and was given permission to enter.

"Yes, hello, Nick," said Will, politely. He sipped tea and gnawed on cashews. "Come on in and have a seat."

For someone who claimed to make productive, billable time a top priority, Phil spent an awful lot of time in Will's office kissing his ass, and, sure enough, he was there when I arrived and played his part.

"Shut the door," he demanded, his features marked with loathing. I did, and took a seat beside him.

"Nick, I've been speaking with Phil who has been making certain ... observations about you lately."

"What kind of observations?"

"Nick, it seems as though you've been ... dropping the ball lately," said Phil, his chin resting in his hand.

"What? What are you talking about?"

"Well, Nick, it just seems that, at times, you're nowhere to be found. There's a ... how should I say it ... perception that you're no longer giving us the requisite effort."

I remember that moment like it was yesterday—the moment I finally lost it.

"That's ridiculous! I work just as hard, if not harder now, as a partner, than I did when I was an associate!"

"You say that, Nick, but lately I've hardly seen you here over the weekend or even past seven o'clock during the week. There have been times when I've needed to call upon you and you've just been nowhere to be found."

"Call upon me for what? If you need someone, call an

associate—I paid those dues, remember? I can't believe what I'm hearing—this is complete bullshit!"

I looked to Will who sat idly without expression, like an impartial referee letting two boxers kill each other.

"No it's not, Nick, no it's not," he said, raising his hand and pointing at me. "And lower your voice and lose the nasty tone."

"Look, I'm entitled to take a little bit of time here and there when it's conducive to my schedule—I think I've earned it." I peered out the window and took a moment to catch my breath.

"Nick, let me tell you a little story about when I was a senior associate here at the firm working on a *very* important case. I was part of a team that was conducting an important document review. My wife and I had planned a trip to Florida to attend my brother-in-law's wedding and take the kids to Disney World. I notified the partner I was working for, who I'll leave nameless, that I would have to be away for a while, and you know what he said to me?" He paused. I deadpanned blankly in response.

"He said, 'Well, if you want to get married and start a family, that's certainly your prerogative. But as far as your trip is concerned, think about what we have at stake here. What *you* have at stake here. This is a very important case, and, as you know, the document review is crucial.'" He took a breather, but clearly had more to say.

"I'm listening," I said, feeling achy. My face remained impassive.

"So, I took the hint, set my familial obligations aside, and stayed behind and worked. Now, while I admit I practically ruined my marriage over that, you see, Nick, that's the kind of dedication we need here at the firm. That's the kind of dedication it takes to succeed here, making *big money* working on *important* matters. Understand?"

I didn't even have to ask—he was dead serious. *How*

inspiring, I thought. In retort, I peppered him with a series of rhetorical questions.

"Let me ask you something, Phil—what do you expect me to take away from that story? Am I supposed to want to emulate you? Do you even realize how absolutely ridiculous you sound? There were probably thirty other warm bodies working on that document review with you. Do you think the week or two you would have missed would have made any difference in the outcome of the litigation? And what's so *important* about these matters we work on here? What do you think we're doing … God's work? Our matters are about *money*. So don't sit here and pontificate about importance. This new matter—the pro bono matter I'm working on—that's *important*."

Phil glared at me through his glasses in astonishment, then rolled his eyes and looked to Will. "Well, we all make decisions in life, Nick. I've made mine and soon you'll make yours."

"What the hell is that supposed to mean?" I said, glancing at Will.

"Nick, I got a call first thing this morning from Duncan Shaw," said Will.

"About what?"

"You don't know?" said Phil, looking at me enigmatically, eyes squinted as if blinded by the sun, brows arched.

"No, what's this about?"

"He said he gave you his company's luxury box at Shea Stadium for last night's Mets game?" said Phil.

"Yes, he did. Why?"

"What did you do with the tickets, Nick?"

"I thought it would be nice to treat some of the support staff to the game—I thought they'd enjoy it."

Then Will interjected. "Nick, Shaw said he showed up to meet you last night at the game to discuss the consequences of your defeat in court and how to potentially resolve the situation. He said he was greeted by a bunch of riff-raff making a complete mess of the place."

"First of all, they're not riff-raff. They're good, honest, hardworking people—believe it or not, we depend on them here at this firm."

"The tickets were for *you*, Nick. For *you* to go, and perhaps, for you to take your associates—people who generate income for the firm. Shaw was appalled by what he saw when he got there. Kids bouncing off of the walls, loud music booming—the place was a total pigsty, Nick. Shaw's livid. This is terrible, terrible business."

"And losing that motion doesn't help the situation, either," said Phil.

"First of all, I told Duncan when he offered me the tickets that I couldn't go, but he insisted I have them anyway. Second, I did everything I could on that motion—we had little to no chance of winning, and you know it. I refuse to take an iota of blame for that. Ted Wickersham, Duncan's general counsel, was there, and he told me himself I did a great job. He told me that over lunch, which he invited me to—after we got the judge's ruling. In any event, it will be fine. I'll call Duncan and work it out with him."

"No, you will not!" barked Phil, his mug scrunched. I felt my face crease as I stared him down, resolute, as if warding off a stray dog contemplating attack.

"Settle down, Phil," said Will, shooing him off.

"Will, Duncan is my client—I'm the one who brought him to the firm. I have a great relationship with him. I can take care of it."

"Listen, you arrogant son of a bitch," said Phil, incensed, "you might think you're an all-star, but make no mistake about it—Duncan Shaw and ATR came to the firm because of the firm and because of this firm's stellar reputation. If anything, we might lose him because of you. And what, you're bigger than this institution now? You get your picture on the cover of a fucking magazine and you think you're somebody? I don't like your attitude, Nick. You had better shape up, real quick."

"Nick, I'm not saying you don't deserve any credit for bringing Shaw to the firm, but ... well, let me share a little anecdote," said Will.

Oh goodie—this was turning out to be story time at Williams Gardner. Gather round, boys and girls.

"I'm listening," I said, settling into the plush seat cushion and crossing my legs. I couldn't wait to hear this one.

"Nick, my father, may he rest in peace, was once asked, at a time when I was a young lawyer with the firm on the verge of making partner, what it had been like raising me and how I had been as a child. You know how he responded?"

I shook my head, responding as if I gave a shit.

"He said, 'I don't know. I wasn't there.'"

I nodded gloomily, wondering which story would be more pathetic.

"But look around you, Nick. Look where you are. My father built a great firm. An institution! A leader in the legal community! My point is, Nick, that it takes serious dedication ... a full, unbridled commitment to the firm."

I took a moment and considered what kind of person I wanted to be. I loved and revered my father deeply, but his company-guy mentality no longer served me well. I was ashamed of myself. And then, when I thought about it, I realized that, deep down, after everything Dad went through, he wouldn't want me to just sit back and keep quiet. It was time to stand and be counted.

"And what does it say on his headstone?" I asked with an artificial sense of audacity. My superiors were stunned and taken aback.

"I beg your pardon?" said Will, frowning, his eyes level beneath drawn brows.

"His headstone—what does it say on his headstone?"

"How dare you!"

"Oh, shut up already, Phil," I said unflinchingly, staring straight ahead at Will.

"Quite frankly, I don't remember. I haven't been there in a while. And who do you think you are asking me a question like that?" he said, sternly.

"Why haven't you been there in a while, Will? He was your father, wasn't he?"

"I see him every day that I walk into this office, Nick. I see our name—his good name—on the door and on the letterhead. I see the magnificent oil painting of him in the reception area. I feel his presence everywhere."

"Does it say loving father and husband? Or great lawyer, with nothing more?"

"He said he didn't recall, Nick," said Phil, as if he was defending his client at a deposition.

"That's a shame, Will."

"Oh, and Will," prompted Phil, "let's not forget about the pro bono project and Nick's unwillingness to participate in the firm's PR campaign."

"My feelings haven't changed on that—I want no part of it," I said.

"Nick, perhaps it's time that you started ... considering your alternatives," said Phil.

"What?" I exclaimed. I turned to Will, who did not seem surprised by the comment.

"You heard me, Nick."

"I'm an equity partner!"

"So?"

"So that's it? I gave my fucking life to this firm! All the great work I've done, the victories in difficult cases, the countless hours, the revenue I've generated, and all of the personal sacrifices—you know, all the reasons I was made a partner! Amazing. It's as though none of it ever even happened."

"We don't rest on our laurels around here, Nick," said Phil.

"To stay on top, we need to perform each and every day. The past is just that—it's past."

I quickly retorted. "The past is not dead, Phil. In fact, it's not even past."

"What?" he said, brows furrowed in dismay.

"William Faulkner."

He laughed under his breath.

"You see, Will ... he even has time for literature!"

Phil looked to his master for praise.

"I've actually never read Requiem for a Nun. I picked up the quote from a newspaper article, and I liked it so much, I thought it was worth committing to memory. Under the circumstances, can you blame me?"

Silence loomed over us like heavy smog. My tolerance for abuse had reached its limit. "Are we finished here?"

"No, not quite," said Will. "Nick, you can protest from now until kingdom come, but, as far as we're concerned, giving away Duncan Shaw's tickets was a flagrant error in judgment. Now, you have two options. You can remain steadfast about your feelings on this issue, which may give you a certain degree of personal satisfaction, but, from a professional standpoint, I think you are making a terrible mistake. So, with that said, your second option is to redeem yourself. Make things right, Nick, and talk to the press about your pro bono matter. Do the necessary with that, and we'll wipe the slate clean. What do you say?"

I looked at Phil to see if he was on board with the deal. He nodded, though begrudgingly.

"The identities of the parties will be kept confidential?"

Will nodded. I took a deep breath and slowly exhaled.

"Fine."

"Splendid! Here are the contact people at their respective publications. Give them a call. They're expecting to hear from you," said Will, handing me a memo that he had waiting for me on his desk.

"I'll take care of it."

"Good boy," he said in that paternal way of his that never felt anything other than patronizing.

"You were really starting to worry me there, Nick," said Phil. "But I'm confident that I'll be seeing your smiling face much more often."

I forged a placating smile.

"Right," I said, pushing myself to a standing position.

"Let me know how it goes, Nick," said Will.

"No problem."

"Oh, and one other thing," said Will as I was halfway out the door. I turned to face him. His cold, measured eyes were waiting for me.

"Don't ever take that tone with me again," he said, looking toward Phil when he was finished, as if to convey that we were adjourned and that no response would be entertained. I exited and closed the door behind me.

I walked back to my office slowly, my gait more a limp than a stride. My self-esteem had been picked apart, my dignity bagged and tossed out with the rest of the trash amid foodstuffs and other miscellaneous debris. They could do that to me. They literally had that kind of power.

I entered my office and closed the door. On my chair was a message memo from the doctor's office seeking to confirm my appointment for the following afternoon at two o'clock—right smack in the middle of the day, the only available time slot.

I set the message on my desk, sat down, and drew a deep breath. I allowed myself to calm down for a few moments and then, like a good boy, I contacted the reporters and provided a brief synopsis of Dawn's case. They advised me to contact them when the case was resolved so they could finalize their pieces and run the stories immediately. I also provided them with Tom Dooley's contact information. I spoke very highly of Tom and encouraged them to speak with him as well. They said they would and thanked me.

Then I remembered that I had to call the doctor's office back.

I had to keep Phil off my back for a while. Not just for the sake of my status at the firm, but for my sanity. I needed some peace and, both mentally and physically, could feel my strength waning more and more. I thought about the Duncan Shaw problem and how ATR was intensifying as we were approaching the court-ordered deadline for the close of fact discovery. I surveyed my desk and was reminded of various unrelated matters and bar association responsibilities that had been piling up. In light of all of that, coupled with my recent jousts with Will and Phil, the idea of leaving the office for personal reasons, a potential run-in with Phil, missing an important call from Duncan Shaw only to have him ask for Phil in my absence, compelled a simple decision.

I had to cancel the appointment.

Chapter 11

Later on in the week, Evan and I had been in a meeting with a new client—a writer-director Evan discovered at the Sundance Film Festival considered a rising star by Hollywood insiders—when Mike Carroll called about resolving the Nelson matter. It hardly came as a surprise—less than one day after serving the application for *pendente lite* relief, I had faxed Carroll a report containing the fruits of our investigation, which uncovered three separate bank accounts in Jimmy's name containing substantial six figures. Making matters worse for Jimmy, a hearing in family court was scheduled for the following week. After a bit of phone tag, we finally hooked up. Carroll advised that Jimmy wanted to put the ordeal behind him and proposed that, in exchange for Dawn dropping all criminal charges, Jimmy would consent to a divorce and waive custody. After I then got him to consent to a permanent order of protection and no visitation, he insisted we waive child support. Since child support meant Dawn and Jimmy would continue to have contact with each other indefinitely (and I knew that's exactly what Dawn didn't want), I agreed provided Jimmy made a lump sum payment up front. We went back and forth on the number over the next few days and finally arrived at something fair and reasonable—an amount that, by Dawn's standards, provided a nice cushion to help her move on.

"Oh, and one other thing," I said, clearing my throat. "Jimmy relinquishes all parental rights over Jordan."

"I'm sure that won't be a problem," he said, implying he'd get back to me on it.

"It shouldn't be," I said. "I hope your client will realize how lucky he is."

"Clients do strange things, Nick," he said, doubtful.

"Don't I know it," I muttered under my breath. I advised that I would go over everything with Dawn and get back to him. First, though, I immediately called Tom, who was on board with the agreement. Like me, he took comfort in the order of protection, which had a statutory term of five years. The file on the entire matter would be maintained and, if at any point Jimmy violated the order, Dawn could re-petition the family court for further relief. The family court could then modify or issue a new order of protection, hold Jimmy in contempt, commit him to custody, and either send him to prison for up to six months on its own or, alternatively, refer the matter to the district attorney for prosecution in criminal court. A criminal court judge could then release Jimmy on bail, restore the case to the court calendar, and commit him to custody, impose probation, or order imprisonment. Tom instructed that I speak with Dawn to get her approval, which I did.

Mike Carroll scheduled a conference call for early the following week with all counsel, including Rachel Schor, Jordan's court-appointed law guardian, to finalize the agreement. Carroll agreed to prepare all of the necessary paperwork and e-mail drafts to the group sufficiently in advance of the call. The call was fairly short and amicable. A few minor terms of the stipulation were tweaked, but otherwise everything went smoothly. The final version of the agreement was circulated by hand delivery for signatures, and, once the agreement was fully executed, copies were provided to all parties, including a courtesy copy for the judge.

In preparing for the hearing in family court, I needed to meet with Milena and her parents as they would be testifying on Dawn's behalf. Since I couldn't squeeze in a meeting during the day and the three of them all lived and worked in Brooklyn, I spoke to Milena and suggested that I come to the house after dinner when they would be relaxed and have plenty of time to talk without interruption. She appreciated the offer and took me up on it.

Our meeting was set for the following evening. Milena had given me directions, which I followed to a tee, and I enjoyed a smooth ride to Brooklyn with no traffic whatsoever.

It was twilight … another day winding down. The orange sun had nearly dissolved and spread across the horizon like a pool of molten lava. A half-moon dimpled the purplish upper atmosphere and waited on deck, ready to serve its purpose.

My trip to Brooklyn ended on Ocean Parkway, the heartbeat of Brooklyn's Kensington section. It forms a promenade, its central thoroughfare beset by grassy landscaped malls and side roads. Trees are foliaged, large, and thick-barked, shading sidewalks, wooden benches, and playing tables with built-in chessboards; an asphalt bicycle path stretches all the way to the Brighton Beach boardwalk. It is inviting, and fosters peaceful interaction among the residents that include Irish and Italians, Hasidic Jews, and immigrants from Bangladesh, India, Pakistan, the Middle East, and Russia. The homes, set on tiny plots and packed tight like Legos, are just as varied, with prewar mansions, one- and two-family homes and apartment buildings, both luxury and lower income.

I turned right at a cross street and pulled a quick left onto the Ocean Parkway side road. Milena had said it was the fifth house on the right. I rolled up slowly, parked in an empty spot, and turned off the engine. As I stepped out of the car, a gentle breeze eased the transition from artificial chill to summer swelter. A strong afterglow fought off deepening shadows, salvaging another precious thirty minutes or so of outdoor activities. Joggers and cyclists traveled in opposite directions, carefully avoided each other, and nodded, as if part of a secret society. Two elderly women shared a bench and chatted, one's cane and the other's walker within reach. One squinted, studied her watch, and reported the time. They seemed to agree on something—possibly that their TV programs were about to start—and began the arduous process of heading inside. Two houses down, a mother and her young ball-playing sons engaged in a loud discourse. Though spoken in Russian, they were easily comprehensible: she called them in, they pleaded for more time, she insisted, they objected, she threatened, and, ultimately, they capitulated.

Boys will be boys.

Milena's home was a relatively small, two-family house, its façade sheathed in white aluminum siding. I unhooked and stepped inside the gate affixed on both sides to a metal fence that enclosed the tidy plot. The narrow concrete path was bordered with colorful tulips and geraniums; three brick stairs connected the path to the porch. There were two doors, each with its own bell. Milena's parents and her sister Sonia occupied the left side. I pressed the white button on the right, the one for Milena's side.

The even-paced sounds of stomping against wood planks grew louder as Milena bounded down the staircase. The steel door creaked open, and Milena greeted me in a way that exuded her bubbly personality: a big smile accentuated full, red lips, and wide cheeks. Her eyes, big and brown, were decorated in lashes that seemed to flutter. Her long black hair was straight, the sides kept close to her face that looked more oval than round. She was dressed casually, but nicely, in a fitted white, short-sleeved button-down with a beige, knee-length skirt and sandals.

"Hi, Nick," she said, upbeat. "It's so nice to meet you."

"It's nice to meet you too."

"The folks are running a little late … fashionably, of course, but they'll be ready in a jiffy," she said. "Come on in!"

I could hear from the distance that Jordan was giving Dawn a hard time, protesting the fact that Milena's sister, Sonia, would be filling in on bedtime duty because Dawn wanted to sit in on our meeting. I could hear him pleading with a choking cry, "I don't want you to go, Mommy!"

"We're having a little crisis here," Milena whispered. I nodded, my mouth shut tight. A few more steps and we reached the peak of the staircase. The parquet floors gleamed as if they had just been polished. A black iron coat tree with six stems held a variety of lightweight jackets appropriate for the season.

"Come, let me show you the pad," she said, guiding me from area to area, starting with the living room. A plush, red couch and matching chairs faced a low-standing, Zen-like entertainment center. A glass coffee table, set atop a black-and-red, polka-dotted area rug, displayed an assortment of fashion magazines. An Andy Warhol–influenced series of pop art depicting Madonna and Gwen Stefani hung evenly spaced against the stark white wall. The faces in the prints were traced in black against a white background; bright reds dominated their eyes and puckered lips. Three large plastic crates were set in the corner. It looked as if they might have been empty only moments earlier. I pictured a random assortment of Jordan's toys scattered across the floor and Milena accomplishing a hasty he's-gonna-be-here-any-second cleanup.

Though Dawn and Jordan were down the hall behind closed doors, the heartbreaking wrath of a troubled child was loud and clear.

"But I want *you* to read me books tonight!"

"Honey, Aunt Sonia's going to read to you tonight."

"No ... *you!*"

"Sweetheart, I always read to you. It's just for tonight, okay? I promise."

"No, I want *you*, Mommy... *I WANT YOU!*"

They repeated versions of this exchange several times over. I felt guilty about being there ... as if I was an imposition.

Milena quickly showed me her bedroom. A fold-up table in the corner held a sewing machine; a small easel was set up for sketching designs. I asked what they were for, and she told me that she was a "fashionista in training" who had found her calling when Dawn got pregnant with Jordan. She was taking courses at Fashion Institute of Technology and working to develop her own line of chic, yet affordable, maternity wear. I thought it sounded exciting and wished her luck.

I took a further look around, and a framed eight-by-ten of a young man in a military uniform caught my attention. Milena noticed and told all. "That's my honey," she said proudly, sitting on the bed and taking the photo from the table. The picture was of her boyfriend, a soldier in the army named Daniel, who was stationed in Texas; she stared at it with a smile filled with affection, her eyes full of life, until I asked about the length of his commitment.

"Last month, Daniel came home to visit and told me he'd been offered a promotion. He said he couldn't pass it up, that his superiors advised that it would be 'great for his career,'" she said cynically, with emphasis. Her mouth took on an unpleasant twist, her expressive face approached somber. "Supposedly, it's only one year."

I nodded, not knowing what to say.

"I told him I would be here waiting for him," she said.

"Hopefully it will go fast," I said, trying to be upbeat. "He'll be home before you know it." She nodded, flashed me a smile of thanks, and rose from the bed. I followed her to the living room.

"So this is it," said Milena, her arms outspread with a

smile like a *Price Is Right* girl presenting a new item up for bid. I complimented her on her taste. She thanked me and then stepped away for about five minutes until Dawn emerged from the bedroom. Under the circumstances, her composure was remarkable; she ambled gracefully and smoothed her knee-length silk burgundy skirt, her shadow close behind against the wall. A black barrette kept her hair from falling over her face.

"Hi," she said with a smile. I rose from the couch.

"Hey there," I said, smiling back. "It's good to see you."

"Yeah, you too."

"I hope it's not a bad time."

"No it's okay—three stories and he'll be out."

"Are you sure?"

"Absolutely," she said, as Jordan, dressed in baseball pajamas, cautiously revealed himself from behind the wall.

"Hi, sweetie … do you remember Nick?" said Dawn. "He gave you the Thomas toy, remember?" Jordan sulked timidly. Dawn asked Jordan to come over and say hello; he remained silent and twisted his head no.

"I know … Jordan wants to dance with his auntie!" shouted Milena, suddenly emerging from the bedroom, sweeping him off of his little feet and dancing to her own vocalization of "Twist and Shout." Jordan's mood changed instantly; he belly laughed unrestrainedly as she gyrated and spun him around.

"Come on, come on, come oooooon … ba-BY!" she sang, gently laying him on the floor and letting her long hair run across his face, tickling him to no end.

Milena was fun—a total firecracker. Jordan was in much better spirits and said his final goodnights. "I love you, sweetie," said Dawn as Jordan gave her a big hug and kiss. Dawn seemed to feel much better, and so did I. We both smiled.

Moments after Sonia left with Jordan, Milena's parents,

Vicki and Paul D'Angelo, arrived, smiling with genial charm. Vicki, wearing a red blouse and black pants, was the spitting image of Milena, with curly black hair and full makeup over swelled cheeks and lips; Paul, slightly taller than his girls and dressed in a navy blue golf shirt, khakis, and running sneakers, had wiry hair and sideburns flecked with gray.

We sat down at the dining room table, which had been set for dessert with placemats, coffee mugs, and forks and spoons. I removed my suit jacket to get comfortable and broke the ice with pleasant conversation. Milena politely excused herself and returned shortly with a silver platter filled with assorted cannoli and biscotti and a carafe of freshly brewed coffee. As we ate, we continued to bullshit and even had a few laughs.

Our meeting lasted about an hour and eventually was very productive. I walked the D'Angelos through the agenda I had prepared for their testimony, in which I would first establish their credibility by having them discuss their personal backgrounds. Only then would I delve into their relationship with Dawn. I kept it simple for them, and they seemed comfortable and ready to go.

When our work was finished, Milena slipped into Jordan's room to retrieve Sonia, who had fallen asleep while lying with Jordan. We all said good-bye, and, as they left, I advised the D'Angelos to call if they had any last-minute questions. Sonia followed her parents out. Milena said goodnight to Dawn and I and then retreated to her room, leaving the two of us alone.

Dawn excused herself for a moment, and I took a seat on the living room couch. She returned with two glasses of water, set them on coasters, and then sat beside me.

"Well, we're almost home," I said. "How do you feel?"

Dawn smiled, took in a deep breath, and exhaled.

"I'm getting there ... I just want this over with."

"I know," I said, nodding.

"Nick, I know you've worked really hard—for nothing, no less—and I want you to know how much I appreciate it."

"It's okay," I said, smiling. "And it's not for nothing."

A small smile of enchantment touched Dawn's lips as she nodded in response; she sat pensively for a moment.

"I'll be right back," she whispered. "Don't go anywhere."

"Take your time," I said, as Dawn stepped away. While she was gone, I sipped my water and reminded myself that it was time to get going.

Dawn returned with a black-and-white composition notebook. It was banged up pretty good, as if it had labored through an entire school year of daily homework assignments and cafeteria stains. She looked as if she had something to say about it, so I waited patiently.

"Remember that day we met for coffee, I told you I wanted to write?"

I did indeed, and nodded, telling her so.

"Well, ever since I was a little girl, I've been writing children's stories. I used to lock myself in my room and escape to faraway places. I've never shown this to anyone before. In fact, no one else knows it exists. But I want to share them with you."

"Really?"

Dawn smiled and nodded.

"I would love to read them," I said, as I took the book from her and opened it to the first story. It was penned in cursive, the handwriting elegant for its level but with years of development clearly ahead of it. The labored penmanship had left ridges in the fragile paper; I ran my finger across the words as if they were written in Braille. Touching her words in this way made me feel as if I was meeting Dawn as she had been back then, feeling the emotion that underpinned her troubles. She watched me, her face creased with concern about my assessment of its quality. I began to read.

What Does Mommy Do?
by
Dawn Mulcahy

What Does Mommy Do?
Before I go to school, Mommy helps me
buckle my shoe.
Mommy takes me for rides on the train.
Choo, Choo! Choo, Choo!
Sometimes Mommy takes me to the zoo.
Mommy hugs me as we sit and watch the sky
so blue.
She even makes me my favorite dessert.
Yum, yum, Tiramisu!
Mommy gives me pretty dolls, like this one
named Ellen Sue.
At night, Mommy reads me lots of stories,
like the one about the cow that says, "Moo!
Moo!"
Mommy tucks me into bed, gives me a kiss,
and says, "I love you."
"Mommy, I love you too."

"It's sweet," I said softly, looking at her.

"You think so?" she said tentatively, her face still slightly wrinkled.

"Absolutely—how old were you when you wrote this?"

"I think ten or eleven."

"Wow," I said, genuinely impressed, as I flipped through the rest of the book and read a few more stories. Titles like "Happy Family" and "Goodnight Kisses" made the pain that inspired these stories palpable. I flashed back for a moment, fondly recollecting memories of trips to the zoo, and bedtime stories with Mom and Dad. Then I pictured Dawn, alone in her room, while her parents were out doing God knows what.

"They're beautiful," I said, low and smooth. I closed the book and thanked Dawn for sharing her stories. She looked at me and smiled, nodding, as if to convey that she was the appreciative one. Beyond that, I was at a loss for words, which at that moment was okay because I could tell that all Dawn wanted was to be held.

Though I knew better, I couldn't help myself—I wanted to stay.

Nervously, I gathered Dawn into my embrace, her face pillowed against my torso. We snuggled like that for a while, building momentum with each stroke of her fingers against my chest and the brushing of mine against the soft flesh of her leg. Dawn withdrew from my clasp. She looked at me intently and leaned in, pressing her warm, open lips to mine, and kissed me with a yearning that belied her ostensible calm. We continued like that for a while, breaking here and there to stare deeply into each other's eyes. Eventually, we fell asleep on the couch just like that.

I awoke at around five-thirty in the morning. Dawn was still asleep and didn't have to be at work until one, so I didn't want to disturb her. On the other hand, I didn't want Jordan to wake up and find us there together either, so I nudged Dawn and told her I had to go. She asked me what time it was, and the shock of how long we'd slept jolted her awake. We sat up straight and stretched a bit, squinting at each other through glassy eyes. I nodded, indicating it was time. Dawn took my hand and led me downstairs.

We stood in the dark and narrow vestibule and held each other close. Still in wake-up mode, her voice groggy, Dawn thanked me for all of my work and for being there to listen. She then told me she wanted to see me again, but not to discuss the case. I smiled and nodded.

"Me too."

I opened the door and we stepped outside. The cool temperature—close to sixty—felt soothing against my face. The sun had only beaten us by a nose; a faint orange pastel stretched across the horizon and evaporated into a steadily intensifying blue. Like the grass, my car was dampened by the morning dew. Early risers drove by. Along the walking path, a black Rottweiler dragged his master, a tall adolescent whose pained look suggested he regretted asking his parents to get him a dog. A happy songbird chirped delightfully.

Dawn and I enjoyed a long kiss together before saying good-bye. After reaching the sidewalk, I turned to wave, and Dawn's eyes were there to meet mine. She smiled and waved back, blowing me a kiss. I took comfort in her watching me like that; as if she cared about me and wanted to savor every second of our time together. I did too.

But as sweet as the moment may have been, I felt a sharp pang of conscience as I knew I had just taken a step toward crossing that proverbial line—the one that I was well-aware of and that Evan had warned me about. The case would be resolved in a matter of days, though, which would render these issues moot and allow me to not only pursue a relationship with Dawn, but do it with peace of mind.

I got home at a little after seven and was way too wired to go back to bed. I took a hot shower, fixed a pot of coffee, and enjoyed a little peace and quiet out on my balcony. No newspapers. No magazines. Just my calming view of the park in the day's infancy, my warm feelings about Dawn and even Jordan ... my dream of a new life that I was starting to see more and more vividly.

I thought we could be a family.

Chapter 12

The hearing in family court was scheduled for ten o'clock. Dawn and I had agreed to meet outside the courthouse at twenty of, which gave her just enough time to get there after dropping Jordan off at daycare. Nevertheless, I thought it would be a good idea to get down there an hour early, locate my destination, and sit and review the file. I took the subway to Borough Hall, the first stop outside of Manhattan, in thriving downtown Brooklyn. It was a scorcher in the city, one of those ninety-two-but-feels-like-ninety-eight days, and I was thankful to have gone with an undershirt as it had a lot to absorb. The sky was overcast and looked like it might break its fever at any moment.

The workforce was ambitious that morning. New York City buses pulled up every few minutes and unloaded a fresh crop of commuters. Hot dog carts also did breakfast and kept the lines moving swiftly. I took a short walk past my alma mater, Brooklyn Law School, and cut through the ever-festive Fulton Mall, a bustling, six-block retail strip occupied by street vendors, fast-food joints, and neighborhood stores that had somehow avoided death to chains.

The Kings County Family Court is housed at 330 Jay Street, an impressive modern edifice of thirty-two stories. Its eye-level façade is two toned, with tan brick laid horizontally and a gray and black granite foundation chiseled decoratively. Contemporary lighting fixtures are about six feet tall, a border of stainless steel with frosted glass down the middle. Matching flagpoles are perched atop the building like birthday candles. American flags drooped in the morning heat. A series of fluorescent green traffic cones blocked off the inside street lane; knee-high, brown cylindrical fixtures set on the sidewalk provided fortification under the guise of a decorative touch. Uniformed cops were everywhere, with squad cars parked on nearly every corner.

The courthouse is set in the middle of the Metrotech Center complex, home to major corporate and public tenants. It has a campus feel and encircles a sprawling park, with lush gardens, meticulous landscaping, and pavement worth looking at. The lawn often hosts cultural events, and a stage was set that day for a lunchtime rhythm-and-blues festival. Restaurants feature an assortment of cuisine with indoor and outdoor seating.

I picked a nice air-conditioned café, sipped an iced coffee, and thumbed through some papers to kill time. In addition to Milena and her parents, Dawn's boss, Richard Kohn, had also made himself available. Although he'd only been able to confer with me by phone, we'd had a friendly discussion, and I was pleased with what he planned to say. Other than Jimmy, Dawn seemed to be surrounded by great people.

I waited outside the courthouse for a couple of minutes. A cluster of young people congregated outside smoking cigarettes and gabbing on cell phones. A silver-haired, elderly fellow sat peacefully in a wheelchair and looked as if he had no reason for being there; a court officer gave a Hispanic man directions. In due time, Dawn emerged from a sea of passersby with Milena and her parents. Dawn and I greeted each other as colleagues, not even a handshake. She seemed nervous and scanned the vicinity furtively; I smiled with an air of confidence in an attempt to calm her down. As I had suggested, Dawn was dressed conservatively in a beige pantsuit and black heels; Milena played the part as well and wore black. Milena's parents sported their Sunday best; Vicki wore a black pinstripe skirt with matching jacket, and Paul sported a nice summer suit—a solid tan two-button and brown silk tie worn only on special occasions. They were warm and smiled with genial charm. Richard arrived moments later. A handsome older gentleman around sixty, he looked healthy having just returned from vacation, his skin slightly tanned; for Dawn's sake, he had taken his attire seriously—a tailored navy suit and yellow tie. It was his pleasure to be there, and a warmhearted smile said it all. The D'Angelos were longtime customers of his, and they knew each other well. Tom and I had arranged to meet upstairs, so, with our group fully intact, we headed inside.

Like the building's façade, the interior is spectacular. The floors and walls are covered with marble, the judges' daily calendars are digitally displayed on a massive, state-of-the-art computer screen. After passing through the airport-like security, we took an elevator to the sixteenth floor.

Judge Barkley's courtroom was crisp and clean. Like a hatched egg, it was half-shelled in natural bamboo, the pews, counsel tables, bench, witness stand, and jury box all done to match. There were a few accents of black, like the jurors' oversized leather chairs, which had to make jury duty more tolerable. The room was shallow, the pews only four rows deep on both sides. Behind the bench in full view, the words IN GOD WE TRUST were carved in a modern font. Tom, cloaked in an ill-fitted tweed jacket with leather elbow pads, a random tie, and khakis—all of which seemed thrown together with no thought whatsoever—was seated in the front row conversing with Rachel Schor, with whom I'd spoken on countless occasions. A contemporary of mine, Rachel's hair was red. She wore it shoulder length. Her attire, a brown skirt suit, was professional. Everyone was introduced, and we all took our seats in the appropriate places.

Silence fell upon the courtroom until the double doors in the rear flew open.

Jimmy entered, calm and collected. He was fairly good-looking in a rugged way—about five-ten and thin, but as tough and sinewy as someone twice his size. Dark eyes looked out from a square face framed by thick, black hair done in a Brylcreem slick-back. His sideburns stretched to the earlobes. A scar on his left cheek became more pronounced as he neared. He wore an off-the-truck, double-breasted gray pinstripe, red tie decorated with stock market icons poorly knotted against a white, second-day-in-a-row dress shirt, and black wingtips, spit shined and varnished. He was accompanied by his attorney, Mike Carroll. Mike looked fit in a three-button navy suit, and wore a pleasant smile as if to suggest that our battle was nothing personal. I approached and introduced myself to Mike first, then to Jimmy.

"Hi, James Nelson," he said with a harsh voice, full eye contact, and a smile, shaking my hand. Jimmy eyeballed me, his dark brows arched mischievously with a look as if he'd known me from somewhere but couldn't put his finger on it. He spoke slowly, buying himself time for a more careful examination, and then seemed to have an epiphany. A derisive, wide-eyed grin expanded into a full-blown smile—he had the look of a man whose ship had finally come in. He nodded in lieu of patting himself on the back, flashed a quick look at Dawn, then focused back on me and shook his head critically. I felt nervous and uptight and, again, was happy to have worn an undershirt.

"All rise! The Family Court of the State of New York, County of Kings, Part Fifty Six is now in session. The Honorable Samuel T. Barkley presiding," shouted the uniformed court officer, a young eager beaver with a military crew cut and the enthusiasm of someone who had just started a new job.

All present rose and stood in silence as Judge Barkley entered the courtroom. His tall, statuesque frame belied his sixty-one years, evidenced only by a thatch of white hair and the lines on his long, weather-beaten face. He was led out by his law secretary, a young female attorney of average height. She had long, brown hair and was dressed in a navy suit. Like a law clerk in federal court, she was the judge's right hand, conducting legal research, drafting opinions, and presiding over conferences. The court reporter followed and took a seat in the well beneath the judge's bench. He had set up his stenography machine and laptop well in advance. Round and baby-faced, he quickly removed his olive-colored suit jacket and draped it over the back of his chair.

Judge Barkley ascended to the bench and turned and faced the congregation of spectators with an impassive visage, carefully examining each individual before him.

"Good morning. Please be seated," he said as he sunk into the depths of his throne. The law secretary stepped up to the bench, set the file in front of the judge, and sat in the witness chair to take notes. After attendance was taken, the judge got started.

"I understand there is an agreement to resolve this matter?" he asked in a deep tone. All counsel responded in the affirmative.

"Good," he said, firmly. The judge took a few moments and gave the papers a cursory review. He turned the microphone away and whispered something to his law secretary, who approached to confer in private. When they were finished, I respectfully rose and advised the judge that we had several character witnesses who wished to speak on Dawn's behalf. He was indulgent and allowed time for a brief examination of each. I called them one by one. Milena and her parents each testified about Dawn's character and attested to the court

141

that Dawn and Jordan would always have a nice, warm, loving home to live in. Richard testified that Dawn was one of the best workers he'd ever had and that she would always have a job with him if she wanted it; he even said he'd loan her money to finish pharmacy school. Since we had an agreement, Carroll didn't cross-examine the witnesses, but reserved his right to in the future should the proceedings reopen for any reason.

The judge then heard from Rachel, Jordan's law guardian, whose endorsement could make or break Dawn's case. She recommended whole-heartedly that the judge approve the agreement, pleading that it was in Jordan's best interests for Dawn to be his primary and only custodian.

The judge seemed pleased. He took a few moments to study the agreement and conferred briefly with his law secretary. Then he turned and faced Jimmy.

"Mr. Nelson," said Judge Barkley in a low, composed voice. Jimmy looked up straight-faced.

"Mr. Nelson, have you discussed the terms of the agreement with your attorney?"

"Yes," he said. Carroll then quickly whispered to him. "I mean, yes, Your Honor." The judge seemed to appreciate that.

"Do you understand that you are bound by the terms of this agreement?" he said sternly.

"Yes, I do, Your Honor."

"From what I understand, though, you've already crossed the line once before throughout these proceedings—why should I believe you now?" he said with an incredulous stare.

Jimmy shrugged his shoulders casually.

"Verbal response please," said the court reporter.

"I don't know."

"Well, do you have anything to say for yourself?" he said, talking down to him.

"I do," he said. The judge nodded and, after a deep breath, Jimmy proceeded with what sounded like a rehearsed speech, with stammers between sentences.

"I just want to say that I know how lucky I am to be getting this deal ... I feel bad about what I did to Dawn and Jordan and what I've put everyone through ... I made a lot of mistakes, so I wish Dawn and Jordan a good life and all the best ... and I promise, I'm moving on. They'll never see or hear from me again." He exhaled, relieved that the hard part was over with.

"Mr. Nelson, do you understand the limitations being imposed upon you by the permanent order of protection and the potential consequences of a violation thereof?"

"Yes, I do."

"Very well then," he said, ready to move on. Carroll sat down, but Jimmy remained standing. "All right, with—" said the judge, before Jimmy interrupted.

"And, actually judge, I have something else I want to say."

Everyone was taken aback, including the judge, who repositioned himself in his chair, set his arms on the bench, and arched forward in earnest.

"Go ahead, Mr. Nelson."

"Like I said before, I know what I did was wrong, and I am truly sorry. But I'm not the only one in this courtroom who did bad things, especially during these proceedings."

Carroll covered his face with his hands, slowly shaking his head.

"What do you mean, Mr. Nelson?"

"Well, Your Honor, Mr. O'Reilly over here has been getting together with Dawn and doing who knows what."

Noise filled the courtroom. Judge Barkley banged on his gavel.

"Everyone quiet down!"

"Quiet down," reiterated the court officer with the judge's

implied authority behind him, moving closer to accentuate his point. But all eyes were fixated on me.

"What is the basis for this accusation, Mr. Nelson?"

Jimmy straightened himself out and stood upright with poise and self-assurance. "I saw them," he said with conviction. "Just last week, I watched from across the street as Mr. O'Reilly showed up at the D'Angelos. I stayed all night and watched Mr. O'Reilly leave early the next morning—they were kissing and looking real cozy with each other."

For a man whose feathers never seemed to ruffle, Tom was outraged; he glared at me with bulging eyes, his round face red as a beet. I rose to address the court.

"Your Honor, Mr. Nelson was not supposed to be that close to Ms. Nelson. That's a violation of the protective order."

"I realize that, Mr. O'Reilly, and I'll address that in a moment," he said, pausing. "But I am nevertheless concerned about Mr. Nelson's allegations. Are they true?"

"Your Honor, this is the second time during the course of these proceedings that Mr. Nelson violated the protective order ..."

"Mr. O'Reilly, let's try this another way," he said, leaning forward. "Mr. Nelson claims that he saw you enter the home where Ms. Nelson is currently residing—is that true, yes or no?"

My face beaded with perspiration; a panic like I'd never known welled in my throat. I drew a deep breath and exhaled. I could feel my body shaking uncontrollably as I searched for a plausible explanation.

"Yes, Your Honor, but ..."

"Mr. O'Reilly, Mr. Nelson claims that he saw you leave the following day in the early morning. Is that true, Mr. O'Reilly, yes or no?"

"Your Honor, if I may ..."

"Yes or no, Mr. O'Reilly?" he asked as his brow pulled into an affronted frown.

"Yes, Your Honor." Judge Barkley shook his head and sighed.

"You did take professional responsibility in law school, didn't you, Mr. O'Reilly?"

"Yes, Your Honor."

"You do appreciate the ethical concerns and the appearance of impropriety here, don't you Mr. O'Reilly? After all, this is a domestic relations case, and the code prohibits certain relations with clients."

"Your Honor, it's not like that," I respectfully insisted.

"Mr. O'Reilly, I am not going to subject you to any further embarrassment here today," he said, pausing, "however, I am referring this matter to the disciplinary committee for a full investigation. You can plead your case to them. My job here is to determine whether this agreement is in the best interests of Jordan Nelson."

Tom ejected himself out of his chair to address the court. I sat down.

"Your Honor, Thomas Dooley, New York City Legal Services."

"Yes, counsel."

"Your Honor, I would like to assure the court that, notwithstanding Mr. O'Reilly's ostensible iniquities, which, I represent to the court, I knew absolutely nothing about, I believe this agreement is fair and in the best interests of Jordan and all of the parties."

"Thank you, Mr. Dooley. While moments earlier I shared your sentiments, with all due respect, I am gravely concerned about Mr. Nelson's recidivist behavior. He is certainly intelligent enough to understand the terms of the order and the limitations it places on him, as well as the potential consequences that a violation would give rise to, but he chose to cross the line nevertheless. I have no confidence whatsoever that Jordan or Ms. Nelson will be protected by this agreement."

I looked over at Jimmy. No longer wearing the face of a man with the world in his hands, his jaw dropped, his skin turned pale. Realizing he'd just done himself in, Jimmy closed his eyes, ran his fingers through his hair, and shook his head, as if about to say the only possible thing that could have been going through his head: What the hell was I thinking?

"I am inclined to reject the agreement the parties have proposed so long as it provides that the criminal charges against Mr. Nelson are dropped," said Judge Barkley, his words like stabs to Jimmy, who started to shake.

"Mr. Nelson, you are accused of raping and assaulting your wife, and there is overwhelming evidence to support these accusations. These are some of the most heinous and morally repugnant crimes that one could commit. That, coupled with your violations of the protective order, leaves me with no choice but to hold you in contempt of court. Mr. Nelson, if I were to allow you to walk out of here scot-free under these circumstances, then I would no longer be worthy of wearing this robe.

"I hereby order the following: We will take a one-hour recess during which time the parties will contact the district attorney's office. If you can work out a plea that will satisfy me, then I'll approve the agreement. Mr. Nelson, you must be punished. We are adjourned until eleven-thirty."

"All rise," yelled the court officer as Judge Barkley exited, his law secretary following behind. I sat back down and stared straight ahead. Tom looked down at me with anger.

"Good work, *counselor*," he said. I looked down at the table, covered my face with my hands, and closed my eyes, brooding. The lawyers stepped outside to contact the district attorney's office. Richard and the D'Angelos said good-bye to Dawn, wished her luck, and left.

Dead silence filled the empty courtroom, until Dawn approached.

"Nick, I don't understand ... why is this happening to you?"

I removed my hands from my face and opened my eyes, staring straight ahead at the judge's bench.

"That night ..." I said, allowing a moment for Dawn to reflect. "I fucked up, okay? It was too soon."

"Nick, I want to help you—we'll get through this together," she said in a heartfelt plea.

I raised my hand dismissively, shaking my head.

"I'd like to be alone if that's okay."

She breathed in heavily, and then exhaled. "Okay," she said in a broken whisper, rising and proceeding to exit the courtroom.

When the hour expired, everyone returned as per the judge's order. Tom and Mike Carroll advised Judge Barkley of the plea—two to five years—which he accepted as fair. Jimmy agreed to surrender himself immediately to the district attorney, and Carroll said he would escort him personally. Judge Barkley then approved the civil agreement.

We were adjourned, and the matter was closed.

But a new matter was opened—the matter of what to do with Nick O'Reilly.

A host of thoughts raced through my mind. I considered all of the potential outcomes, but, invariably, I came to the same conclusion: disbarment.

Chapter 13

The night had been long and restless. I had dozed off for an hour, maybe two, tops.

I woke up feeling achy. As I got out of bed, I painfully maneuvered myself and planted my sweaty bare feet on the carpet in a way that felt different. I felt, I thought, the way a newly convicted felon must feel on sentencing day. I resigned myself to the reality of a scary new world. I was a solid citizen branded a villainous persona. I took a slow, savor-every-last-second-of-freedom walk to the closet and took extra time to carefully select, if not my best, my most appropriate suit—the one that, in the minds of my final arbiters, would give the best shot at leniency—an innocuous olive green with brown tie and shoes. It was the sort of outfit worn by a guy you subconsciously feel sorry for.

I strategically arrived at the office at eight o'clock—as late as possible without the risk of an awkward and seemingly endless elevator ride with colleagues to whom I had nothing to say (eyes affixed on the digital floor counter, tight-lipped smile to ease the tension, a lengthy time-killing stare at the floor and then back to the counter for the home stretch).

The seat of my chair was a reservoir of message memos from clients, colleagues, and adversaries on unrelated matters followed by messages from Ruth Davidson, Schmidt, Addison, and Evan. My red voice mail light flashed like an ambulance in hot pursuit. I listened as Will demanded I meet with him at ten o'clock and, with every utterance, could feel myself shiver with panic. I attempted to steel myself for the conversation, visualizing the worst scenarios. Somehow I managed to calm myself down a bit until one of the guys from the mailroom dropped off my copy of the *Law Journal*. Sure enough, there it was—front page news:

Williams Gardner Drops the Ball on Pro Bono Matter

WGS partner Nick O'Reilly, assigned to represent a domestic violence victim pro bono, was accused yesterday in open court of having intimate relations with his client. At a hearing yesterday before Family Court Judge Samuel T. Barkley in Brooklyn to approve a settlement agreement, the husband of O'Reilly's client represented that he saw O'Reilly and his wife in what was described as a compromising position. O'Reilly did not deny the allegations. Judge Barkley forwarded the matter to the disciplinary committee for review.

On display in black and white, I was disgraced—details about my private life exposed for everyone to scrutinize. Friends, colleagues, adversaries, judges I'd appeared before, law school classmates and professors ... their impression of me was now distorted by a third-party's out-of-context account. The faces of random acquaintances I hadn't seen (let alone thought about) in years flashed across a mental screen.

I wanted to pick up the phone and call each one, maybe send an e-mail: It's not what you think, let me explain ....

I felt queasy, my stomach churning with anxiety. Then the phone rang—a single tone indicating an inside call. With trepidation, I glanced at the screen: Schmidt, W.

After three very long rings, I took a deep breath and picked up the receiver.

"Hi, Will."

"I'm waiting for you, Nick," he said, disturbingly calm. I put on my suit jacket and stepped in front of a glass-framed print that doubled as a mirror. I checked my hair and adjusted my tie as if it would make a difference. With the awkward gait of a wounded soldier, I ambled slowly, hands in pockets, my head downcast. When I reached Will's office, the door was closed, and I knocked twice.

"Come in," said a familiar voice that didn't belong to Will. I opened the door. Will sat upright, his face marked with the look of death. The desk was clear but for a copy of the *Law Journal*; the paper drew the attention of a masterpiece on exhibit with an entire wall all to itself. Will ordered me to close the door and be seated. I desperately needed a deep breath, but didn't want to draw any more attention to myself.

Phil and Ruth were also there. They sat in matching chairs facing me. I felt as if I was on the witness stand.

Silence enveloped the room, the tension among us increasing rapidly by the second. The phone ringing off the hook didn't help, a painful thanks-to-you nod by Will following each one.

"This is devastating, Nick," said Will, his voice low and emotionless. "We're in shock."

"Nick, what were you thinking?" said Ruth, an octave higher. I asked for a chance to explain, my voice cracking slightly.

"Please do," said Phil, his jaw clenched.

I knew what I wanted to say, just not how to say it in a way this group would appreciate. I swallowed hard, struggling for a response. Chastened, words failed me. For the first time in my career, I didn't know how to plead a case—my *own* case. I was numb.

"Did you sleep with this gal?" asked Will. I buried my head in my hands, my elbows dug deep into my knees. I shook my head and then unmasked myself.

"Absolutely not."

"Well then, what *did* you do with her?"

"Not what you think," I said, with defiance in my tone. Sighs and headshakes followed.

"Not only are you personally disgraced here, Nick, but you're bringing the firm down with you," he said. "My *father's* firm."

"Ironic, isn't it, Will, about how adamant Nick was about not talking to the press about the matter because this girl was 'our client' who was 'putting her trust in us'?" said Phil. "Talk about double standards!"

"Touché," said Will, pointing at Phil. Ruth interjected and told me that she had spoken with Tom Dooley, who had called to inform her that NYCLS was no longer interested in working with the firm. I drew a long, deep breath and then asked if he'd said anything else.

"Not really, though he did mention that he was disappointed, mostly because he thought you were a good lawyer and a good guy."

"I still am … *both*."

"No one's disputing that, Nick, but I'm sure you appreciate the gravity of what you must admit was an egregious error in judgment and lack of professionalism," she said, pausing. "And not just as an attorney, but as a member of this firm. This is very serious, Nick. You're under investigation and may very well be disciplined."

I remained silent.

"Nick, after Ruth got the call from ... what's his name?" Will asked, looking to Ruth, eyes squinted in confusion.

"Dooley, Tom Dooley," she responded. Will continued.

"After Ruth spoke with this Dooley fellow and he warned us that he intended to be completely candid with the press, we called an emergency partners' meeting. Conveniently, you had taken the rest of the day off. While there were some who felt our handling of this situation should be punitive in nature," said Will as I looked at Phil, his face split into a wide, malicious grin, "the majority were sympathetic and felt they owed you a certain degree of respect."

I mentally took a sigh of relief, but only too soon.

"So, rather than terminating you in a cloud of shame," he said, pausing, "we'll let you resign and go out with dignity."

"But I'm confident that I'll be cleared," I pleaded. "Can't you at least give me time to resolve this?"

"I'm very sorry, Nick, but that was considered ..." said Will, as Phil cut in, delighting in my misfortune.

"And rejected as an alternative," he said with pride, like the kid in the school play with one lousy line whose big moment had finally come. My knees jittered.

"So, go to your office and write a memorandum to all personnel announcing your departure ..." said Will.

"Write it in draft and show it to us first," said Phil.

"Why? I thought you're letting me leave with dignity?"

"It's okay," said Will. "Just do it as tactfully as possible."

"And your computer is being monitored, so don't even try to take anything," said Phil.

I didn't respond. Will briefly advised me of the necessary arrangements for me to divest my equity in the firm, assuring me I'd get full value without concern.

"And wherever it is that you go from here—if anywhere— don't even think about contacting any of our clients," said Phil. Silence loomed for a few more moments.

"All right, Nick," said Will, brooding, with the look of a disappointed father. "That will be all."

I rose out of my chair and exited, the creak of the door cueing folks to scatter. I stopped at Evan's office and found him chatting with a junior associate in our group; she stopped mid-sentence and excused herself, dashing past and shutting the door without asking if Evan wanted it closed or open. I took her seat and moved it up to the desk. Evan arched forward in earnest for the final huddle, fourth and goal, the clock near expired with no timeouts remaining. He closed his eyes in deep contemplation and slowly shook his head. Just as family members grieve with each other, it was as if my pain was his pain. His role in my transition was a given.

"So what now?" he asked. I told him about the investigation and that I needed time off to clear my head. Appreciating that it was too soon for specific ideas, he kept his blessing-in-disguise speech brief, but gave me just enough to open my mind and get me started. Then he rose and came around to hug me.

"I'm here for you, brother," he said. "For anything."

"I know," I said, nodding. "I'll be in touch."

I returned to my office for the last time. From the seat of the couch, I looked around. I reflected on victories, hard work paying off, and praise from legal scholars. I remembered when Will extended his hand to offer me partnership, how good it felt to know that I would make enough money to help my mother. And though I had serious issues with the firm's culture, the clients, folks like Phil, the dreadful hours—this was no way to go out.

After trying (unsuccessfully) to unwind, I sat at my desk and wrote my farewell memo:

Brian Cohen

Dear Colleagues:

I joined Williams Gardner & Schmidt twelve years ago as a summer associate. After graduating from law school and completing a federal clerkship, I eagerly returned to the firm to begin my career in private practice. Approximately five years ago, the firm rewarded my efforts and made me a partner, an honor and a distinction of which I have always been very proud. After making partner, I did not rest on my laurels, but continued working long hours and making countless personal sacrifices for the firm and its clients. I was not alone, however, and I want to say that I could not have accomplished all that I have here at WGS without the assistance of many, including partners, associates, paralegals, and support staff. It has been a great ride.

As you probably know by now, I have recently been accused of certain misconduct in connection with a matter I have been handling pro bono. I want to let you all know that, despite whatever you might read and/or hear, I do not believe that I have done anything wrong or committed any violation of the Code of Ethics. I have always acted according to the highest standards of professional conduct, and the situation at issue is no exception. I intend to contest these allegations vigorously and am hopeful that, in the end, I will be cleared of wrongdoing.

*Nevertheless, after meeting with my
partners, I have decided that it would be in
the best interests of the firm for me to resign,
effective immediately. I am saddened to be
leaving the place to which I have given the
best years of my life, and would like to thank
those of you who have been good to me during
my tenure here at WGS. I wish you a lifetime
of peace and prosperity.*

All the best,

Nicholas O'Reilly

With Evan's help, I cleaned out my office. I also tended to
a few administrative issues, including faxing a letter resigning
from my post at the bar association. I said good-bye to Janice
and a handful of others. Evan escorted me out, walking by
my side for all to see.

When I got home, I left my things by the doorway,
exchanged my suit for a T-shirt and sweats, and stepped out
onto the balcony. Sitting splay-legged on my cushioned wicker
bench, I considered what to do next. Leaving law wasn't an
option as I'd been an attorney my whole working life and had
never considered a different path. I lived and breathed the
law and had worked tirelessly to improve my craft. All that
knowledge and experience for nothing? I couldn't imagine
leaving it behind. I thought about what my alternatives were
within law. As a career litigator, I didn't have many. But, with
the investigation pending and a wave of negative publicity, no
firm would touch me. Besides, even if I could, returning to
another Williams Gardner, peopled with sociopaths like Phil
Addison, was definitely not happening.

After ruminating a little longer, I crashed.

I awoke a few hours later, stepped inside, and found

two messages on my machine—one from Mom, the other from Dawn. I called Mom back and told her about what had happened. She said the ordeal brought back memories of what happened to my father. She also invited me to come and stay with her for as long as I needed, and, as much as I appreciated the gesture, I declined.

Then I played Dawn's message: "Hi, Nick, it's Dawn. If you're there, please pick up ..." There were three or four seconds of silence, and then she continued, "... Nick, I tried you at the office and your secretary told me you weren't with the firm anymore .... Nick, I want to tell you how truly and deeply sorry I am about what happened to you. I feel terrible. You deserve so much better than this .... I'm here for you and I really ... I really want to be a part of your life ... I want to help you get through this.... Please don't be a stranger, Nick. Good luck, and hang in there. And thank you for everything you did for me. Bye."

Staring at the machine, I smiled faintly, but with a hint of sadness.

Then I lowered my head and held it in my hands, my eyes drawn shut. At that moment, I didn't have a clue as to where in life I was headed, let alone what, if anything, would happen with me and Dawn. I wondered why she would even want to be with me.

I couldn't bear to call her back. I wouldn't even know what to say.

Upon receipt of a directive by Judge Barkley, an investigation was officially commenced by the Departmental Disciplinary Committee of the Appellate Division of the Supreme Court of the State of New York, Second Judicial Department. The transcript of the hearing before Judge Barkley reflecting Jimmy's allegations served as the basis for the notice of charges in a formal proceeding styled "In the Matter of Nicholas O'Reilly, Respondent." The pleading was served upon me by first class mail, advising of the nature of the allegations and the facts alleged as well as my right to state my position in response. I was ordered to appear before a hearing panel in about a month's time and advised to retain counsel.

I consulted a practitioner with experience in these types of matters, an attorney named Debra Schwartz. She came highly recommended, and her credentials were impressive. After a pleasant discussion during which I got a good feeling, I formally engaged her, and she immediately filed a written notice of appearance on my behalf. Debra suggested hiring an expert on professional responsibility—a professor at Fordham Law School named Ann Marshall—to prepare an affidavit opinion. I gave the go-ahead despite the hefty price tag.

In the meantime, the committee would be interviewing Dawn and Tom Dooley, as well as Evan, whom I had designated as a character witness.

I agonized over what would become of those interviews. Driven by an undoubted sense of betrayal, Tom would be out to hang me. And as for Dawn, though she would only try to help, sometimes things just come out the wrong way, especially when emotions take hold. I didn't think twice about Evan.

That got me thinking about Dawn again—the good times we'd had together, our nice talks, how we bonded over the intimacies of our personal lives, the recognition of our deep connection, her beautiful smile, the emotional fulfillment I derived from our togetherness ... and how, for all of these reasons, I couldn't stop myself from developing feelings for her.

And for that, I was guilty as charged.

Chapter 14

I spent the next few weeks leading up to my hearing alone.

Other than when Mom and Evan called to check in, I spoke to nobody. At times, I found myself wallowing in self-pity, the victim of a raw deal.

To quell my sense of gloom, I freed my mind by keeping my fingers moving. When I first sat down at the piano, the tone seemed a little off, and I immediately called in a tuner. After opening the top for the first time in years, he only needed a quick look inside to determine that it needed both tuning and restoration. He replaced the strings and soundboard, resurfaced the cast-iron plate, and re-felted the key beds. I was surprised at how much work it needed, but was happy to have it back and brought up to pitch for a more enjoyable sound. I thought it played better than ever.

I picked up sheet music from artists I admired and took the opportunity to learn new material. It felt good to play full-time, and I even booked a couple of late-night gigs at local bars; they were quiet and low key with crowds small enough to share a bottle of wine. For the first time in well over a year, I gave pickup basketball a shot, though after twenty minutes of full court I realized a slow walk in the park was all I could handle. As for food, I put thought into every meal; over time,

I'd accumulated a long list of restaurants to try, and I treated myself. The Mets were on a ten-game home stand, and there was no better time to take in a couple of games over hotdogs and beer.

But this was no vacation. Like an antidepressant, the pleasing effects of my newfound leisure eventually wore off, and reality abruptly resurfaced. The stress of the investigation and appearing before the disciplinary committee weighed heavily on my conscience. Busy-looking suits, their briefcases swinging and BlackBerries buzzing, charged the streets and served as a constant reminder of the world from which I'd been banished. Being out of work and feeling unproductive left me miserable, ashamed—in a dreadful rut to say the least. I was in such a bad way that I wondered how Dawn would even want to be with me.

Time finally passed, and the hearing panel convened to interview Dawn, Tom Dooley, and Evan.

Then, it was my turn.

An hour before the meeting, I met with Debra to prepare. Long curly brown locks fell over the jacket of her navy skirt suit, and, with the heels, I'd say she was about five-six. With dark eyes, high cheekbones, a dainty nose, and square chin, there was both fragility and strength in her face. Debra had attended the other interviews and had not only had a chance to cross-examine the witnesses, but had gotten a feel for the members of the panel. She said they were tough as nails, which wasn't what I wanted to hear, but at least I knew going in.

The hearing took place at the offices of Manning Boggs Sullivan & Strong, a large law firm ranked a tier below Williams Gardner. One of the members of the committee serving on the panel, Paula Mittenhoffer, was a Manning Boggs partner.

Debra and I arrived at the reception desk. The firm's extravagant interior—mahogany crown moldings, marble floors, wainscoted walls, and fancy artwork—was painfully familiar.

After waiting for ten minutes, we were escorted to a lush conference room, its views obscured by blackout shades pulled low. I felt trapped. John Black, the committee chairman and the dean of a local law school, was an imposing presence. He sat in the middle of the conference table flanked by Paula Mittenhoffer, Judge Reed Saunders, and seven empty chairs. But only two chairs were set directly across on our side. The other eight had been deliberately removed and lined up along the perimeter of the room. A court reporter licensed to take oaths, a young woman with long black hair and dressed in a pantsuit, was already set up at the head of the conference table and ready to transcribe.

"Have a seat," ordered Dean Black, his voice deep yet clear. He spoke with the air of a man who'd grown accustomed to getting his way. He was shiny bald on top with white around the sides and back. His face was long and pale and square of chin, and he was dressed for a state-of-the-union address—a solid navy suit, white shirt, and red tie that matched the American flag pinned to his lapel. With barely a glance, he pointed at our chairs. A thick Mont Blanc nestled between his fingers like a fat Cohiba. Hardly skipping a beat, Dean Black turned his attention to the file spread out before him. In advance of the hearing, Debra had submitted an answer, a responsive pleading formally responding to the allegations (with mostly denials and a few admissions to basic uncontested facts) along with the affidavit submitted by our expert, Professor Marshall. I recognized those documents on the table.

Though Paula looked small next to Dean Black, by reputation she loomed just as large as the heaviest hitter in her area of white-collar criminal defense. In her mid-fifties, she used makeup sparingly and kept her tawny coif short and side parted. She dressed in style—a black skirt suit, white-collared shirt, and pearls. Judge Saunders, an African-American in his late sixties, had retired from the bench about five years earlier. His copper-colored hair was cropped tight; his face was full and freckled. With broad shoulders that filled his gray suit jacket, he sat sternly and arched forward, his hands locked and resting on the table, thumbs tapping anxiously, eager to get back into the game.

Debra and I sat and faced the panel, their faces stone cold reflecting minds already made up. They had no time for niceties as they were there to regulate and possibly to punish. Hardly appearing out of obligation, they served with an aim toward cleaning up the profession, preserving its integrity, and setting examples for others. Before we began, Debra advised that Professor Marshall could make herself available, if necessary. Though he didn't seem to care, Dean Black nodded politely and then proceeded with the inquiry.

"Mr. O'Reilly, we've interviewed your former client, Ms. Nelson, as well as Mr. Dooley and your former colleague, Mr. Berger. We've also read the transcript of the hearing before Judge Barkley. While we have ideas as to what direction this is headed in, since you are our last interview, this is our opportunity to do a little more fact finding and for you to plead your case," he said. I nodded, and he turned to Paula.

"I believe you had some questions, Paula, so why don't you begin," he said. She cut to the chase with zeal.

"Mr. O'Reilly, the original settlement proposal provided that all criminal charges against Mr. Nelson would be dropped," she said, pausing. "Mr. O'Reilly, knowing what happened, the horrific crimes that Mr. Nelson had committed, his violations of the protective order, how could you agree to just let him walk?"

I took a moment, face down to free myself from distraction, and carefully gathered my thoughts. I looked up as six impatient eyes assessed me critically, their expressions stilled and serious.

"First, as compelling as Dawn's testimony could potentially be, proving rape in a marital context is extremely difficult. And, second, I didn't have the final say. Given the financial terms, the permanent order of protection, and the immediate ramifications of any such violation, and ultimately that it was in line with my client's wishes in terms of achieving both full custody and Mr. Nelson's relinquishment of parental rights as quickly as possible, I thought the deal was fair and reasonable and one that I could bring to my colleague, Mr. Dooley, for approval."

"Really?" asked Paula.

"Yes," I said. I responded with intensity, abandoning all pretense. "I didn't make a single move in this case without going through Tom first. Family law is not my area of expertise. I relied on Tom to guide me, as if I was his associate. That was the nature of our relationship."

"Speaking of relationships, Mr. O'Reilly," said Judge Saunders, leaning toward me, his eyes cold and measured, "tell us about your relationship with Ms. Nelson."

"Sure. I met her for the first time at Mr. Dooley's office. She was there with her son, Jordan."

"What did you think of her when you first met her?" said Paula.

"What do you mean?"

"Were you attracted to her?" said Judge Saunders.

"As a matter of pure fact, Your Honor, Dawn is an attractive woman, but to answer your question, no, I was not attracted to her in the way that you're intimating. All I could think at the time was how different she looked in person compared to the pictures of her that were in the file. We were briefly introduced, and then I listened to her tell her story. So, to be honest, all I was feeling at the time we first met was sympathy. I just wanted to make a difference in her and her son's lives. That was my job."

"Why the distinction about telling the truth, Mr. O'Reilly?"

said Dean Black. "Are you not always telling us the truth here?" Mentally, I sighed to myself.

"It's just a figure of speech. Of course I'm telling you the truth—every word," I insisted with a vague hint of annoyance in my tone. My lips thinned with irritation.

"Mr. O'Reilly, do you remember what Ms. Nelson was wearing that first day you met her?" said Paula.

I turned to Debra dismayed, eyebrows arched in bafflement. But Debra wanted to keep her participation to a minimum. She felt that frequent objections would give the impression that I had something to hide. In a private whisper, Debra advised that it was okay and that I should just tell my story. She wanted me to get comfortable and get some momentum going. I briefly reflected on that day and responded, narrowing my eyes and shaking my head with a slight shrug, perplexed as to the question's relevance.

"Is that your type, Mr. O'Reilly?" said Paula. I clenched my jaw, raging inside. I struggled to maintain an even, conciliatory tone.

"Ms. Mittenhoffer," I said, pausing. "It wasn't until after I got to know Dawn on a personal level that I realized that maybe she was my type—at the very least, I saw what I had been missing in my life."

"Well, how exactly did you get to know her on a personal level?" said Dean Black. "Did you pursue her in that way? Did you take her out on dates?"

"No, I did not pursue her, and I did not take her out on dates," I said, before recapitulating our discussions and meetings in chronological order—the Jimmy and Jordan incident, the afternoon we met for coffee, and so on.

"Did you kiss her?" asked Paula. I gritted my teeth.

"Once."

"So, you had feelings for her at that point?" said Dean Black.

"At the point when we kissed, we had feelings for each other."

"Mr. O'Reilly," said Judge Saunders harshly, his green eyes blazing with sudden anger, "you had an attorney-client relationship."

I took a deep breath and exhaled. "I understand."

As the panel took a few moments and caucused, a long, drawn-out silence loomed like a heavy mist.

"Tell us what happened the night you slept at Ms. Nelson's home," said Paula. I responded with a brief description of the evening, recounting the meeting with the D'Angelos. Then Judge Saunders asked me what happened after they left.

"We talked for a while and then kissed a little, and eventually, we fell asleep on the couch."

"That's it?" asked Paula. "Just kissed?" I nodded. Dean Black asked me if we touched each other, and I felt my face flush with humiliation.

"Well, we held each other," I said, softly. "We held hands and hugged."

"That's not what I meant," said Dean Black, pausing. "Did you fondle her?"

I took a deep breath and thought about the question.

"I understand how this whole thing looks now, but ..."

"Mr. O'Reilly, please answer the question."

"Absolutely not," I said with conviction. "I was aware of the rule, but I also knew that I wasn't taking advantage of Dawn. I always looked out for her best interests, and, at the time that this happened, short of court approval, the matter had been resolved. I wasn't out to exploit a vulnerable woman. Dawn and I want the same things, share similar dreams and values. We make each other laugh."

"But you were aware that you were having relations with your client, right?" said Judge Saunders, his voice firm, final.

"In my heart, I didn't feel as if I was doing anything wrong. In my mind, I realized how, to outsiders, the situation could be misconstrued. Did I have 'sexual relations' with my client? I don't believe so."

"Since you mention it, why don't we take a close look at that, Mr. O'Reilly," said Judge Saunders. He reached over the table and passed two copies of Professional Disciplinary Rule 1200.29-a over to Debra.

"Why don't we all review this for a moment, with careful attention paid to subsections (a) and (b)(3)," said Dean Black, as everyone silently read the following rule:

§ 1200.29-a. Sexual Relations with Clients.

(a) "Sexual Relations" means sexual intercourse or the touching of an intimate part of another person for the purpose of sexual arousal, sexual gratification, or sexual abuse.

(b) A lawyer shall not:

(1) Require or demand sexual relations with a client or third party incident to or as a condition of any professional representation.
(2) Employ coercion, intimidation, or undue influence in entering into sexual relations with a client.
(3) In domestic relations matters, enter into sexual relations with a client during the course of the lawyer's representation of the client.

I looked up and nodded, indicating that I was finished.

"So, Mr. O'Reilly, do you think, based on your interpretation of this rule, that you violated it in any way?"

said Judge Saunders. I thought back to our times together ... the kissing. I didn't know what to say.

"Well, Mr. O'Reilly?" said Dean Black.

"No."

"Did you ever undress each other ... ever touch each other?" said Paula.

"I answered that question already," I said, frustrated. I seethed with anger and could feel my features harden. "Again, the answer is no—we kissed—that's it. That was the extent of our relations."

"*Sexual* relations, Mr. O'Reilly," said Dean Black, his voice stern with no trace of sympathy.

The members of the panel took a minute and huddled one last time. After taking their seats and getting comfortable, Dean Black posed the final question.

"Just so we're clear, Mr. O'Reilly, you don't believe you made a mistake?"

"Actually, I do," I said with an air of confidence, my eyes focused directly on his. "Several, in fact."

"Well, what are they?"

"For starters, my career path—the best years of my life are a total blur, and, other than a collection of money, I have nothing to show for them. The fact is that I made a name for myself successfully defending blatant acts of fraud and getting good cases dismissed. I allowed guys like Will Schmidt and Phil Addison to treat me like their lackey.

"I know I'm supposed to say that I shouldn't have gotten involved with my client, but I can't and I won't. Dawn Nelson is a beautiful person, and, no matter what happens here, she changed my life for the better. She showed me who I want to be."

Chapter 15

"I'm going to be disbarred," I said, my voice fading, as Debra and I exited the building.

"I wouldn't go that far, but they certainly didn't pull any punches back there," she replied. Debra seemed to want to spend a few minutes rehashing the interview, playing up positives, and minimizing the negatives. But it was over, and I wanted to leave it at that. Instead, I thanked Debra for her efforts. "I'll let you know when I hear something," she said. We shook hands and parted in opposite ways.

The interview had been in midtown, not far from my apartment. I walked north on Fifth Avenue. It was late August and still quite humid. I removed my suit jacket, rolled up the cuffs of my shirtsleeves, and loosened my tie. As if I were walking on the beach, I kept my pace slow and steady as others shuffled by.

On my way, I reflected on what I had said to the panel about Dawn at the end of the interview, about the influence she had on my life. For a moment I thought about calling her, as the sound of Dawn's voice was always a boost, but the distress from my state of affairs was excruciating and had left me low. I couldn't even stomach a quick hello, and, at that moment, with the way things were going, I wasn't sure when I would speak to Dawn again, if ever.

Continuing on, I passed a bookstore and stopped in. I had amassed a growing reading list, I had plenty of time to kill, and I found the thought of an air-conditioned rest stop appealing. I checked out the careers section, which offered an overabundant selection on alternatives for lawyers. After selecting a volume that I thought might be helpful, I browsed the rest of the store, skimming dust jackets and excerpts. I left with a nice assortment of fiction and nonfiction, which included novels, jazz biographies, how-to primers on starting your own business, and an inspirational self-help tome authored by a famous basketball coach.

I was in no rush. There were several Starbucks nearby, and I chose one that seemed the least trafficked; even with employee chit-chat and a consistent take-out line, it was relatively quiet. Tracks from a Ray Charles compilation fostered a soothing environment.

I ordered myself a large drip. After running it through the fix-it station, I sat down and got comfortable on a cushioned banquette that ran the length of the west side of the cafe. Along the row, five circular tables were spaced comfortably.

I picked one of my new books and started reading. My interest grabbed from the get-go, I was a strong ten pages into it when I was suddenly distracted by a man, short and frail and probably in his seventies. He stood by the entrance, his head oscillating like a surveillance camera as he took in the lay of the land in a way that made me nervous. And he came dressed for the occasion in classic old-timer attire, an ensemble of pale blue, short-sleeved button-down (blotched with sweat), white and blue pleated seersucker trousers, a gold-buckled black leather belt with shoes that matched, and a gray fedora. He helped himself along with a traditional-style cane made of wood. Mistakenly, I fixed my gaze on him a little too long; his eyes caught mine for just a second, which was all he needed. Slowly heading in my direction, he settled two tables away and set his book down. It was a really thick one, covered in library plastic with a bookmark jutting out about a quarter deep. Though I cast my eyes downward, from the corner of my left I watched as he removed his hat and set it by his side, pushed the disheveled gray tresses of his half-bald head back into a part, and got comfortable. Then, as moments passed, I could feel him eyeing me. I became increasingly edgy, anxious to escape.

"Excuse me," he said, his voice squeaky, almost cartoonish. I turned just enough to connect with his stare. His mouth broke into an open, friendly smile. His eyes were clear and observant. "Are you studying for the big medical exam today?"

I smiled courteously. "No."

"Oh, the reason I ask is that lately a lot of people in here have been studying for it, and you look like maybe you are."

"No, I'm sorry, I'm not." I could feel the aloofness in my face.

"Oh, okay." With his belongings holding his place, he let me be and ambled to the coffee bar, my concentration taken in tow.

He soon returned with a small cup of something hot. Feeling restless under his gaze, I glanced uneasily over my shoulder. He clenched the cup tight with both hands, nursing his drink one slow sip at a time as he people-watched with steady attention.

He later returned to the bar, this time for a bottle of spring water. On his way back, I feigned a deep focus, looking down with my forehead resting on my hand, which served more as a visor. Nevertheless, he stopped in front of me and waited patiently. I looked up with a narrowed glinting glance.

"I'm sorry to disturb you, young man," he said, "but would you mind opening this for me?" His arm outstretched, he offered the bottle. I smiled at him.

"Not at all," I said. I took the bottle and twisted the cap that was so loose a light stroke of a feather would have just as easily done the job. I handed the bottle back to him, smile intact. He then sat down at his table and asked me what I was reading. I told him I was reading a novel.

"Oh, that's wonderful. I wrote a book many moons ago, you know ... never tried to publish it, though. I wrote it for my daughter. It was after my divorce. I got married too soon. Married a rich gal. It was a big wedding ... smorgasbord, Viennese tables, the whole shebang," he said, taking a breather. I respectfully indulged him, smiling closed-mouthed and nodding impersonally.

"I wanted to stop it, but you don't just call off big weddings like that—at least not in those days ....

"When I got divorced, I gave up everything ... I let my ex keep all of our material things. All I wanted was my daughter ... but, as the father, especially back then, you know how that turned out. Of course, I saw her every other weekend before she went to college, but it's not the same ....

"Anyway, I learned later that the family had a lot more money than I thought. They owned stores ... retail stores. It was a good thing I had gone into the business. I picked up a trade ... learned how to run a shop ... so I opened my own place ... a men's clothing store ....

"I never remarried. I dated here and there, but never any sparks ... and the store didn't help ... I mean, if I wasn't watching it, then who was? But at least I had that ... until about ten years ago when the landlord decided he'd rather have the Gap as a tenant. You believe that? Almost thirty years of paying every month on time and poof! ... lights out."

He prattled on a little longer, his stream of consciousness taking him every which way. I wanted to give him the time of day he needed, but deep down I knew better. Like the lesson learned after feeding the birds, just when you feel you've done something nice and dropped a handful of breadcrumbs, they hound you for more and even invite their friends to join—the quintessential good deed that would not go unpunished. I needed to be alone and wasn't up for entertaining. I sent the message by saying nothing of substance—only lots of dry yeahs and uh-huhs.

When he appeared to realize that the conversation was going nowhere, he wrapped up.

"Well, I won't keep you," he said, smiling. "Thank you for listening."

"You're welcome."

I continued reading for a little while until the arrival of new company. Early-twenty-something, she was dressed in a simple white tee and tan shorts, her blond hair quickly put back in a "whatever ponytail." She had an overloaded black knapsack slung over one shoulder and a heavy laptop case hanging from the other. Together, the burdens weighed her down and seemed more than her petite frame could handle. She made a beeline for one of those rectangular workstations coffee shops all seem to have these days as if it was part of her regular routine. In day-before-the-exam mode, she hustled to get herself settled: a quick setup of her computer and the methodical layout of textbooks in a way that spoke of a focused agenda. After loading up on caffeine, she sat down, slipped off her flip-flops, crossed her legs on the seat of her chair, and seemed to pick up right where she had left off from her prior session.

Yet to take a sip of his water, my old acquaintance had been sitting patiently. When study girl was right where he wanted her, the man waited for the best moment and moved in for the kill.

"Excuse me," he said faintly, drawing a step nearer. The girl looked up. "You know, you remind me a lot of my daughter when she was your age."

"Really?" she said. The man smiled as if this one had more

potential than the last dud, to whom talking had been like pulling teeth.

"Yeah—she was pretty like you and wore her hair the same way."

"Oh, thank you—I actually have a twin sister."

"Really?" the man asked. "Was she here yesterday?"

"No, that was me," said the girl, smiling thin-lipped and tapping her textbook, a subtle hint.

"Oh, because I've been coming here a lot and I've been seeing the same people. I used to sit in the lobby of my building. You know the supermarket a few blocks over?" said the man, pointing. The girl gave a forced smile and a maybe-but-so-what-look.

"That's my co-op. It's a beautiful lobby, but the rules are so strict they said I couldn't hang out there anymore. So someone on the board told me to hang out in Starbucks."

Helpless, the girl quickly glanced over at me; I smirked, forging an instant bond, and then looked away.

"Well, I have a lot of studying to do—it was nice meeting you," she said, her open books fortuitously spread out to corroborate. He asked if she was studying for the big medical exam, and she shook her head. "Child psychology."

"Oh, that's interesting," said the man. "What are you going for?"

"A masters—social work."

"Oh, that's wonderful," he said. "Lots of good luck to you, doll."

The man returned to his table, and, after staring at his book for about five minutes, he left. It wasn't long, though, before I noticed him peering through the window. No doubt, he'd be back later for a second shift of patrons.

I returned home and read voraciously into the night, breaking only for a quick Italian take-out dinner. But my mind wandered at times, the lonely man intruding my thoughts. I figured he'd gotten divorced in his early thirties and, other than his daughter on occasion, had been without love and companionship ever since. And though he at least had been able to immerse himself in his work and enjoy daily interaction with customers, even that had been taken away. Now, he had nothing and was reduced to scrounging for small talk with random strangers.

Then I thought about Dawn, about how sweet and special she was, and I realized right then and there how much I loved her.

I reflected back on the moment the old man and I parted company. I realized with fearful clarity that, when I peered up and our eyes connected, I was looking at myself. I knew that, despite our age difference, I was traveling very close behind him on the very same road. But I'd finally seen the Last-Exit-for-100-Miles sign, and this was my one chance to get off—my one chance to rewrite my fate.

The next morning, I anxiously awoke and immediately called Dawn at home. I was excited to hear her answer the phone. She asked me how I was feeling.

"I'm not sure."

"How did everything go?" she asked, her tone marked with concern.

"I went before the panel yesterday."

"Lovely bunch," she said, tersely.

"Yeah, tell me about it," I said, affably, attempting to lighten the mood.

But an uncomfortable silence lingered for what seemed like an eternity.

"So?" I said, feeling uneasy.

Dawn remained quiet. I thought quickly to myself as tension mounted.

"Remember Miss Maudie ... from *To Kill a Mockingbird*?"

"You read it," she said, sounding somewhat pleased.

"Miss Maudie said there are some men 'who're so busy

worrying about the next world they've never learned to live in this one.'"

"I remember."

"Well, I think I've learned … and I really need to see you."

"I never thought I'd hear *that* again," she said with a tinge of attitude that made me nervous.

"Really?"

"Well … why didn't you call me?" she said, her voice calm but intense, clearly upset.

"Dawn, I'm sorry, I—"

"I thought we had a connection," she said, firmly.

"We do."

"Really? I haven't heard from you in weeks."

I tried to explain myself to her … my reasons for being out of touch … my lowliness and feelings of humiliation, but she wasn't hearing it.

"Think about everything I've been through in my life, Nick—my childhood, my parents, Jimmy. Yet somehow, some way, I managed to let my guard down and allow a *man*—my *lawyer* no less—into my world.

"No offense, Nick, and I don't mean to shortchange what happened to you—it's awful, and you know how badly I feel about it—but your *career* hits a bump in the road and all of a sudden you fall off the face of the earth?" She paused to catch her breath.

"Dawn, I wouldn't exactly call it a bump in the road. What I—" I cut myself off as I realized that, no matter how I characterized what had happened to me, she was right. Under the circumstances, the fact that Dawn could expose herself to me the way she did was remarkable—sharing the personal reasons she had hooked up with Jimmy (which, as her lawyer, I did not need to know), letting me in on what was happening in Jordan's life, showing me her private writings, which reflected intimate thoughts about her childhood that she'd never shared with anyone else. When juxtaposed with the way I had handled myself, I looked and, at that moment, felt, very weak.

"Dawn, I feel terrible," I said, apologetic.

"You should, Nick. I wanted to be there for you. You know I did—I called. After everything you did for me, didn't it cross your mind that I would want to do the same for you? I thought you would have wanted to lean on me, but you didn't—you totally shut me out."

"I want us to be together, that's where you stand," I appealed in earnest, with no holding back.

"Not if you're going to skip town when the going gets tough, Nick—that's no relationship. Not that I'm an expert in that area, but that's the way I believe it's supposed to be."

"Dawn, I—"

"Oh, and let's not forget that night in the club," she said, sounding a bit more relaxed, as if her defenses were starting to subside and, with her points made and out of the way, having me in the hot seat was more of a fun thing now. "Remember, up on stage with Sharlene and the rest of the gang? You think I do that every day?"

She was good. Maybe she should have been the lawyer and I should have gone for pharmacy—might have kept me out of trouble (I think).

"Dawn, I was wrong and I'm sorry. There is nothing more that I can say other than that I'm better for it and that it will never happen again. Whatever the future brings, we're in it together."

She paused for a moment and then replied, "For real?"

"I wouldn't have it any other way," I said with conviction.

She let me hang for a brief moment, breathed in, and exhaled. Responding in mock surrender, she said, "All right, all right, I suppose I can give you another chance."

I felt relieved, my face creasing into a sudden smile.

"So does this mean that I can come see you tonight?"
"I'll think about it," she said playfully.
"Okay, think about it until eight-thirty."
She chuckled. "See you then."

Chapter 16

I couldn't wait to see Dawn.

I felt relieved that everything was behind us, and excited about moving forward with our relationship, free of stress and inhibition. Ironically, Phil had been right about one thing (at least in this context): The past is just that—it's in the past.

Unusually concerned about my appearance that night, after considerable thought, I selected a deep blue dress shirt and black slacks that fell over black leather slip-on shoes. After a long, hot shower, I broke in a fresh new razor that left my face feeling smooth. I made sure my thick, dark brown hair, tapered neatly, was perfect.

The weather reminded me of why I loved fall. It was mid-September, a comfortable low-seventies temperature with no humidity. The slight nip in the air portended the change of seasons.

A perfect parking space was available in front of Milena's house. Milena had taken Jordan to her parents' for dinner, so, when I arrived, all was quiet. It was almost eight o'clock, and darkness was fading in. I ascended the porch with a beautiful autumn bouquet—lots of sunflowers, which I knew Dawn loved, their bright petals sweeping outward like rays of sunlight, some lilies, and a couple of others I couldn't remember (or pronounce, for that matter), with yellows, rusts, and oranges predominant.

I rang the bell, and, moments later, Dawn arrived to greet me. Euphoria filled me as Dawn drew closer; her soft, engaging smile reminded me of how I felt when we were together. And then I heard her voice.

"Hi, handsome," she said, projecting the warmth and comfort of an old friend. I held open the screen door as she stepped outside, her long black hair fluttering in the soft breeze. She looked radiant in a pink halter sundress that had kind of a retro look—a low-cut v-neck tied behind the neck à la Marilyn Monroe, a tapered waist, and an above-the-knee finish. Pink flip-flops were thick-soled with sparkled straps; her nails were done in pearl. A hint of clear gloss gave her full lips a shimmery finish. Her perfume set my heart thudding with excitement. I loved that smell; how it invoked memories of the way we'd held each other, and when, even after good-bye, with Dawn's fragrance affixed to my clothing, I could still enjoy her presence. I leaned in and gave her a soft peck on the cheek and was psyched when she smiled with an air of pleasure.

"Hi," I said as a gulp of saliva pooled in my throat. "You look beautiful."

She smiled appreciatively. "Oh, thank you."

I opened my arms and invited her in. My arms encircled her, bouquet and all, locking her into my embrace. After a few moments, a slight adjustment of our positions enabled me to kiss her cheek. As we drew apart, the flowers caught her eye.

"They're beautiful," she said after a careful look. "My favorite."

I smiled and responded with an expression that conveyed I felt the same way about her.

"I'm happy you're here," she said, her hands on my shoulders, gazing at me with relief. Dawn took my hand, led me inside and up the stairs, and then walked me to the couch. I slid between the couch and the table set before it and took a seat, settling deep into the red cushions.

"I'll be right back," she said, waving the flowers. I watched as she walked away, one fluid stride after the other. Moments later, Dawn emerged from the kitchen, the flowers packed tightly in a glass vase filled with water. She set the vase center table and sat beside me, took my hand, and held it gently.

"What's going on?" I said. Dawn frowned. I sat forward and looked at her intently.

"Daniel called Milena today," she said, her voice strained. I thought back to the night Milena told me about her long-distance relationship with her boyfriend, who was serving in the military down in Texas. "They're sending him to Iraq."

"Oh, no," I said, feeling my face crumple. She told me that Milena was a wreck; we were quiet for a moment before Dawn relayed what Milena had told her about her conversation with Daniel. "The gist of it is that he loves her, and that, as soon as the war is over, he's going to retire from the military and come home so they can begin their lives together."

Clutched by a terrifying realization, we went silent.

But then something had clicked. As we gazed at each other, our expressions gradually morphed from sadness to contentment, as if our nearness was a consolation to each other ... as if we appreciated what we had together, a palpable bond. It left me feeling that, no matter what happened with the investigation, I had a lot to look forward to in my new life and much to feel lucky about.

"I've missed you," I said. "I hope you didn't think my distance meant I wasn't interested."

She shook her head gently.

"I understand," she said. "I've also been feeling bad."

"About what?"

"Like all of this happened to you because of me."

My heart and soul unlocked. I paused for a moment and then responded.

"Dawn ... I fell in love because of you."

A grin overtook Dawn's features; her eyes brightened with delight. Nevertheless, I felt bad putting her on the spot like that, unsure if she was ready to reciprocate. I brushed a gentle kiss against her lips, rendering words no longer an option.

"I'm going to be fine," I said, "no matter what."

With her eyes, she told me she was there for me. I gazed at her with fulfillment.

"I know you will," she said, her soft hand taking my face and holding it gently. "I'd just really like to be there with you ... no matter what."

I smiled, beaming approval. "That's exactly what I was hoping you'd say."

We stepped outside onto the porch. After Dawn locked the door, I held out my elbow, she took it, and I led her to the car, our feet dropping gently down the pathway. I opened the door for her and, by the way she looked at me, I could tell how much it meant to her that such romantic gestures didn't just happen in old movies. Dawn checked her dress and held it close to her leg as she entered the car; we took a moment and gazed at each other, her gaze as soft as a caress. She thanked me; I smiled and eased the door to a careful close.

"So tell me, do you eat sushi?" I asked as I pulled away from the curb. She shrugged her shoulders in a way that suggested she didn't, but felt bad about throwing a wrench in whatever I had planned. I told her I knew a great place and that they'd have all kinds of cooked dishes if that was more to her liking.

"I'll try it. I mean, I like fish. It's just the thought of it raw like that ... I picture it coming out swimming on my plate, you know?" she said reluctantly, followed by a quiver and a sweet chuckle. I had once felt the same way; I nodded with a tight-lipped smile, telling her so.

"But I'm always up for trying new things."

"I figured," I said, smirking. Then she asked me where it was. Ironically, it was downtown, not far from where we had gone the last time.

"Uh oh," she said with a mischievous grin. I smiled. "Listen, I can't take my top off this time, so if that's the kind of place we're going to, you're on your own."

"That's a chance I'm willing to take," I said. Dawn playfully tapped my right forearm, which was close to her as I liked to grip the transmission as I drove. The touch of her hand, with the softness of her fingertips and slight graze of her nails, was unbearable in its tenderness. I turned to look at her, but only for a moment. I hated the fact that I had to watch the road so carefully. It was torture.

We had a great time at dinner. I ordered a nice assortment of sushi and maki rolls that I thought Dawn might enjoy, which she did. After a brief orientation, I slowly fed her a few pieces. Dawn told me she'd love to return the favor, but didn't know how to use chopsticks.

"It's okay," I said. "I'll teach you some other time."

I studied her profile carefully and loved every little thing about her, her cute dimples and even the way she chewed. But it was the way she looked at me—a look that suggested an undeniable magnetism between us—that caused my heart to pound.

After dinner, we thought it would be nice to take a walk. We strolled aimlessly until stumbling upon a small café nestled into the cleft of a crooked cobblestone side street. Five tables, set alfresco, were sheltered beneath a navy blue awning; clear amber glass holders, centered atop beige cloths, held flickering tea light candles and fostered a warm ambiance. Another couple sipped lattes and nibbled on biscotti. It was quiet, so we sat for a while; we ordered cappuccino and passed on dessert.

Dawn and I sat as close as physically possible, enjoying playful banter and tasting our drinks on occasion.

I leaned in to Dawn, kissed the top of her head, and whispered into her hair, "I'm crazy about you." Her sensuous eyes beamed approval. A rush of pink flushed her cheeks as she nodded with a sense of happiness. She smiled and looked deep into my eyes.

"Me too," she said with a sigh of bliss. She cupped the back of my head, bringing me closer. I placed my hand just below her neck and proceeded to explore the hollows of her back; I rubbed her lightly with my fingertips, her skin prickling at my touch. I moved in and brought my mouth to hers, gently stroking her lips with mine before sliding my arm down further, clenching her waist.

We stayed at the café for about an hour. Just before we left, Dawn called to check in on Jordan. Milena said he had fallen asleep in Sonia's bed and that she'd bring him home in the morning after breakfast.

Though we were in no rush, we thought it made sense to walk in the direction of where the car was parked. On the way, we passed a small jazz club called Clive's.

"Come, let's make one last stop," I suggested. Holding her hand, I led Dawn inside the club, an unpretentious black box with a bar, stage, and affordable cover charges—a great spot to chill out and enjoy live jazz. A decent-sized crowd sipped cocktails over live cuts of John Coltrane that played from a sophisticated sound system. The owner, Clive Nash, a slender gentleman in his late forties with a black Wayne Newton–mane combed back, was leaning against the well-burnished bar and sipping what looked like a diet cola with lemon. He wore a white Don Johnson/Miami Vice suit with a black silk button-down. Clive smiled gap-toothed from behind his mustache and set his drink down when he saw us enter. I had become friendly with Clive over many years of sneaking out of the office and stopping in to play or just relax and unwind from a long day with a beer and good jazz. His wife, Sandra, used to help run the joint but has since abandoned those responsibilities in favor of their son, Clive Junior. The club was Clive's passion; a musician himself, he played a mean tenor sax and always kept an extra one around just in case.

"The master of the keys, Nick O'Reilly," said Clive with a rasp in his voice that, despite having quit smoking years earlier, seemed permanent. After he greeted me with a hearty long-time-no-see hug, I introduced him to Dawn, and they exchanged pleasantries.

"Hey, Stevie," said Clive to his bartender. "Bring my friend here a Guinness, would you?" Well-groomed and blue-eyed, Stevie looked about my age and in search of a better offer; he did as he was told with very little emotion, and a perfunctory no-problem nod that was more exhausted than enthusiastic. Then Clive asked Dawn what she'd like. She asked for white wine, and Clive barked a follow-up order. Stevie set the drinks atop coasters and retreated to the other side of the bar, an overzealous patron hailing him down the way he'd hail a taxi if he were late for an important meeting. Stevie took it nice and slow anyway, running his hands through stylishly unkempt black hair as he ambled over to serve.

"Ever hear this kid play?" asked Clive, looking at Dawn while pointing at me.

"No, I can't say that I have," said Dawn, keeping her eyes on me; Clive seized an opportunity for a quick up-and-down.

"He's the man." I shrugged in dismissal and rolled my eyes, as if to say, Okay, whatever.

"Hey, what ever happened with that kid I had in here?" he asked. Clive was referring to a talented horn player fresh out of Julliard he referred to me for representation. I smiled and gave the thumbs-up.

"I got him signed to an independent label—they're cutting

his debut as we speak." Clive seemed proud of himself, as if he might have discovered the next Miles Davis.

Then I pointed to the classic Steinway perched upon the stage. "Is it open?" I asked. Clive checked his watch.

"I've got a new quintet I'm real excited about going on in about thirty, so go ahead—knock yourself out." I took one last sip of beer and set it down.

"How 'bout a little Monk?" asked Clive.

"Thelonious Monk it is." I took Dawn's hand and walked to the stage, which was readied for the gig with sound equipment, a five-piece drum set, and a bass crafted of spruce and maple resting on a stand. Dawn seemed uncomfortable beneath the spotlight.

"I need to have you close to me," I insisted as we settled onto the cushioned piano bench. Clive faded out the Coltrane and introduced me as an old friend who had popped in to warm up the crowd. He pointed to me, indicating that I was good to go. I loosened up with a few chords before launching into a harmonious, off-balance melody for which the legendary pianist was known. Playing Clive's brought back memories, like the night I had jammed with Pops Jackson.

The passionate tapping of the keys and the riveting sounds they produced made me feel alive and well, especially with Dawn seated beside me, the way her eyes bathed me with pride and admiration. I didn't tell Dawn at the time, but that was a first—something I always fantasized about doing with someone special and, when I had seen Clive's, I couldn't resist. I played for about fifteen minutes, and, when I finished, Clive and his patrons gave a generous round of applause.

I took Dawn's hand and helped her down. Clive convinced us to stay for the quintet's first set, and, after hanging out and enjoying the music, we were ready to head out. Over Clive's objection, I insisted on paying for the drinks, and left Stevie a generous tip.

"I'll try to stop in again soon," I promised Clive.

He winked at me. "I'd like that, kid."

It was a pleasant night … a crisp breeze in the air. I powered open the sunroof and front windows. My hands were fully occupied—the steering wheel in one, Dawn's hand in the other. I took advantage of an open straightaway on the Prospect Expressway to safely glance over at Dawn; she looked angelic, calmly facing out the window, eyes closed, hair blowing in disarray. She wore a pleasing smile, one more delicate than ever, and seemed deeply engrossed in her own reveries. I hoped she was thinking what I was thinking.

I pulled up to the house at around one in the morning. Neither of us wanted the night—a perfect night—to end. Dawn invited me up, as I'd hoped she would.

"I would love to," I said as I shifted into drive and pulled into a spot.

I met Dawn on the sidewalk, put my arm around her, and leaned in for one soft kiss. We remained in that embrace all the way to the porch. Dawn dug through her pocketbook, fumbling for her keys. I stood behind, my arms around her midriff, playfully pecking her neck. She giggled and pleaded for me to stop. After I cut her a break, Dawn found her keys, and we went inside. She was careful to lock the door behind us.

We entered the dark living room, and Dawn led me to the couch. A cluster of oversized, ivory candles were decoratively arranged in the center of the coffee table. Dawn lit the candles, setting the mood for intimacy, and then stepped out of the room. Moments later, she returned with two glasses of water and set them on coasters. Dawn then sat beside me on the couch. We locked hands and rested them on my leg.

"So, how soon will I get to see you again?"

"As soon as possible," she said, smiling. "I had the best time tonight."

"Me too." I leaned toward her and met her lips halfway. We kissed for a little while before Dawn pulled back.

185

"When did you learn how to play the piano like that?" she asked, her eyebrows arched with interest. I told Dawn all about my playing as a kid, that my mother had taught me the basics and I had picked it up from there, starting first on classical before moving on to jazz.

"Are you close with her?" she asked, her eyebrows arched with interest. I felt guilty about answering that one, but smiled thin-lipped, nodding.

"That's really nice," she said. A mirthful smile curved her mouth.

"I think she'd really like you," I said.

Dawn smiled and looked into my eyes, lightly tapping my chest. "I'm sure I'd really like her, too … I'd love to meet her one day."

"You will …," I promised, leaning in and kissing the tip of her nose, then her eyes, her cheeks and her chin, before finally pressing my lips to hers, massaging her mouth. Dawn then rose and took me by the hand and led me to her bedroom. We removed our shoes and lay down, quickly returning to the dreamy intimacy we'd been enjoying moments earlier, our eyes locking as our breathing came in unison. We kissed intensely, our tongues exploring the recesses of each other's mouths, while our hands pursued each other's tops.

We fooled around for a while and eventually fell asleep. When I awoke, I didn't allow myself to touch her again, as I knew I had to leave and drive myself home. So I quickly replaced my shirt and shoes and struggled to do it quietly.

When I was ready, I sat on the edge of the bed and watched Dawn as she slept; her blissful expression was enchanting, like something out of a fairy tale. I lowered my head to hers and gently touched my lips to her cheek. She lay there still for a moment and then opened her eyes, the corners of her mouth pulling into a smile as she reached for my hand.

"I love you," she said in a whisper, leaving me feeling a

bottomless peace with the direction in which my life was headed.

"I love you too."

Chapter 17

One week later, I got the call from Debra.

Though the disciplinary committee had the right to privately reprimand or censure me without penalty, it had gone a step further and notified the Appellate Division of the matter via a formal petition that described the prior proceedings, transmitted a report and the record, and requested that the court take serious action. It was now up to a judge to decide my fate. We were ordered to appear before the court in ten days' time.

The Appellate Division, Second Department, is located on Monroe Place in Brooklyn Heights. The building's façade bears classical details, with white limestone and a pink granite base. The lobby is magnificent—a domed ceiling supported by green marble columns, with bronze enhancing everything from the doors to the vents.

Debra and I entered the empty two-story courtroom, half-paneled in walnut and stone. The coffered ceiling is accented with gold leaf and holds four oversized chandeliers. A uniformed courtroom deputy emerged and advised that Associate Justice Rita Garbus would be out momentarily. We took seats in the front row of the pews.

Justice Garbus, a short woman of about sixty-five years,

cloaked in black robe with big-rimmed glasses, pearl earrings, and hair back in a bun, stepped out from behind closed doors, and we were ordered to rise. The court reporter, an older, gray-haired gentleman, followed behind and made a beeline for his station, the equipment already set up just beneath the bench.

Wasting no time, Justice Garbus advised that she had considered the committee's report and recommendations and had undertaken an independent review of the record, including all of the testimony and Professor Marshall's affidavit. She expressed concern over the fact that I was aware of the disciplinary rule regarding sexual relations with clients, had concerns about my behavior, and had taken steps to conceal it. She then articulated what she deemed to be "mitigating circumstances" in my favor—the fact that I worked closely with Tom, who guided me step-by-step throughout the proceedings, as well as what she'd characterized as my "impeccable and distinguished" reputation as a member of the bar.

"However," she stated, slowly and with conviction, her words spread far apart, "a knowing or reckless violation of an ethical rule cannot be countenanced."

Having laid the foundation, she proceeded to rule: "Mr. O'Reilly, you are hereby suspended from the practice of law for a period of two months. In addition, you are ordered to satisfy an additional fifteen credit hours of legal ethics above and beyond the mandatory continuing legal education requirements for a period of three years."

I was devastated. Filled with a deep sense of shame, I looked down at the table and closed my eyes.

A two-month suspension, though not disbarment, was, for all intents and purposes, a ban from practicing law as I'd known it. Even if I wanted to, no firm would touch me.

I had been suspended—my record blemished forever.

As much as, deep down, I had known this was coming and

had convinced myself that my life was still better off ... that everything happens for a reason and I was moving onward and upward and all that good stuff ... hearing Justice Garbus' ruling was far more painful than I had imagined. I would now be associated with the shysters of the legal profession, the sleazeballs who inspire the joke books, the Jimmy Nelson counterparts—illegitimate, dishonest, and shady.

An outcast.

I hopped in a cab with Debra but asked to be let out as soon as we crossed the Brooklyn Bridge. Though lower Manhattan was a long way from home, I was in no rush to lie around my apartment and think. I needed distraction and started walking. From my BlackBerry, I called the three people who needed to know—Dawn, Mom, and Evan—and left messages. Their unavailability—that their lives were active and productive—got to me.

I tried considering my alternatives again. After my suspension was over, I could hang up a shingle somewhere and start a solo practice, switching sides and representing plaintiffs, all on contingency; good, honest company people, like my father, disenfranchised by the machines they were so dedicated to and for which they'd labored so long and hard. And small investors, too, folks who relied on the integrity of the companies they invested in, only to see their nest eggs squandered by the Duncan Shaws of the world. I had always been fascinated with constitutional law, especially since my days as a student and a law clerk, and the idea of taking on civil rights cases was intriguing.

But I wouldn't even know where to begin. I felt lost and disoriented.

On my walk, I got a call from Dawn, whose words were beyond apology. In no uncertain terms, she conveyed that she believed in me. Despite what I'd accomplished, my self-esteem was at rock bottom, but Dawn's infusion of confidence gave me new life. I fell in love with her even more. She was like a best friend.

"I love you, Nick—we'll get through this together."

"I hope so."

A little later, I spoke to my mother.

"Oh, Nickie, I can't ..." she said, her voice trailing off, shivering.

"Mom, are you all right?"

"I ... this is just ... it's so unfair, honey," she said, crying. "I can't believe this is happening again."

Again.

At that moment, as Mom relived my father's tragedy through my own misfortune, I was far more worried about her than I was about myself. For both of our sakes, I needed a quick exit strategy and a little bit of luck.

As it turned out, a couple of days later, they both fell into my lap.

I was at the piano when the phone rang. The caller-ID said "Williams Gardner," and I initially thought it was Phil, perhaps suffering from withdrawal pains from not being able to fuck with me anymore. I answered with trepidation. It was Evan.

"I got your message," he said. "How are you holding up?"

"Barely."

"Uh huh," he said, pausing. "Listen—what happened to you is total bullshit, and you know I'm here if you want to talk about it, but I need your help with something first."

"Of course, anything."

"Great. I need you to get down here right away," he said. I chortled in surprise and asked if he was kidding. "No," he said in earnest, "I'm not, actually."

"Why?"

"I need you to help me clean out my office."

"Why, what happened?"

"I mean, it's only fair—after all, I helped you clean out yours, didn't I?"

I shook my head in shock. "What's going on?"

"I gave notice, bro."

"What? Where are you going?"

"I'm joining a start-up entertainment law firm called Berger O'Reilly LLP. I hear it's a real up-and-comer—cool client base, lots of stars on the rise, and two really handsome name partners," he said, dead serious. "Ever heard of it?"

"For real?"

"Absolutely. I'm tired of toying with the idea, Nick, so I'm not going to ask you again. You're doing this with me, whether you like it or not."

"Why are you doing this?"

"Because life's short, I'm tired of living like a miserable prick … and because I refuse to let top talent like Nick O'Reilly go to waste."

Biting back tears, I held the phone away for a moment. If I hadn't appreciated what true friendship was all about before, I sure as hell did then. I took a deep breath, gathered myself together, and asked Evan, "What about my clients?" I assumed that he had cleared the move with his own clientele, but half of the practice consisted of my music clients, and, before I left the firm, Evan had had very little, if any, contact with them. But on my last day, I'd brought him up to speed just enough to carry on business as usual—the complete roster, contact information, and a brief summary of the status of all open matters.

"They're on board—every single one," he said, firmly.

"But what about my situation?"

"What about it? I told them you're head over heels in love."

"That's it?"

"I told them all about what happened—the case, the

fallout with the firm, and the suspension—and none of them cared … they think you're the man."

"And what about Phil?" I asked. "The guy was obsessed about me not taking clients."

"First of all, you're not taking any clients, I am. Second, it's the Duncan Shaws and ATRs that Phil was getting his panties in a twist over. And, anyway, I advised your old buddies of my intentions, and they couldn't have cared less. You know how they felt about our entertainment practice—the talent side's not really the firm's business model. Now, if we were on the corporate side and represented Twentieth Century Fox and Sony Music, we'd have a fight on our hands, but we don't, so it's a clean break. So what do you say, O'Reilly? Ready to rock?"

It was practically handed to me. I was on my own whether I liked it or not, and, now that leaving behind the security of Williams Gardner was no longer an issue, the idea of starting an entertainment boutique with Evan was exciting. No more bullshit—our focus would be on building something special and doing it our own way.

"There's nothing to think about—I'm in."

"Sounds good, buddy," he said. "Hey, keep your chin up—better days are ahead."

"Evan, I don't know what to say."

"No worries," he said. "You'll have plenty of time to tell me how wonderful I am."

Chapter 18

Evan and I spent the next few weeks setting up shop. With Evan more in control of his own schedule, he and Julie decided to move out of the city to give the girls the suburban childhood their parents had both enjoyed. Having settled on Westchester County where Julie grew up, an office close to Grand Central Terminal was ideal. After much disappointment, we finally found the perfect location four blocks away.

Since our practice would be limited exclusively to entertainment law, we wanted the office to reflect the creative vision of our clients, and with this space, we got lucky. The prior tenant, a burgeoning media buying agency, had created a modern and innovative workspace, with natural materials like metal and timber—the kind of avant-garde design a couple of stuffed shirts fresh out of Williams Gardner would never have envisioned. The suite had everything we wanted—a reception desk faced with black Corian, corner offices with smaller ones for associates and paralegals, an updated kitchen, a large conference room with a respectable view, and secretarial stations. We had both accumulated a great deal of memorabilia over the last few years, like movie posters and gold records commemorating our clients' successes, and it felt great to take it all out of storage and use for decoration. The atmosphere exuded excitement and inspiration. I couldn't wait to start.

With nothing left to do but get to work (at least for Evan, anyway, since I still had another four weeks of suspension to go), we took Dawn and Julie out to dinner to celebrate. It was the first time that Evan and Julie had met Dawn, and it couldn't have gone better; the women hit it off right away and, before the night was through, had already made plans to get together on their own. Evan said I seemed like a completely different person ... that I looked happy in a way he'd never seen before. For the first time in my life, things felt perfect.

I couldn't remember the last time I had taken a vacation, so, when Milena and her parents volunteered to watch Jordan, Dawn and I took a major step in our relationship and went away together on a five-day trip to New England.

It was just before noon when we arrived in Newport, Rhode Island, the "City by the Sea" known for its wharves and yachting. Personifying the Gilded Age, back when Newport was a summer haven for railroad tycoons, robber barons, and steel kings, immense oceanfront mansions punctuate the shore and remain the area's greatest attractions. Our hotel was located in the heart of the picturesque Historic Hill district, only a short walk away from everything.

After settling in and dropping off our things, we headed out to enjoy the day. The blazing sun and frosty New England draft were ideal for fleece pullovers and khakis. Hand in hand, we strolled along Bellevue Avenue, visiting quaint antique shops and the Newport Art Museum. Down by the harbor, a seafood festival was taking place; we lunched on fresh crab and shrimp salad as luxury liners and lobster boats glided by. Later on, we took mansion tours, Cornelius Vanderbilt's The Breakers being our favorite; we sat snugly on a bench out back and kept each other warm, gazing out at the Atlantic Ocean, but more so at each other.

By mid-afternoon, I was physically drained, and, since Dawn had awoken early herself, we returned to the hotel and napped for a good two hours.

Feeling rejuvenated, we got ready for a romantic dinner. Though we wanted the vacation to be casual, we had planned for one evening of elegance and had packed the requisite attire; we weren't sure when it would be, but, while in town, we had passed a waterside restaurant and decided to make it the one. I dressed in a black, three-button blazer, white dress shirt, and herringbone slacks. Dawn wore a black, spaghetti-strap dress trimmed with lace at the neckline and knee-length hem. Her feet looked elegant in ankle-strap heels, and her hair was as silky as her dress. Expecting a chilly night, Dawn had brought along a matching wrap. I thought she looked stunning.

The dim restaurant was a pocket of calm, the tables lit by candles. The maitre d' saw to it that we were tucked away at a quiet table in the corner. Set against the wall of windows, we sat close and enjoyed the view—magnificent yachts slithering along the glistening water against the onyx backdrop of nighttime. After the waiter poured our first glasses of red wine, I rested my arm on the top of Dawn's chair and dove deep into her eyes, triply illuminated by the flickering candles, her own natural radiance, and the pale light of the moon. I took my glass and raised it to make a toast, but then quickly set it back down; Dawn's smile retracted a bit as she followed and did the same.

"I just realized something," I said.

"What?" asked Dawn, her curiosity piqued.

"A long time ago, it started out as a dream—like a one-dimensional photo depicting a fictionalized view of the way I always wanted things to be. But you know how, sometimes, a movie opens with a drawing or a cartoon sketch that suddenly transforms and the people and places portrayed become real?" Dawn smiled and nodded, a peaceful serenity settling into her features; with arms folded on the table, she leaned closer to me.

"That's it," I said, "but with one difference. It's not about what I'm seeing, but what I'm feeling."

Dawn nodded, tears of pleasure welled within her eyes. We raised our glasses, and I made a toast. "To my postcard from heaven."

"And to mine," Dawn replied, clicking my glass. With her perfunctory sip out of the way, she set her glass down and leaned in for a slow, thoughtful kiss. Withdrawing ever so slightly, she raised her lids, the spark vivid in her eyes.

"I love you so much," she said.

"I love you too, babe."

After a relaxing dinner and a short walk, we arrived back at the hotel. I opened the door to the suite with my cardkey and invited Dawn in for a surprise. Crackling flames glimmered from thick logs ablaze in the fireplace. Romantic classical music sang through the open doors of the mahogany armoire. Rose petals were strewn across the room and over the bed. I had arranged for the hotel staff to set it up just in time.

"Oh my God," said Dawn, hand over mouth, relishing every detail. I offered not a word, but a closed-mouthed smile. I took her purse from her hand and set it on the chest of drawers.

"Come," I said. I took Dawn's hand and escorted her into the middle of the room. I didn't consider myself much of a dancer, but I'd learned the basics by watching my parents. I held her closely, rested my forehead against hers, and dove deep into the smoldering depths of her eyes. Our lips brushed against each other's as we exchanged I love yous. We continued like that until the album ended; it automatically shifted to something similar.

"Let me show you something," I said. I led Dawn to the bathroom and opened the door—a large tub was revealed, silver votive candles surrounding it as if it were a fortress. We stood at the threshold. I smiled and then left Dawn's embrace to turn on the faucet, careful to avoid the shimmering flames, their shadows dancing on the walls. I adjusted the water to a comfortable, soothing heat and poured in a small amount of lightly scented foaming bath oil.

Before long, the tub was ready. I told Dawn I'd be right back, stepped out, and quickly returned.

Dawn and I faced each other. Our features settled into embarrassed grins as this would be our first time seeing each other naked. We undressed each other slowly, giggling nervously as we alternated article after article from top to bottom, our clothes jettisoned to various corners. Our gazes journeyed from head to toe as we appraised each other, the experience culminating with a long embrace.

After Dawn put her hair up, I stepped into the tub so I could assist her. Making it safely, I helped her down, leaned back against the tub's marble shell, and eased her against my chest. We snuggled as our bodies adjusted to the temperature, enjoying the tranquil ambiance and comfortable silences. I caressed her body, moving my hands upward over her midsection and cupping her breasts. I planted my lips on a sensitive spot on the side of her neck, kissing her incessantly as she quivered, laughing. We rested like that until the water turned lukewarm, losing its appeal. The votives were nearly extinguished.

I rose and reached for a towel that hung on the closest rack but insisted that Dawn stay in for just a moment.

"I'll be right back," I said, exiting the bathroom, a trail of drips trickling behind. I soon returned with a warm towel

I'd carefully draped near the fireplace. I held it open and, as Dawn rose, wrapped her quickly.

"Oh, that feels so nice," she said. "That was so sweet, thank you."

I responded with a smile. We dried ourselves off, donned the courtesy his-and-her terrycloth robes, and sat in front of the fireplace. I uncorked a nice bottle of Chianti and filled two glasses halfway; we nursed the drinks nice and slow, having already polished off a bottle at dinner. We talked about important things, like family and our lives together, our hopes and dreams. The moment was so perfect, I wished that time could just stand still.

We relaxed in front of the fire until it was time. Standing beside the bed, we stared at each other with longing; the anticipation was nearing unbearable.

I tossed the pillow shams onto the floor and removed the duvet cover, careful to spill some rose petals onto the sheeted mattress. After we removed each other's robes, I lifted Dawn and laid her down gently with unthinking ease.

We took our time, our kisses protracted, intense.

I pushed myself upright for a full view, admiring the freshly bathed body that lay bare beneath my gaze. Tracing a path from head to toe, I slowly massaged the peaks and valleys of her torso, her flesh swelling at the intimacy of my touch. I appraised her even further, caressing the skin of her silken belly, the soft lines of her waist, her hips, and thighs. All I wanted was for Dawn to feel beautiful, and I told her so.

Carefully, I maneuvered myself. Fixing my eyes on hers, I noticed they were bordered with tears.

"What's the matter, babe?" I said in a whisper, breathy.

"Nothing, it's just … this is the first time since …" she said, biting her lip in an attempt to control herself, sniffling.

"It's okay, we don't have to," I said. "We can wait."

"No," she insisted, her head shaking a bit. "I want you to make love to me."

"Really, it's okay."

"I know ... you're so sweet," she said, brushing away lingering tears, pulling me toward her. A smile reassured.

With a tormented groan, she brought me inside, her body warm and moist.

Making love to Dawn was special ... as if, like everything else we were experiencing together, it was the first time all over again.

The next morning, Dawn and I awoke in the secure embrace of each other's arms. Blades of morning sunlight shot through gaps in the drapes we'd forgotten to pull tight. Basking in the change of scenery, we left them as such and picked up from where we had left off the night before. We took our time and fooled around for a while until we brought our bodies together once again.

After a late breakfast in the suite, we checked out of the hotel, packed up the car, and headed for Nantucket for a couple of days before finishing up in Martha's Vineyard. The vacation went too fast, each day as blissful as the first.

On the way home, we had been driving for about twenty minutes when, nervously, I made a suggestion.

"Listen, I'll understand if you don't want to—I know you've been away from Jordan and are anxious to get home, but I was wondering if we could stop by on the way home to visit my mother," I asked, my forehead creased.

Dawn seemed flattered by the suggestion.

"Of course," she said, smiling, "You know I'd love to meet your mom."

"You're sure?" I said, eyes narrowed.

"Positive," she said, her sincerity palpable. I felt relieved.

I called Mom and gave her the heads-up that we were coming. She was thrilled, and promised nothing less than one of her vintage feasts.

"So, is this a big deal for you ... you know, bringing a girl home to meet your mother?"

I turned to Dawn, who was smiling flirtatiously. I played it cool, wrinkling my nose and shaking my head. "No, not really," I answered, very ho-hum, la-de-da-da.

After driving for just over four hours, we arrived. The front door was open. I followed Dawn inside and announced our arrival.

"Hello? Anybody home?"

"I'm out back," Mom yelled. Moments later, she emerged, brushing a wisp of hair from her face.

"Hi, honey," she said, followed by a kiss and a hug. She quickly pulled off to introduce herself to Dawn, smiling and embracing her with a hug. "I've heard such wonderful things about you."

"Same here—it's really nice to meet you, Mrs. O'Reilly."

"Oh, it's so nice to meet you, honey," she said, doting, "and please, call me Charlotte."

"Okay," she said. I could tell Dawn felt comfortable immediately.

"These are for you," said Dawn, handing Mom a beautiful bouquet of fresh sunflowers for which she had insisted on paying. Mom thanked her.

"Come, let's go put them in water," she said, beaming with delight, clasping Dawn's arm and escorting her into the kitchen.

"Just gonna' run to the bathroom," I said. "I'll be right back."

Dawn twisted her neck around just enough to catch my eye.

"That's okay, take your time," she said, reinforced with a wave.

After a quick pit stop, I protracted my excursion with a visit to my old bedroom, its childhood décor unchanged—the carpet a tight-woven brown, the walls papered in beige, the furniture done to match in an oak wood finish. The same old crinkly posters drew immediate attention—athletes representing my favorite teams and musicians that sampled my taste, featuring jazz legends Thelonious Monk and John Coltrane and a really cool shot of Bruce Springsteen live at The Stone Pony. An assortment of sports equipment, including my old baseball glove and bat, hockey sticks, and basketballs, filled the corners. I had moved back home for law school to save money on room and board, and textbooks and bar review materials filled the bookcase along with required reading accumulated from high school and college, the genesis of a home library I envisioned I'd start one day. Horizontal shelving above the desk displayed Little League trophies and game balls, all of which I had always insisted on keeping; I hoped one day I'd pass them on.

I took a load off and sat down on the full-sized bed, back to the wall, legs over the edge. I stared at the collection of pictures displayed beneath the lamp on my end table, particularly the one of me and my father on my first day of college. With his arm around me, Dad could not have looked happier, a boyish smile ear-to-ear as he proudly sported his new "Binghamton Dad" baseball cap as if it was a crown atop the head of a newly-minted beauty pageant winner; my achievement was his achievement.

I sat pensively, reflecting on certain sacrifices Dad had made to give me a better life, family vacations and nights out with Mom foregone, all so I could have a top-notch education and start out adult life free of debt. Though Dad had died young, I knew that what he had been able to give me was far superior to what a lot of other fathers had been able to give.

"Hey, you," said Dawn, startling me out of a trance. I looked up and found her lounging nonchalantly against the door frame as I slouched on the bed, picture in hand. "We were afraid you might have fallen in."

"Hey, babe," I said with a smile, extending my arm, inviting her to come sit. She asked me what I was doing. "Oh, just taking a walk down memory lane." Dawn looked around, studying every detail.

"This is definitely a boy's room, no doubt about that. It's really nice."

Dawn sat beside me and noticed the picture. She looked into my eyes and ran her fingers through my hair. "You okay?"

I glanced at the picture and then up at her, smiling.

"I wish you could have met him—he would have loved you."

"I'm sure I would have loved him, too, especially if he was anything like your mother. She's so sweet." I nodded.

"I knew you two would get along."

"She asked about Jordan."

"Really?"

"Yeah. She said, 'I hear you have the cutest little boy.' I thanked her, and then she asked to see pictures."

"Which you have, of course."

"Of course," she said, referring to her mini "brag book" filled with twenty pictures.

"Your mom told me she thinks we make a cute couple," she said, taking me by surprise.

"Really? She's never said that to me about anyone before."

"Good, I'm glad," she said with that smile of hers that drove me crazy. Dawn's face morphed into a devious expression, as if she had me busted. I smiled, my eyebrows raised inquiringly.

"What?"

"Your Mom said that this is the first time you've ever brought someone home to her." I chuckled, shaking my head slowly in mock defeat.

"Sure, leave it to Mom to blow my cover."

"I didn't need your Mom—I could tell."

"Oh really?" I said with a smirk. Dawn nodded, seemingly pleased with her intuition. "Speaking of my mother, what's going on down there?"

"I was helping her prepare dinner and we got caught up in conversation before we realized that you were still up here, so I came to check and see if everything was all right."

"Everything's great," I said. "Are you hungry?"

Dawn nodded with a smile.

"Good, let's go eat," I said. "I'm starved."

Chapter 19

During the last few weeks of my suspension, Dawn and I were inseparable. I had dinner at the D'Angelos' regularly and got to know Milena and her family quite well. On days when Dawn was working, I took opportunities to bond with Jordan. We had fun, bouncing from one activity to the next and covering everything several times over—the park, the zoo, gym classes, children's museums, and even paint-your-own pottery. I also brought Jordan to visit my mother, who ate him up as though he were a piece of her famous apple pie.

Dawn insisted I set limits for Jordan, that he needed to learn to follow rules and deal with frustration from not getting his way, that I had to act more like a parent because just being his pal wouldn't serve him well. I enjoyed the challenge and derived a great deal of reward when it seemed to work—watching him closely and intervening in situations, insisting that he share and play nicely with other children, and explaining how one afternoon snack meant one, not three. It was as if he wanted the discipline ... that it meant I cared about him. He'd take my hand and even ask me to carry him, his head on my shoulder, arms and legs wrapped around my neck and waist, like a koala bear clinging to a tree for safety.

When my suspension finally ended, I was raring to get

back to work. Upon my return, we sent announcements about the formation of our new firm—Berger O'Reilly LLP—to all of our personal and professional contacts. We issued a press release and took out full-page advertisements in *The New York Law Journal* and *The American Lawyer* as well as various entertainment publications like *Variety, The Hollywood Reporter,* and *Billboard.* For a start-up, we were extremely busy, with a full roster of clients whose careers were flourishing.

Dawn and Mom had been spending a lot of time together and were gradually developing a close relationship; Dawn didn't think twice about picking up the phone to call, either for a specific reason or just to say hello.

Mom and I were invited to celebrate Christmas with the D'Angelos. We had joined them for Thanksgiving, so everyone was already well-acquainted. Mom and Vicki were cut from the same cloth and got along great.

The winter was brutal that year. Just when the last layer of snow seemed to be melting away—an enduring process on account of a long stretch of near-zero temperatures—another storm would hit and leave its mark. When it warmed up a bit (I'm talking low thirties), we bundled Jordan up for a little outdoor playtime. We built snowmen and castles in the D'Angelos' front yard and tobogganed along the sidewalk. To my surprise, Jordan was fully familiar with the game of snowball fights. I learned the hard way, glancing up at just the wrong time. "Hey, Nick, look!" I took it right in the kisser. "That's it, I'm gonna' getcha!" I said, making a snowman out of him.

By May, it started to feel like spring again. Dawn and I had known each other for over ten months, but it felt like a lifetime—though in a good way.

Feeling that we'd run out of activities for Jordan, we asked around for ideas and someone suggested The New York Botanical Garden.

Set on two hundred and fifty acres in the Bronx, the park boasts one of the world's great collections of gardens and plants, its scenic terrain including a river and waterfall, rolling hills, and ponds. It was clear and sundrenched that afternoon, though a mild breeze kept us in long sleeves and jeans. With Jordan in the middle, we walked hand in hand in hand, playing one-two-three, jump! along the way. We spent time in the Children's Adventure Garden, which catered to adventurous toddlers like Jordan, with flowers thrice his size ("Pick me up, Nick! Pick me up!" he'd plead for a better view), a boulder maze for climbing, a touch tank to experience plants close up, and an indoor lab that offered experiments, microscopes, and art projects, like make-your-own-birds' nest.

But this particular day was exceptional in that it wasn't all about the kid.

After Jordan exhausted himself, I suggested to Dawn that we do a little exploring of our own, escape the crowds, and enjoy a little peace and quiet. With a multitude of gardens to choose from, I selected one where most of the four hundred or so trees are evergreen, and the landscape is calm, thought-provoking, and rich in color no matter the season.

It represented everything I hoped for in our future together.

We took the curving path and picked the perfect spot for a picnic—under a giant golden green pine set atop a plateau offering a panoramic view of the vista. I spread out a navy cotton blanket and unpacked my canvas tote bag, which I had filled with sandwiches, cold drinks, and snacks. We removed our sneakers and got comfy.

I started tickling Jordan, setting his laughter beyond control. Dawn and I exchanged sinister glances, and she joined in too. When he'd had enough, we eased up, and Jordan's hysteria faded to a breathy giggle. Then I tapped him on the shoulder and brought him closer. I had a secret and whispered to him, my hand a half-moon over his ear and my mouth.

"Tell Mommy that I love her very, very much."

He giggled, a smile full of baby teeth.

"Go on, buddy, tell her."

"Nick said he loves you, Mommy."

Dawn stayed focused on Jordan, gently stroking his bowl of a haircut.

"Well, I'm glad, honey," she said and whispered into his ear. Again, he giggled.

"Mommy loves you too," he said. I quickly responded.

"Tell Mommy to close her eyes."

"Why?" Jordan asked.

"Because I have a surprise for her," I said. He told her.

"Okay," said Dawn, hands over face. I reached deep into my bag and retrieved a large card enveloped in white and a small black velvet jewelry box.

I whispered into Jordan's ear, "Tell Mommy I want to know if she'll marry me."

"Mommy, Nick wants to know if you'll marry him!" Dawn was seated like a mermaid. She dropped her hands, and her luminous greens widened at the sight of the diamond engagement ring sparkling in the box. I helped her to her feet, and, in the spirit of tradition, remained on one knee. With my other hand, I held Dawn's leg. She ran her fingers through my hair, already unkempt from the breeze.

"So, what do you say, babe? Will you marry me?"

Mesmerized by the sight of the ring, Dawn was too startled to respond. She stood there amazed and shaken as she wept aloud; eventually, she pulled it together ... just barely.

"Of course I'll marry you," she said, kneeling down for a long kiss. Withdrawing, she fixated on the ring as I slid it onto her finger.

"Oh, my God, it's so beautiful ... I can't believe this," she said, shaking.

"I can't wait to be your husband," I said, taking her attention away from the ring for a moment. Nodding in agreement, she was smiling and radiant.

"I can't wait to be your wife … and for us to be a family."

"I feel like we already are."

"You're absolutely right, we are."

Through watery eyes, Dawn looked to Jordan, took his hand, brought him within our circle of intimacy, and said, "Sweetheart, Mommy and Nick are getting married. Isn't that great, honey?"

Jordan smiled and nodded coyly.

"I love you, buddy," I said to Jordan, giving him a kiss and a hug.

"I love you too, Daddy."

As Jordan's words resonated deep within me, an unexpected blush filled my cheeks; my insides rippled in a tidal motion. Tears of pleasure broke through and found their way to my eyes, tracing paths down my face.

For a long time, I'd abandoned hope of ever feeling that way.

After finishing our lunch and enjoying the moment with Jordan, we packed up, took our time through the gardens, and headed out. We thought it would be nice to surprise my mother at home. Mom opened the door to the sight of Dawn's ring. Needless to say, it was an emotional moment.

"I'm so happy for you, honey," she said, tears trickling down her cheek, securing me in her embrace. "Your father would be so happy."

Then Mom grabbed Dawn and held her tightly. "You're the daughter I always wanted. I waited such a long time and now I finally have one, and you couldn't be sweeter or more beautiful."

"And you're the mother I always needed," said Dawn,

withdrawing from Mom's embrace to face her. "I love you, Mom."

Then Dawn knelt down to Jordan, who looked as if he was starting to feel deprived of attention. "Guess what, pumpkin?" Dawn asked. Jordan liked guessing games; his mouth curved into a smile. "What?" Dawn pointed to Mom.

"Charlotte's going to be your grandma!" she exclaimed with cheerfulness. He grinned, then twisted his neck and seemed as if he was in deep thought, absorbing the concept.

"Yaaaaay!" he sang, his arms in the air as he jumped up and down. Mom got down and took him in for a tight embrace.

On the way back to Milena's, Dawn reached into her bag for something and realized that she'd forgotten to open the card I'd given her with the ring. She nearly tore the seal before I stopped her.

"Don't open that yet." Dawn cocked an eyebrow.

"How come?"

"Because … you already know how I feel," I said. "I want you to tuck that away for a while."

"But when will I get to read it?" she asked with a smile, as if it was some kind of game.

I paused, thinking for a moment. Having a little fun with it, I gave a lopsided half-smile, my left cheek engorged like a water balloon.

"Save it for … I don't know … a rainy day."

Over the next few months, we spent a lot of time planning the wedding. After looking at a handful of spaces, we booked a quaint hotel on Long Island in the Village of Roslyn with a beautiful ballroom that we'd heard was modeled after one of the fancy hotels in Manhattan. The ceremony would take place at Mom's church, with the same priest who officiated at my confirmation, which made it extra special. We didn't want to wait too long to get married, so we settled on the first Sunday in December.

It would be a small affair, as neither side had much family. I would pay for the wedding, and Dawn would plan it with Mom, with help from Vicki and Milena, who Dawn thought would be great to have around when it came time to go for a dress.

With most of the wedding plans behind us, we spent the early part of the summer looking for a house on Long Island, which we chose so we could be close to my mother. In July, we found something on Nassau County's North Shore that we both fell in love with at first sight. It was a center-hall colonial on half an acre, with four bedrooms, two and a half baths, and a finished basement we planned to use as a playroom for Jordan. The timing was perfect, as we were able to move in just in time for Jordan to start preschool. As soon as we went to contract, I put my apartment up for sale. Manhattan apartments moved quickly, and it lasted less than a week on the market.

Dawn and I enjoyed decorating our new home together. Fortunately, we had similar taste in neutral colors and contemporary furniture. Appreciating the need for a feminine touch, I gave Dawn creative license.

The firm continued to prosper. We got good publicity, and the phone rang off the hook with new clients looking to retain us for a mix of services, including new deals and litigation that, as champions of artists' rights, we considered significant and potentially groundbreaking.

Jordan loved preschool. We took pride in providing him with a healthy environment, one in which he could flourish. It seemed like the trauma he'd experienced with Jimmy and whatever issues they engendered were long behind him.

Through Jordan, Dawn met a lot of other young mothers and made some nice friends; a few times, we went out as couples with them and their husbands. Mom was only twenty minutes away, and was a big help to us, especially as a Saturday night babysitter.

Having more flexibility, Dawn found enjoyment in cooking. She made some interesting dishes and enjoyed the tradition of sitting down together for a family dinner. I loved the warmth and comfort of a home-cooked meal—it was reminiscent of my childhood.

It was the life I had always dreamed of: a family I loved, a beautiful home, and a fulfilling career.

I was, as they say, living the Life of Riley.

Chapter 20

"All right, honey, I'm out!" I yelled from the marble foyer on a beautiful October morning. It was Saturday, and I was heading over to Christopher Morley Park for my weekly basketball run. Mom would be by any minute to pick up Dawn to take her for a fitting for her wedding dress.

"Okay, have fun. I love you."

"I love you too, babe. Say hi to Mom."

I hadn't had a regular run since law school, and it was good to be back, although I definitely noticed a difference in my stamina and physical shape, particularly my left knee. I made sure to tape it up, as did most of my contemporaries.

After exchanging pleasantries with the guys, I stretched and shot around before we split into teams. I sat and waited through the first game and continued stretching. My knee still throbbed a little, but not enough to keep me down.

The first game ended, and my team was in. We'd been running full court for about ten minutes and I was starting to build up a good sweat until I collapsed on the hunter green asphalt, wincing in pain.

"Ahhhhhhhhhh! Fuck!" I yelled, screaming inexorably; the sound was disturbing, like that of a torture victim. The pain was excruciating, as if my knee had literally popped from its cap. The games on the other three courts stopped dead in their tracks, bouncing balls caught midstride and cradled. I'd suffered knee pains in the past, but this was different. It felt as if my leg was literally about to snap in two.

My friend Jason Katz rushed me to the emergency room at one of the local hospitals. On the way, I called Dawn on her cell phone to let her know what was happening. My message was choppy, delivered through heavy breaths and sighs.

"I'm sure it's nothing, babe. Routine sports injury."

"Are you sure? I can reschedule ... really, it's okay."

I spoke calmly and went to great lengths to assure her that everything was going to be fine and that she should finish with her fitting before rushing over to the hospital. She told me that, as soon as she dropped Mom off at home, she'd be right over.

I sat in pain for over twenty minutes before a male nurse, short and stout and goateed and dressed in royal blue scrubs, finally came and took me down via wheelchair to a windowless room in the basement for X-rays. I was convinced that I was going to need either arthroscopic surgery or some other similar procedure that was typically used to fix sports-related knee injuries that I had always read about. I even flirted with the cachet in bragging about it: Yeah, ripped up the old knee playing ball, but don't worry ... I'll be back out there in no time.

After the X-rays were taken, I sat and thumbed through a magazine as the pain continued to worsen. I reflected on the problems I'd had with my knee over the years, how tape and Ace bandages never seemed to help during basketball, and regretted ignoring them. In the midst of those thoughts, I was greeted by one of the hospital's attending radiologists, Dr. Sarah Goldstein, who wheeled me into one of the small private offices that lined the perimeter of the basement. She looked a tired forty. She was tall and had cropped dirty blond hair. Her black reading glasses were perched on her head. Her white lab coat was fully buttoned, and her picture ID was clipped to the front pocket. Her credentials were framed on the wall, and I was pleased: top schools and prestigious residency and fellowship. She parked me beside the desk and closed the door behind us. After hanging the films to an illuminated screen against the wall, she took a seat and delivered the news. "Mr. O'Reilly, you have a tumor above your left knee," she said, pointing despite the obvious, even to a layperson. "I've consulted with one of the hospital's attending oncologists, Doctor David Lampkin, who immediately ordered a full set of X-rays starting with your chest. We'll need you to get undressed and put on that gown over there."

My body stiffened in shock, my eyes blinked with bafflement. A tumor? Cancer? Still feeling the invincibility of my youth, I assumed that, at my age, there was no way I could have such a serious health problem. But then I thought back to the way I'd been feeling recently ... all the fatigue, the sweats. *This couldn't possibly happen to me*, I thought. I had Dawn and Jordan to love and support. I always thought that I would grow old peacefully with my wife beside me, and die old and happy.

It would take a while to get the results. The thought that I had cancer completely horrified me, and so those next few hours seemed like an eternity. They made the long and depressing hours at Williams Gardner seem like paradise.

When the results were in, Dr. Lampkin, the head of the oncology department, came into my room and introduced himself to me. I asked that he locate Dawn and escort her to my room so that he could discuss the prognosis with us together. He stepped out and, about five minutes later, returned with Dawn. They found me seated by the windowsill and staring out expressionless, my bad leg resting on a matching chair. Dawn walked briskly to me, bending down for a long hug. She pulled over a seat, took my hand, and squeezed it tightly as we faced the doctor, whose bedside manner was about as warm and fuzzy as a prickly porcupine in fright. Dr. Lampkin was five-four and thin, with hollow cheeks partially concealed by a rugged brown beard. Beneath caterpillar eyebrows, he wore owlish gold-rimmed glasses that lay perched upon his slightly oversized nose. He spoke in a flat, dreary monotone. "A CT scan and follow-up ultrasounds revealed a large malignant tumor on the left kidney. The tumor has invaded the surrounding tissues, and it would not have done so if it were benign. You have what is known as renal cell carcinoma."

Kidney cancer.

"We'll need a biopsy to confirm, but, nevertheless, the first form of surgery you need is the insertion of a metal rod into your leg to give it strength. Then, during that procedure, while we have you under, we'll perform the biopsy and see to what extent the tumor may have metastasized, or spread, to other organs through the bloodstream or lymph vessels."

Before either of us could manage a question, Dawn broke down. With her hands wringing in her lap, she closed her eyes and cried, the tears breaking through her lids like rain through the crevice of an old windowsill. I took Dawn's head and gently brought it to rest on my shoulder as if she were Jordan, in need of comfort in the wake of a nightmare.

"Everything's going to be okay," I said, gently, as Dr. Lampkin excused himself. "They haven't done a biopsy yet. These scans show false positives all the time."

I wasn't afraid of cancer per se, knowing that many have successfully beaten it and gone on to live long, healthy, and prosperous lives; I also knew, though, that advanced cancer was most often incurable. I was suspicious that such was the case with mine, given the preliminary results and how much pain I was enduring.

But Dawn and Jordan gave me strength to move forward and fight. I had so much to live for.

We sat quietly for a bit before Dawn left to use the restroom. I sat alone pensively by the window and stared out at the crowded thoroughfare below where throngs of people were carrying on with their day ... the usual hustle and bustle of daily life, some at work and some at play. It was a world that, up until that morning, I'd felt very much a part of, yet from which, in an instant, I had felt an immense separation.

Dawn came back from the restroom, her expression darkened, her eyes moist and bloodshot; it was obvious that she hadn't been able to stop crying.

Shortly thereafter, Dr. Lampkin returned. With his hands stuffed into the front pockets of his lab coat, he discussed the procedures that would follow. He mentioned the orthopedic surgeon who would assist him with the operation, which we then went ahead and scheduled. After wrapping my knee, advising on care, and prescribing painkillers, Dr. Lampkin said I was free to go. A nurse transported me in a wheelchair, and, upon reaching the exit, I switched to crutches.

The sky was heavy and gray; rain spilled hard and fast. A kind security guard sheltered us with an oversized umbrella as we made our way to the car. After helping me into the front seat, Dawn quickly closed the door and scurried around the rear to the front driver's side.

The hard pour pounded like bullets from an Uzi, rendering windshield wipers useless. On the short ride home, I incessantly reiterated that everything was going to be okay ... that people survive cancer all the time, and that, whatever it took, I was going to get better.

We parked in the driveway and picked up Jordan from our friends' house next door. Upon inquiry, we played it down and chalked it up to a mild, no-big-deal injury. After putting Jordan to bed, we sat down on the brown leather living room couch to relax and spend some quality time with each other. I sat at the corner with my legs resting on the ottoman. Dawn sat next to me, with one arm around my shoulder, and the other hand holding my hand.

"Hey, how did everything go with your dress today?"

"Oh, it's so beautiful. I can't wait for you to see it."

"You're going to be the most beautiful bride."

Dawn smiled and then drew her lips in thoughtfully. Something in her expression concerned me.

"Everything okay?"

Excitement added gleam to her eyes. "Well, I have something I want to tell you."

As if there hadn't been enough news for one day.

"What?"

With tears spilling down her face, she broke into a wide, open smile.

"I'm pregnant."

Chapter 21

"We're having a baby?"

"We sure are," she said, smiling.

"When did you find out about this?"

"I'm almost two weeks late, so this morning after you left I took two tests, and they were both positive. I scheduled a doctor's appointment to get a blood test to confirm it, but these things are ninety-nine percent accurate, so it's safe to assume that I'm with child."

Just then, hope sprang eternal.

"This is unbelievable! I'm so happy," I said blissfully as I reached over for a hug.

"Me too," she said. We smiled at each other as Dawn held me, her hands on my cheeks. She stroked my left earlobe, something she loved to do.

"You didn't tell my mother, did you?"

"No, of course not. I wanted to tell you first."

"Good. I can't wait to break the news."

Then there was a pause after we quickly realized that we had both good news and bad news to share.

Everyone gathered at our house at around eleven on Sunday morning. Milena and Sonia entertained Jordan upstairs in his room while the rest of us relaxed in the living room and had coffee. Later, I summoned Milena and Sonia downstairs. They left Jordan at play.

"Just sit with us for a minute. We have some things we want to tell all of you," said Dawn. They all sat up, leaned forward in earnest, and faced us. We were looking at each other funny, not knowing who would initiate the conversation until I did.

"Well, we actually have some good news and some bad news. Which do you want first?"

"The good news," said Milena.

"Okay, the good news is … we're pregnant!" said Dawn, wide-eyed and smiley-faced.

"I knew it! I knew it!" shouted Milena, grabbing Dawn and holding her tight. Everyone rejoiced and celebrated for a while. They were all so happy, but I couldn't put it off any longer.

"I hate to break up the party, but we have something else to talk about."

The room went silent. Everyone watched me warily as they returned to their seats. I pointed to my leg, elevated and resting on the ottoman.

"This is not exactly a routine sports injury," I said, as tension mounted. "It turns out I have a tumor in there."

My mother lost herself. She arched forward with a worried expression, elbows on knees and hands over mouth.

"But that's not all. I actually have some in other places." Keeping my voice firm, I shared the diagnosis. Mom's mouth opened in dismay, her eyes darkened with pain, tears choked her voice. The sadness from the others was palpable. I told them about my forthcoming knee surgery and that we would know a lot more after a biopsy.

"Listen, everyone. I'm gonna' fight this thing tooth and nail," I said confidently, attempting to suppress the mood of despair. "People survive cancer every day!" Dawn sat next to my mother, placed her arm around her, and held her hand.

"This is another one of life's challenges, which I will overcome. In the meantime, we have so much to look forward to—a beautiful wedding in two months and a brand spankin' new baby in less than nine. Let's celebrate and have a good time, and I'll worry about this other stuff. I'm going to be fine."

I pushed myself up off of the couch and hobbled over to hug my mother, who held me tighter than ever before.

"Oh, wow, look who's here … it's Spider-Man!" said Sonia, as Jordan entered dressed up as the famous comic book character.

I went back to the hospital the following week for surgery on my knee. The doctors nailed my leg and secured it with screws. During the procedure, they performed a biopsy on the tumor in my kidney. After revealing the results, the doctor advised, "I'm afraid we're going to have to remove it." Although the wedding was approaching and I would have preferred to have the procedure afterward, we were racing against the disease. A week later, Dr. Lampkin removed my kidney. Unfortunately, he also confirmed that the tumor was, in fact, malignant. He also took chest X-rays, which raised concerns about the potential spread of cancer. Further tests were scheduled.

After my leg was nailed, I was treated with radiation and chemotherapy. At first I felt okay, but then the pain came back with a vengeance because, according to the doctor, they had used screws that were too long; they had eroded the skin adjacent to the bone. With the wedding only a few weeks away, and considering that I was still fairly strong, I declined follow-up surgery and decided to live with the pain at least until after the honeymoon. I had several radiation treatments to the left thighbone, which, in the end, only complicated the future orthopedic legwork and did nothing to diminish the size of my tumor.

Thankfully, I felt well enough to sit down at the piano. Easing my mind, it turned out to be the best medicine, and I played every chance I could. If Dawn was home, she'd come and join me at the bench. Those times reminded me of the night I took her to Clive's, mostly because she continued to look at me the way she did that night.

And the firm was growing at a rapid pace. We were signing a lot of new and interesting clients and really enjoying ourselves. It turned out to be a great partnership—Evan and I were flexible and always covered for each other so that we both had plenty of time to spend with our families. Evan was very understanding when it came to my treatment. If I needed to get out, he was there for me.

It was only a couple of weeks before the wedding. Dawn had just had a final fitting on her dress and, aside from lethargy, was free of the typical first trimester symptoms. I picked up my new tuxedo, and all of our bridesmaids and ushers were ready to go.

Then came the day that my hair started to thin. Concerned that the eventual discovery of it on my pillow or clogging the shower drain would happen on our wedding day, I embraced the transition, and, with an electric razor, gave myself a crew cut. As I stared in the mirror, I started to get used to my new look and had a little fun with it. "Pretty tough, O'Reilly," I whispered. "All you need is a goatee and you'll *really* be badass."

I walked into the bedroom to show Dawn and found her seated on the far end of the bed, hunched over, head in hands, brooding. I went over, sat beside her, and asked if everything was okay. Without looking up, she exhaled a sigh.

"Hanging in there," she said. I realized that it wasn't the

right time to talk about my hair. But it was too late. As Dawn looked up at me, the color drained from her face.

"So, what do you think?"

"Oh, I'm sorry."

"Don't be sorry," I said. I shook my head and put my fingers over her lips.

"I think it's pretty cool, actually." The tense lines on her face relaxed a bit.

I maintained an iron control over myself as I thought about my last conversation with Dr. Lampkin. With the wedding approaching, I didn't want Dawn to worry any more than she already was. I wasn't going to keep it a secret for too long, but just enough so that Dawn could enjoy the wedding and honeymoon free of trepidation, especially when there was nothing she could do. Without a doubt, if she knew that Dr. Lampkin had given me six to twelve months and advised me to ensure that my affairs were in order, she would have been devastated and everyone around us would have sensed it. I didn't want to put a damper on our wedding. I didn't want to ruin it for our family.

Chapter 22

The big day had finally come. It was a cold and crisp, yet sunny Sunday morning in December. Everyone awoke without alarm clocks. The women in the bridal party had early beauty appointments, and, before Dawn left, she gave me a very long kiss good-bye as it would be the last time we would see each other before the big moment.

"I can't wait to marry you," I said as we stood in the foyer, holding each other while the others waited for her in the car.

"Me too—I love you."

I spent the morning relaxing and caring for our ring bearer, who couldn't have looked cuter in his little tuxedo. Immediately after the wedding, the adoption papers were going to be filed. His name would be changed to Jordan O'Reilly, and he would legally be my son.

At one o'clock, the small crowd of guests gathered at the church, and the ceremony started promptly. Evan was the best man and Milena was the maid of honor. Mom wept aloud as she escorted me down the aisle, overwhelmed by so many emotions coming together at once: her pride and joy was getting married, Dad wasn't around to enjoy it, and I was sick. I walked with a slight limp.

After Evan's daughters, Jenny and Rebecca, made their way down the aisle and left a trail of petals for the bride, Milena's parents, Vicki and Paul D'Angelo, emerged from behind closed doors as they would be giving Dawn away. It was a long aisle, and I watched Dawn make every step from the moment the doors opened and she emerged. Her dress was stunning, and she was beautiful—light makeup accenting her natural, florid complexion, and her hair was pinned up in a mass of soft curls. As soon as she reached the front pew, I extended my arm and escorted her the rest of the way. We stood looking at each other throughout the entire ceremony, giggling to each other at times, unable to believe that it was actually our wedding day and that we were getting married.

The priest's prayer for "a lifetime of good health and happiness together" struck a nerve and brought tears to my eyes, which I let fall unchecked as we were pronounced husband and wife. I took a long look at my wife, smiled, and kissed her tenderly. The small crowd cheered as we led the procession down the aisle.

And with the ceremony complete, it was party time.

The ballroom was exquisite, with fifteen-foot-high ceilings, European-inspired design, glorious chandeliers, and hand-painted murals. Set atop an elegant patterned blue carpet, the tables were covered in ivory floor-length cloths and elevated floral centerpieces done in autumn colors. Beautiful china and silverware made it classy. The dance floor of gleaming maple wood was laid in the center of the room, a seven-piece band set up behind.

I had the first dance with my bride. Everyone turned their chairs to face the center of the dance floor to watch, though, at the time, it felt as if we were the only two people in the entire room. At least until Jordan, who could only hold out for so long, yielded to his enthusiasm and scooted to join us.

At the end of the reception, we danced a traditional Italian tarantella, which the band played upon the D'Angelos' request. It was agonizing, but worth every bit of pain I endured. Nothing was going to stop me from enjoying my one-and-only wedding day to the fullest.

After the reception, Mom took Jordan home with her for the night so Dawn and I could have the house to ourselves. When we arrived, I went to sweep Dawn off of her feet and carry her inside as we entered our home for the first time as a married couple, but with my leg feeble and deteriorating, it was an unattainable endeavor.

"It's okay, honey," said Dawn with a gentle smile of empathy. Filled with renewed humiliation, I looked away, but Dawn took my hand and led me up to the bedroom and made me feel very much like a man.

Two days later, we were off for an eight-day honeymoon to Aruba. We had a suite with a full ocean view, and we spent each day at the beach where we relaxed under a shaded, makeshift hut. I stretched my body on the towel-covered lounge chair. Vacationers were lathered in lotion, bathing under the scorching sun. I had brought a couple of good thrillers to read, but couldn't seem to focus. All I wanted was to lie and imbibe the roaring and crashing sounds of the ocean waves and the giggling of children building sandcastles in close proximity. I took labored deep breaths and inhaled the edible fresh air, dug my feet into the sand, and felt the texture of the grains as they nestled between my toes. I appreciated every moment I had with Dawn, to rub the soft skin of her legs, smell her, feel her, and make love to her.

As I stared out at the water, I thought about how long it had been since my last trip to the beach. As a child, my family had shared a cabana every summer with neighbors. I realized then how much I missed it.

"I'll be right back, babe," I said, smiling. Dawn set her paperback down for a long kiss good-bye. I limped down to the ocean and eased my way into the water, slowly drifting out farther and farther until I caught a decent wave to bodysurf back to the shore. I felt incredible.

Afterward, Dawn and I took a slow walk along the lip of the ocean. The sand was cool and mushy, and we were careful to avoid clumps of broken seashells. It was late in the afternoon, and high tide was on its way. After going as far as the neighboring hotel, we stopped and rested on a wall of rocks. Dawn, wearing a pink bikini with a matching sarong, leaned against my chest and rested her head on my shoulder, locking herself into my embrace. We kissed and held each other within feet of the crashing surf. A couple of times, the waves snuck up and nearly drenched us. We relaxed there for a while and waited patiently for the orange sun to melt into the horizon.

Then I thought about my cancer. After briefly speculating as to whether I'd been exposed to radiation at some point during my life, whether I had stood too close to the microwave, drunk contaminated water from the sink, or used my cell phone excessively, I channeled away such negative thoughts as my hands made their way down to Dawn's exposed belly, rubbing it gently as she turned to me to enjoy the moment. That was our child in there.

I was determined to make it.

I was determined to hold our baby.

Chapter 23

"Listen, there's something we need to talk about," I said in earnest as Dawn and I sat in the kitchen the day after arriving home from our honeymoon. Jordan was upstairs taking a nap. He had awoken at six and had been playing for hours.

"Okay," she said, tucking her hair behind her ears. Stirring uneasily, she placed her hands on her legs, arched forward and eyed me.

"You know I would never keep anything from you—you always know everything about me, even before it happens," I said, pausing, as she nodded along. "But this time, with the wedding and the honeymoon, I thought it was best for me to wait to tell you this now."

Dawn stared impassively, biting her lower lip, as I revealed the doctor's prognosis. Her features contorted with shock, and she gasped, panting in terror.

"NO!" she screamed, her voice inflamed. "NOOOOOOO!"

She bowed her head and covered her face with her hands, sobbing. I took her in my arms as she trembled with fear. We stayed that way for a very long minute.

"I can't believe this is happening," she said with an edge to her voice.

"It's not a guarantee. These doctors are wrong about this stuff all the time. I can go for other opinions."

She withdrew from my embrace; eyeliner coursed from her eyes like dripping paint. She shook her head slowly, as if wondering what she had done to deserve this.

"Dawn, I'm a fighter ... I'm in this for the long haul," I pleaded, brushing a wisp of hair from her face, catching a tear. We hugged ... words were not enough.

"I'll sit down with Evan and talk about taking a leave."

She nodded, agreeing. "Whatever it takes," she said with desperation.

"I'm not going to let this defeat us," I said, doing my best to be upbeat. "We've both come way too far."

I spent a lot of time doing research and was referred to a doctor who had experience with a fairly new, but very promising, form of treatment. It consisted of three cycles, each of eight weeks duration, which, except for the chemo, were self-administered at home. I'd heard it had been successful for others, and it seemed to be my best option.

The first four weeks required several daily injections; each dose was grueling, resulting in violent shuddering and sickness. Prescription drugs helped reduce the side effects but also brought diarrhea. With each day that passed, I weakened. I lost saliva and my sense of taste, and, although I was famished, eating was arduous; even liquid food was insipid and difficult to swallow.

One night, Dawn and I put Jordan to bed on the earlier side so we could enjoy a quiet dinner alone. Dawn had gone the extra mile, preparing a full-course meal with chicken marsala as the centerpiece; she had even set the dining room table especially for the occasion, breaking out our fancy new china for the first time and lighting a candelabra. But things didn't work out as planned. Two bites into my entrée, I had to excuse myself; I vomited and collapsed in the bathroom, shivering with chill. Since this reaction had become fairly common, Dawn left me alone.

When I finally returned to the table, I sat myself in my chair and glanced at Dawn who remained focused on her food, her eyes downcast.

"Are you okay?" she asked with staid calmness, as if for the thousandth time.

Overwhelmed with guilt, I lowered my head. As if taking care of a handful like Jordan wasn't enough responsibility, Dawn was now a caregiver to her newly wedded spouse, her emotions were exacerbated by the raging hormones of pregnancy, and her moods swung like a weighted pendulum. She deserved better.

"Are *you* okay?" I asked.

"I have a headache … and I'm really tired."

During those painful next few weeks, all I could do was sleep and take fluids. The bed was my only place of comfort. I lay with my knees drawn to my chest, my body as still as the room, dark and silent. I felt empty and drained, and all I wanted was to be left alone.

But my world continued to move apace.

"Hey, bud," said Evan, who was calling again to check in, which he did regularly. I felt bad for him, forced to take time away from his family to cover for me at the office. "Whatever it takes for you to get better, brother," he'd say. He asked how I was feeling.

"About as good as I sound," I said, my voice throaty, fatigued. "What's up?"

"Listen, it's okay. If you're not up to it we can speak later."

"No, no, talk to me," I said, mustering the strength to sit up and proceed with the conversation.

"All right, I'll make it quick—it's about the Cowen deal," he said.

When I got sick, I had been in the midst of a transaction for a singer-songwriter named Scott Cowen. I'd met him at a folk/rock festival where another client of mine had been appearing. Scott was about to cut his debut album, and, because he had no track record in the industry and very little bargaining power, we had to fiercely negotiate every clause in the recording contract. I was focused on key clauses for a new artist, like tour support, for example—a subsidy to cover the costs of touring, the primary way for a musician to promote an album. As a newcomer with no real earnings to speak of, Scott had minimal funds of his own to invest, so we needed to squeeze as much as possible out of the label to launch a successful tour. And the packaging of the album was also an issue, particularly the visual appeal of the cover, which is often critical in drawing consumer interest. As much as the label thought it knew what was best, Scott wanted to project a certain image and had to have some degree of creative control.

Although Evan understood the concepts, he had no familiarity with negotiating record contracts—he was the film guy, and music was my thing. But, equally if not more important than knowledge and experience, the label would know that Evan was a novice, and that, by itself, would give them the advantage. As a consequence, my presence was critical. Scott's career was riding on this deal, and I had to rally and interject myself into the process, even if just to make a superficial appearance to level the playing field.

"All right, set up a conference call for next week," I suggested. I figured that would enable me to get Evan fully up to speed while also buying some time for me to recuperate and run with the negotiations myself.

"That's perfect," said Evan, sounding relieved. "Listen, I'm sorry I had to drag you into this, but, my hands were tied."

"No, don't be sorry," I said. "I know you need me—that's a good thing.

Later that evening, I was lying in bed watching sports on ESPN. Covered in sexy black lingerie, Dawn slipped in, molded herself into the contours of my body, and brushed a gentle kiss across the back of my head. Her scent, the same one that had excited me when we first met, was riveting. Initially oblivious to her eager affection, I asked if she wouldn't mind grabbing me a snack from the kitchen—an insensitive request, for which I paid the consequences. Dawn instantly withdrew and pushed herself up. Staring me down like I was the enemy, she snapped. "What? That's what you have to say to me?" she yelled, pelting the words at me like stones, her voice thunderous.

I was so caught off guard by Dawn's rage, my mind floundered. I tried to calm her, but she wouldn't hear it. "Dawn, I—"

"I'm up at five-thirty every morning with Jordan, taking care of him all day and meeting his demands!" she said. Mimicking his voice, she continued, "Give me this, I want that, I'm hungry, I'm thirsty—every other freakin' second!"

She paused to catch her breath and then continued. "I'm waiting on you hand and foot, running the errands, taking care of the house, and, on top of it all, I'm *pregnant*! And by the time Jordan's asleep and you and I can spend a little bit of quality time together, you're usually out cold, leaving me all alone for a measly hour of TV before going to bed and waking up to repeat the same miserable routine! Day, after day, after day ....

"But tonight, for the first time since who-knows-when, you're wide awake, so I figured ... maybe we'd have *sex*! Look at me, Nick! *Look* at me!" She paused for me to appreciate her thought and effort, which I acknowledged.

"I'm really sorry, babe—you look amazing."

"Really? Well, thank you for clarifying that because I

didn't get that impression when you asked me to go fetch! Oh, and as for your order, unfortunately, the waitress punched out for the evening, so, if it's okay, she'd rather spend her time off being intimate with her husband ... the father of this baby," she said, pointing to her belly. Her voice broke miserably. "Give me something to look forward to, goddamit! That we're going to go back to the way things were!"

She wept aloud. Hot tears slipped down her cheeks and fell onto mine as she looked into my bloodshot eyes, which sagged above darkish, puffy rings. Dawn hadn't been herself lately; she seemed uptight, which caused me to wonder if her unexpected role as my nursemaid was breeding a bit of resentment. I now knew that it had; the water had been boiling, and had finally spilled over. It pained me to weigh her down with such sorrow.

"I feel terrible. I know how hard this is on you." I stroked Dawn's hair and pushed it back from her face.

"I'm sorry I yelled at you," she said, her voice resigned.

"It's okay," I said. "I needed a good kick in the ass."

I gathered Dawn into my arms and held her snugly. With my lips, I seared a path down the side of her face. I moved my mouth over hers, devoured its softness, and forced it open with my tongue. A wave of passion flowed between us as we yielded to needs that had been neglected for quite a while. I placed my hands on Dawn's shoulders, eased the thin straps aside, and gently stroked her bare flesh before removing her top altogether. With reckless abandon, Dawn removed my shirt and kissed me with a savage intensity. She took my hands and guided them to her chest. With my fingers, I began outlining the tips of her breasts, until an untimely interruption came knocking at the door. We scrambled to cover up, and, once we were decent, Dawn invited our guest inside. Jordan opened the door and stood before us. Wearing his blue and red Spider-Man pajamas, he stood glum-faced, frowning.

"Daddy, you're not going to leave, are you?" he asked, managing to get the words out before starting to cry. He ran over and climbed onto the bed, placed his head in my lap, and wrapped his arms around my waist. Dawn whispered to me that our argument may have brought back memories of prior domestic disputes, and I assured Jordan that everything was great. Nevertheless, since he was old enough to sense that something was wrong, we decided to talk to him about my condition. I leaned forward and pointed to a spot on my back.

"I've got something inside me that's not supposed to be there. It's called cancer."

"*Can*-cer?" he repeated. I nodded.

"The doctors took it out in the operation I had. Now I'm going to have treatment so it doesn't come back."

Jordan gave me a hug. "I love you, Daddy."

Dawn and I looked at each other and exchanged closed-mouthed smiles. She offered to walk Jordan back to his room and tuck him into bed, which he accepted. Jordan took the lead, hopped off the bed, and scooted to the door. Before following, Dawn turned to me and grinned mischievously.

"Make sure you keep that fire burning—I'll be back in a sec."

By the end of my eight-week treatment, Dawn was over four months pregnant. I responded favorably to the treatment, so my doctors signed off on another round, which also went well.

I made the best of my treatment by involving Jordan. Every night, Dawn administered my shots and, upon completion, called in our little specialist. "Hi, I'm Dr. Jordan," he'd say, making his grand entrance costumed in a mini white lab coat and scrubs. He'd open his toy doctor's kit and lay out the contents: plastic syringe, blood pressure gauge, auriscope for my ears, laryngoscope for my throat, reflex hammer, thermometer, cotton swabs, and Band-Aids.

"Hi, Dr. Jordan, I'm Daddy. Nice to meet you."

"I'll make you all better, Daddy."

First he'd survey my arm for freckles and methodically apply the syringe. Then, carefully placing his stethoscope on my chest, he'd check my heartbeat. "Bum-bum, bum-bum, bum-bum!"

Feeling reinvigorated, I eased back into my normal routine, starting with a call to Evan.

"Hey, buddy, how are you feeling?"

"Great, actually. Physically, I'm getting stronger by the day, and, mentally, my outlook is bright. I'm ready to get back in the game. What's happening over there?"

"I don't want you to worry about this stuff."

"I want to worry. Come on, you know me—I never have enough on my plate."

With that, Evan provided updates on current matters and what our clients were up to in general. Then we turned to the Cowen deal and initiated a call with Stu Miller, the lawyer representing the record label. I hadn't spoken to Stu in a while, so, before we got down to business, he expressed sympathy for my falling-out at Williams Gardner.

"I appreciate the thought, but, if anything, you should be congratulating me. We rep a few Oscar-winning screenwriters who couldn't have scripted this any better."

"That's great, Nick," Stu said. "Glad to hear it."

With the ice broken, we turned to the negotiations. I took the lead and worked out a great deal for our client, one that laid a solid foundation for future success. It felt great to be back ... to once again be a contributor in my professional life. Helping unveil a promising new musician was great stuff, and I was pumped. While Cowen was in the studio cutting the album, there would be a lot of work to do on his national tour (which I got the label to agree to finance), including negotiating merchandising and promotion deals and agreements with his manager and road crew. I eagerly told Evan that I would take care of it.

A few of our clients were also in litigation, and one of the matters was starting to heat up. It was a breach of contract case we brought on behalf of an actress against a cosmetics company in connection with an endorsement deal. The defendant filed a motion to dismiss, and, with a family vacation planned close to our deadline to respond, Evan asked if I would mind writing the brief. Mocking my erstwhile nemesis, Phil Addison, I said, "Well, Evan, getting married and starting a family is certainly your choice, but perhaps you need to think a little harder about what we have at stake here … what *you* have at stake here." Evan laughed and, doing his best Will Schmidt, replied, "At Berger O'Reilly, we do not rest on our laurels, as it were, and, as such, we remain one of the entertainment industry's elite law firms which, of course, is a testament to the fine reputation we have enjoyed over the course of our long history!" I laughed.

"Fuckin' pricks," Evan said.

"All kidding aside, it's no problem," I said. "E-mail me the papers and I'll get cracking."

"Are you sure?"

"Absolutely—I'm all over it."

"All right, bro. Kid O'Reilly stays in the picture."

"Thanks, man."

"No, thank you," he said, clearing his throat. "Hey, on a more important note, how's Dawn?"

"So far so good. Starting to show and basically feeling okay."

"Great, send her our love."

After I hung up with Evan, I sat down at the piano and thought about my situation. According to the doctor's original prognosis, I now had almost four to ten months. Given the improvement in how I felt, I was starting to have my doubts. I reflected on all of the personal sacrifices I'd made, how I had hardly traveled. I was eager to make up for lost time. After the baby was born and things settled down, I thought that maybe my mother could watch the kids so Dawn and I could take a few days in Paris.

Over the course of the next eight weeks, as Dawn's belly continued to grow, I underwent the next round of my treatment. It was taxing, but I rebounded when the time came to accompany Dawn to the hospital to view sonograms of the baby. When I visited the hospital for my own appointments, my stomach churned with anxiety with each step through the automatic doors; on this occasion, though, I was without a care.

I stood beside the table on which Dawn was lying as the technician entered the room.

"Hey, folks, how we doing?" she cheered. In her mid-thirties, she was heavyset, wore purple scrubs and white sneakers, and had her black hair tied up. After getting acquainted, she set herself up in front of a fancy computer system. As Dawn lay there, looking up at me with a smile, I couldn't help but think about how beautiful she was. I couldn't get enough of her. She was the sweetest thing in the world, I thought. I felt so lucky to have her in my life.

"How have you been feeling, sweetie?" the technician asked with a comforting smile, as she pulled Dawn's shirt up to expose her belly.

"Really good, actually. Knock on wood, it's been a great pregnancy so far. I can't complain."

"Good, that's what I like to hear."

She reached for a clear squirt bottle containing some kind of jelly.

"This is a little cold and squirmy, but I'm just gonna' put

a little bit on your belly." Dawn's mouth curved into a smile. Her left cheek dimpled as the tech applied the goop. Taking nothing for granted, I savored every single one of Dawn's smiles.

"Do we want to know the sex?" asked the tech, her eyes affixed to the screen as she typed.

Dawn and I glanced at each other and both responded with an emphatic No, having already decided that we wanted to be surprised.

"Okay, let's see what we've got here." The tech rubbed the joystick-shaped sensor over Dawn's belly. Suddenly, our unborn child appeared on the screen. It was amazing.

"Oh, wow," I said, staring in awe.

"Look at its little hands and feet!" Dawn exclaimed.

"So far, everything looks good. I'm just going to take some pictures and measurements." The tech zoned in on all of the baby's vitals, punching in data on the keyboard.

"Beautiful. Everything looks fine, folks."

I stood completely numb, my eyes fixated on the screen. It was a moment I had been fantasizing about. All those early mornings on the balcony overlooking Central Park, daydreaming about having a family and children, and here I was. It was finally happening. That was my baby up there on that screen.

After printing out all of her pictures with all of the measurements to send to Dawn's obstetrician, the technician printed a couple for us to keep. She smiled, wished us good luck, and left us alone in the room. Dawn wiped the goop off her belly with paper towels, and then I helped her carefully climb down off of the table. I placed my arm around her as we stared at the pictures.

"I can't wait to have this baby."

"This child is going to be very lucky to have you," Dawn said. We took our time and enjoyed a long, passionate kiss. I pulled off, exhaling.

"I feel like you just added years to my life."

Satisfaction pursed her mouth as she looked at me. "I'll be sure to keep them coming."

As we exited the hospital, I thought about how excited I was to hold the baby, to lie on the couch with it sleeping on me, its little hands clasped to mine, and for it to look to me, its daddy, for comfort and security.

For as long as I could, I would always give it that.

Chapter 24

I continued to fight aggressively, persevering with treatment. It appeared as if the doctor's prognosis had been inaccurate as I had already passed the six-month mark. Aside from my leg, I felt good and was putting in more and more time at the office.

Dawn was getting bigger, too. "Ooh, come here," she would say, grabbing my hand and placing it on her belly. "Do you feel that?" she'd ask as the baby kicked and adjusted itself. That was exciting.

But my leg still hurt persistently, to the point where I could hardly walk. I was dependent upon crutches, putting my weight only on my good leg and dragging the bad one along. The first operation had been a somewhat careless nail job, but had later been cleaned up in a subsequent procedure that ultimately failed when the nail snapped at one of the screw holes. As if things weren't bad enough, I now needed a knee replacement.

I scheduled the surgery on the same day Dawn returned to the hospital for a second sonogram. First we went for the sonogram. Seeing my unborn child thrive in Dawn's womb gave me a boost. We were less than a couple of months away, and I was confident that I had beaten cancer.

But I wasn't so lucky in surgery, which failed because of an infection I had picked up in the hospital. Within a week, the doctors followed up with another knee replacement operation, which also failed because a surplus of scar tissue prevented the knee from bending.

After running several tests, my team of oncologists told me that I was officially in remission. I celebrated the incredible triumph with family and friends while undergoing two more procedures on my leg. Dawn was now in her ninth month, and the big day was approaching. Everyone was beaming and couldn't wait to welcome our child into the world.

That was when, with Dawn at my side, I sat down with Dr. Lampkin, who would deliver another devastating blow.

"Nick, we've been through six surgeries and, unfortunately, we're at a point now where we really have no other alternatives but one. I'm sorry to say this, Nick, but … we're going to have to amputate."

My mouth dropped open. I sat stone-faced.

"You're going to remove my leg?"

Dawn drew a deep breath. She squeezed my hand with one of her hands and my shoulder with the other.

"From just above the knee."

I lowered my head, shaking it in dismay.

I was devastated. Cancer was something that, in the past, I'd thought about on occasion, seeing how common it was and knowing people or friends or family of friends who had had it. But the thought of having part of one of my legs removed—of being physically handicapped—had never entered my mind. I was too startled to search for words to keep the conversation going, to say how I felt at the moment, or to even ask questions.

"Nick, prosthetics have come a long way. Don't get me wrong, there will be limitations on what you can do …"

"I'll never run again? No hope of even playing half-court basketball?"

241

"Not the type of competitive basketball you were used to, but, with the right prosthetic, you should be able to play. It'll just be a lot slower. In fact, there are special leagues that you can—" I snapped, looking up for the first time.

"Special?" I thought of "special" leagues for "special" people, even the Special Olympics. It wasn't that I didn't care about these folks; I've always been sensitive to their needs and problems. But the shock of being so categorized got me riled up. All my life, I had been a healthy and productive member of society, but not anymore.

Now, I was "special."

"What, handicap leagues? Like, wheelchair leagues?" I asked matter-of-factly.

"Not necessarily. Like I said, with the right prosthetic, you won't need a wheelchair. Assuming you remain cancer free, you should be able to continue to live a happy, productive life. You can go back to work. You can drive a car and play with your kids, take walks, exercise. The two of you can still have very satisfying and healthy relations. It's going to take time, but, once you get used to it, you'll be fine."

Then I cast an angry eye on Dr. Lampkin. I was about to take him to task, but Dawn beat me to the punch.

"Why did he really need this?"

"I beg your pardon?"

"All of these surgeries? Why did it lead to this? All he had was a tumor!"

A shadow of irritation crossed Dr. Lampkin's face. He began to explain himself before Dawn lost it. "How the hell ... did a screw ... just snap?"

His eyes hardened, Dr. Lampkin retorted. "Dawn, with all due respect, I resent the implication. I'm one of the top surgeons in the area, as is the orthopedist who worked with me. As I tried to explain, the resulting complications were not my fault. The knee was deteriorated. This wasn't just some little tumor that we discovered in its infancy. It's been growing for many years. Do you know what kind of damage was done to that knee over all this time from all the activity on it? Basketball, jogging, walking to and from work every day …." His voice trailed off.

At this point, Dawn was spent. She shut her eyes, gritted her teeth, and drew a deep breath. Her hands shook. "I'm sorry, I'm just … I … whatever."

I cut in and took over. "Let's cut to the chase. Where do we go from here?"

Dr. Lampkin recommended that I have the surgery as soon as possible. The longer I waited, the more pain I would endure. Dawn was due in a couple of weeks and could very well go into labor any day, so we decided to wait until after the baby was born. Since my hair was starting to grow back, I thought it would be nice to at least have some pictures with the baby while I still looked mostly like my old self.

After advising the doctor of our plans, he suggested that we call him to schedule when we were ready. He then wished us luck with the baby and encouraged me to call or page him at any time. I thanked him.

"That's quite all right. Take good care." Like a bat out of hell, he excused himself and left us alone in the examining room. A couple of minutes later, a nurse came by with a wheelchair to escort us out.

Stiffened in shock, Dawn struggled to drive home.

"We'll get through this," I said, putting my hand on Dawn's leg. "The cancer's gone. I'm healthy. I'll learn to adjust. We have each other. We have our family … and, hey, maybe I'll train for a triathlon or something. Plenty of people with prosthetics compete in those kinds of events!"

Dawn drew a deep breath and turned to me, revealing tears.

I spent the next few days learning about prosthetic legs, scouring literature and picking the brains of industry professionals, and was encouraged by the advancement in technology. Despite certain limitations, Dr. Lampkin had been right—for all intents and purposes, I could still enjoy most of the things I used to. I drew inspiration from the legion of success stories I read.

That was when I thought about the story that my father used to tell me—the story of the man with no shoes who felt sorry for himself until he saw the man with no feet. While technically I would soon fall into the latter category, I nevertheless appreciated the fact that my situation could have been much worse. I could have been counting my last days.

But I'm in remission, I thought to myself. *Remission! I beat cancer! And I have Dawn and Jordan, and any minute we're gonna' have a new baby!*

With the encouragement I got from my research findings, and with the passage of a few days, I came to more easily accept my fate. As my knee continued to deteriorate and the pain grew more and more unbearable, I felt more and more ready to make it happen.

And then came the magical moment.

"Nick!" Dawn yelled, on a bright and sunny afternoon in June. She was in the bedroom lying on the bed, and I was in my office responding to a work-related e-mail. I asked if she was okay.

"No!" I got up, grabbed my crutches, and quickly made my way down the hall to the bedroom to find Dawn sitting up in bed, her hands resting on her engorged belly.

"I … think … it's … happening," she said, uttering each word in between huffs and puffs, wincing in pain. "The contractions are starting to get really painful."

"How often are they?" I asked, applying what we had learned about labor from Lamaze class.

"Every ten minutes."

"For how long?"

"Like an hour now," she said, wincing in pain.

"This is it, babe, it's time. We're gonna' have a baby." My heart thudded in my chest. Dawn asked me to call our next-door neighbor, Lynn Jacobs, who was on standby to watch Jordan until my mother could come to pick him up.

Since we knew the labor was going to come any day, we had packed our bags for what would be a forty-eight hour stay at the hospital. We had also packed our list of names and numbers of people we wanted to call from the hospital.

I stood beside Dawn, applying weight to my good leg so that I could lend support, counting for her to push, just as we had been taught. This was against my doctor's directive to stay off of my feet. The pain was excruciating, but, at the moment, I didn't care. There was no way I was going to miss out on this—a miracle and an opportunity to help Dawn get through the delivery.

"This is it—I see the head," said the obstetrician, a short older woman with curly gray hair. "Come on, honey, I need another hard push! This baby's ready to come out!"

"Come on, babe," I said, after taking a peek at the baby's exposed head, it's black hair damp and squishy.

"Okay, one, two three, *push!*" the doctor and I yelled in unison. Dawn gave it her everything, and the doctor carefully delivered our baby, who greeted us with a scream.

"It's a beautiful baby girl!" the doctor pronounced, as she held up the baby, all wet and wrinkly and still attached to the umbilical cord, which I immediately cut at the doctor's request.

Dawn and I looked at each other in amazement.

A little girl.

"Oh, my God, Jordan has a sister," said Dawn, continuing to breathe hard in and out, exhausted from the labor, sweat dripping down her face. I held my wife and stared at our beautiful, healthy new daughter and began to cry. I had been dreaming about this moment for so long.

"I love you so much," I said to Dawn, smiling and kissing her as tears continued to trickle down my face. I wiped a coat of sweat from her forehead.

"Can you believe we have a daughter?" she responded. I felt an unending peace.

"She's beautiful, just like her mother." I ran my fingers through her hair, pushing it back from her face.

We told the doctor the name we'd picked out so she could tag the baby and attach an alarm to her foot. Then we spent a few moments with our new daughter before the nurses took her to get cleaned up and weighed. The doctor also had to administer all of the necessary tests, so that was my opportunity to go downstairs and break the news.

"I'll be right back, babe."

"Hurry, honey ... bring everybody!"

When I emerged from the elevator I saw Milena's father, coffee cup in hand, heading back toward the waiting room from the cafeteria. He ambled toward me with a spring in his step and greeted me with a big smile, as if he was having a grandchild himself.

"Wait, tell us altogether," Paul suggested while putting his arm around me. The rest of the gang saw us through the clear glass window that lined the perimeter of the waiting room. They ran out to greet us.

"Guess what, buddy?" I said to Jordan, anxious to hear the news. "You have a little sister."

"It's a girl!" Mom yelled, rousing cheers and excitement so loud that everyone nearby looked up and smiled, sharing in our happiness as we all hugged together. Mom asked about her name, and everyone got quiet.

"Nicole," I said softly. "But, Mom, if you want, you can call her Nickie." She started to cry.

I led my entourage back to Dawn's room where she was sitting up in bed, our daughter cradled in her arms. "Hey, guys," she said with a smile. Mom was the first one there, and Jordan snuck in next to her, wiggling his way as near to his mother as he could.

"Hi, sweetheart, say hello to your sister, Nicole," said Dawn. Paul lifted Jordan and propped him onto the bed. Jordan didn't know what to say. He just stared for a few moments and smiled; everyone watched and ate up the moment before he carefully leaned in and gave her a little kiss on her forehead.

"You're going to be the best big brother, right?" said Dawn. He smiled and nodded. Sonia, as the designated photographer, broke out her camera and asked the four of us to get together for a picture. I went around the bed and leaned in close to Dawn. Jordan sat beside her with Nicole resting quietly in her arms.

"What a beautiful family," said Mom, her hands bunched beneath her chin as she beamed with pride.

And there it finally was. The faceless picture I had had in my mind for so many years was no longer faceless. The blanks were filled in.

No matter what the future brings, I thought, *my legacy is intact.*

Chapter 25

We welcomed baby Nicole into a home filled with color—flowers and balloons sent from well-wishers filled every corner of the house. We'd made a beautiful nursery. All of the furniture that we picked out in advance—crib, chest of drawers, changing table, and rocking chair, all in a matching soft white—had been delivered. The wallpaper had been hung, and the pink carpet laid. The base of a mobile was affixed to the side of the crib and played sweet lullaby music.

One month later, things had settled down and we had gotten used to taking care of the baby. Business continued to thrive at the firm, and I kept busy, even managing to commute into the city a couple of times a week.

Then with everything behind me, I could no longer put off the inevitable.

It was time for surgery.

I had been fully prepped. I was lying on the stretcher, a cap over my head, my arm hooked up to an IV, when my family came to wish me luck for the last time. I could not have had more love and support. Taking one look at them made everything easy. The surgery would make me better. It would allow me to enjoy my life even more.

After I said good-bye and the nurses started wheeling me to the operating room, I lifted the blanket for one last look at my legs. It was the last time I would ever see two full legs affixed to my body.

And then, shortly after arriving in the operating room, the anesthesiologist put me under.

I woke up from surgery feeling free of pain. Nervously, I lifted the blanket and, for a moment, could not believe what I saw. It was then that I finally came to terms with the fact that I was legally handicapped.

I left the hospital after a few days of recovery—wearing my new prosthetic. I had received lessons on usage, treatment, and removal. I walked out of the hospital on crutches and started to get used to my new leg.

Dawn and I had talked to Jordan in advance about what was going to happen to my leg. We had told him that I was going to feel better, and that made him happy.

Each day thereafter, I spent as much time at home as possible. There was nothing better than the feeling of Nicole opening up her little hand and clasping it to one of my fingers while I held her in the rocking chair and sang lullabies. "Hush a bye, and goodnight, my sweet lit-tle girl …"

Each early morning, after Nicole woke to be fed, I would lie with her on the living room couch. I loved it when she'd fall asleep on my chest. I loved the feeling of her little breaths against me.

I was grateful for little things, like being able to bathe Nicole and change her diaper. Each night, long after she was sound asleep, I would quietly sneak into her room, stand over her crib, and stare in amazement at the life that I had helped create. I loved her smell, the fresh amalgam of powder and baby wash. She was so precious. As I stared, I couldn't help but think about how I would have missed everything if I hadn't been assigned to Dawn's case and if I was still at Williams Gardner. I couldn't understand how they do it there … how they live like that.

Before it got too cold outside, I took advantage of the basketball hoop I'd installed and played with Jordan in the driveway. Propping myself up with a crutch, I taught Jordan the proper form for a jump shot and gave him pointers on dribbling. But with my physical infirmities still very new to me, my movement was awkward. I couldn't shoot the way I used to, and it was obvious. I felt ashamed.

"That's okay, Daddy," he said. "We'll practice together."

While we played, Dawn sat out on the porch, nursed Nicole, and peacefully watched her boys. Despite my cancer and everything that we'd been through, Dawn loved her life and was appreciative of what she had. She told me that, once in a while, to keep things in perspective, she'd look back and think about where she had come from—her old house, her parents, and Jimmy and the abuse—and she'd find it hard to believe that the life she was living was real.

"I wouldn't change a thing," she said.

I was happy to have been able to give her a better life, just as she'd given the same to me.

Several months passed, and we found ourselves in the dead of winter. Vulnerable and exposed, trees stood naked through snowstorms and fluctuations in temperature. Each bitter morning brought aches and pains that were eerily reminiscent of when I was first diagnosed; certain aches and pains that, at the time, I didn't associate with cancer, but upon diagnosis, I realized were all related.

I started to feel sick again, often with chest pains, fevers, and night sweats. I suffered from fatigue and was tired and haggard, requiring regular, mid-afternoon naps. I lost my appetite and dropped weight as a consequence.

I tried to sit down at the piano, and, when I couldn't even manage that, Dawn insisted that I immediately call Dr. Lampkin. When I finally got him on the line and described my symptoms, he summoned me to the hospital and ordered a CT scan of my chest. My mother had planned to come over that day to visit and arrived right after I hung up the phone. Dawn greeted her at the door.

"Hi, Mom," she said, embracing her in a hug. They spoke almost daily so there was no need for catching up. Then she walked over to me and asked how I was feeling, holding my face as if savoring every opportunity. I shrugged, indicating not so hot.

Pointing to the living room couch, she told me to sit and rest. She excused herself for a moment and then returned with a cold compress, which she gently applied to my forehead.

"Do you remember how I used to do this?" she asked with a smile, reflecting on a happier and more carefree time. I smiled thin-lipped and nodded. Then I told her about how I'd been feeling and that the doctor had instructed me to come back for a scan. Her eyes turn a dark, cinnamon red, as if every blood vessel in her eyes had burst. I thought about what it must be like for her, faced with the possibility of outliving her one and only child.

Mom stayed to watch the kids so Dawn could take me to the hospital. I took the test and then sat with Dawn in the examining room where we waited anxiously. During the last ordeal, the hospital staff had taught me certain relaxation techniques; I tried using the breathing exercises and counted the seconds in between breaths. Dawn held my hand and counted along. After a while, I started to get nervous, thinking that we had been waiting way too long. The news could not be good. When the doctor finally pushed his way through the door, there was no need for an oral report. His solemn-looking face told the story. He pulled up a chair and sat down next to me.

"Nick, we found a small mass on your lung."

Chapter 26

I drew a deep breath and closed my eyes. Dawn sat beside me, legs crossed, pocketbook grasped tightly against her chest. She tried to be the rock, staying strong for me, yet couldn't help but seem subdued upon hearing the news. She set her bag down, untied her legs, and got closer, putting her arm around me and resting her chin on my shoulder.

"We're gonna' fight it, babe. Just like the last time. I'm gonna' be okay."

Then I thought about my family and looked up at the doctor.

"So what do we do now?"

The doctor explained that I would need to undergo immediate surgery.

"... a thoracotomy, where we'll open the chest wall by cutting through your rib cage," he said. I could have used anesthesia just for the news. I could almost feel my ribs cracking, like a wishbone breaking in my hands.

"A pneumonectomy, Nick, is a removal of the lung, but what we do when your chest is opened will depend on what we observe."

I knew what the doctor meant, and, rather than trying

to educate myself further, I scheduled the operation for the following week.

It was mid-morning at the hospital. Dawn and Mom had already wished me luck and said good-bye. I was sitting up in bed, cloaked in nothing but a front-covering gown tied behind my back. Dr. Lampkin entered the room with an audience of bleary-eyed, white-coated interns and residents. They lined up against the wall and faced me expressionless, some with hands behind their backs, others holding clipboards. Dr. Lampkin glanced at me, his mouth tight and grim, as he neared, quickly turning his attention to the monitors surrounding me. He then began to lecture his protégés, reciting my medical history and beginning with, "This is a case involving ..."

That's all I was now: a *case*—not a person with a life and a family, and not even a patient, but a case ... an academic subject, something to study and learn from if confronted with similar issues in the future. I felt like a guinea pig.

After surgery, I awoke in the recovery room hooked up to an IV pole; a plastic tube dripped fluids and chemo drugs into me through the crook in my arm. I was drowsy and squinted slightly, the light too bright to fully open my eyes. A young Asian nurse named Sue kept me company, feeding me ice chips and making nice conversation while I waited for Dr. Lampkin. I was in fairly decent spirits and hoped that the worst was now behind me.

Later on, Dr. Lampkin came by and dismissed the nurse. I thanked her for her kindness, and, on her way out, she curtained my section of the room for privacy. Dawn had joined us a few moments before.

"Nick, we were able to remove the mass, and, as far as we can tell, your lungs are clear. But while we were in there, we looked further and found that the cancer has spread to your lymph nodes, so, at this point, I'm going to refer you back to the radiologist."

"Well, what does that mean, doctor? What are we looking at here?" said Dawn, standing by my side and squeezing my hand.

"Nick, given the complications you've already had and, based on our findings during this surgery, unfortunately, I would say your chances of surviving a year are ... fifty-fifty, at best. I'm sorry." I trembled.

Something in the way the doctor issued his prognosis set Dawn off. She had already expressed doubts about the hospital, but there was never one thing that she could put her finger on. But rather than instigate another ugly confrontation, Dawn flashed Dr. Lampkin a look of disdain and thanked him dismissively. He excused himself and closed the door. Dawn became petulant, and a sudden anger lit her eyes.

"Nick, we're out of here. I've had it."

I sighed and took a deep breath. A part of me appreciated how she felt, yet I also didn't have the strength to make such a rash decision.

"It's time to go to the city for new opinions. We gave them a chance, but now it's time for a change."

"I don't know, babe. I just don't see how anyone else could have done more."

"I can! You have nothing to lose. I mean, did you see the way he told you what your chances are? It was ridiculous. It was like he was handicapping a sporting event or something. And, anyway, don't you remember his first prognosis?"

I took a deep breath. "I understand, babe, but I know my own body. Something feels different this time."

We were silent for a bit.

"You're okay driving back and forth to and from the city?" I asked.

"I'll drive to China and back if that's what it takes." I

smiled with satisfaction. "I want you to try this. Please," said
Dawn, pulling back and facing me.

"Let me sleep on it."

After the nurse removed the IV and helped prepare me
for discharge, I got dressed and was escorted to the exit in
a wheelchair. A rush of tears nearly choked me and when
I looked up, I made eye contact with a receptionist, who
quickly turned away. I just kept moving along, feeling as if
everyone was staring. Up ahead stood Dawn waiting silently
as I approached. She tried to forge a smile in a futile attempt
to cheer me up.

"Thank you. I'll take him from here." Dawn looked me deep
in my eyes, her hands on my shoulders. Her lips stretched to
a smile, but her eyes revealed sadness. "I love you."

Dawn wheeled me through the automatic doors. Surly
clouds filled the sky, only an occasional ray of sunshine
breaking through. I sat in the passenger seat and stared out
the window. Dawn moved slowly through the parking area of
the hospital and out onto the thoroughfare. There were other
cars out on the road, and, although I couldn't make out the
faces behind the steering wheels, I thought about how there
were so many folks out there, going on with their routines
and normal lives.

And then there was me.

Just me.

I felt as if I'd been placed in a bubble, totally separated
from the world of the living, excruciatingly forced to watch
what I was missing.

I'm not ready to go, I thought. Tears ran down my cheeks
as I thought about how, for all I knew, I soon might not get to
see my baby anymore. I thought about how I might not get to
watch her grow into an adult. No recitals, no graduations, no
wedding, no grandchildren, no important milestones. How
she might soon be without her daddy.

We drove through town, passing all types of boutiques and eateries. I looked in the window of a restaurant as we passed, and I could see a man sitting and having lunch, reading the newspaper, and enjoying a relaxing afternoon. I wondered what he was doing. Perhaps he was on his lunch break? Maybe he had a big interview that afternoon for a great new career opportunity that he'd been looking so long for. Were this guy's dreams about to come true? Or maybe he just had time to kill, to do absolutely nothing other than be alone, eat a meal, and read. Do I have that kind of time? If I did, could I afford right now to waste it sitting alone, when I have a wife and two children to see?

Then we drove up a little further and passed a ladies' clothing store. I could see that a couple of middle-aged women were trying on dresses, modeling in front of a full-length mirror and asking for each other's opinions.

Why were these women shopping? Was it just for fun? Did they just feel like buying clothes today and simply had nothing else to do with their time? Maybe they were shopping for a special occasion several months from now.

Several months from now ....

Then I wondered what I had to shop for. A coffin? A cemetery plot? *What do I have to plan for between now and when my lungs fill with fluid and I die in my sleep?* I asked myself. I wanted my children to be creative and enjoy the arts, so maybe I could upgrade the piano. I pictured the kids ten, fifteen years later, playing for Dawn. Maybe they'd fall in love with it. Maybe they could play in Carnegie Hall one day.

But while those things were all well and good, I knew that what they needed most was their father. I had so much to offer, so much love, support, nurturing, and experience. The void in their lives would be so huge that I knew I couldn't possibly buy enough things to fill it. I'd come to learn that not too long ago. So that would be my project ... to spend my precious time trying to leave my family with something meaningful. Something they'd lodge deep into their hearts for the rest of their lives. After all, they were what I had been longing for over so many years.

Stopping at a red light halfway into the ride, we turned to each other for the first time. My expression felt the way Dawn's looked—gloomy, with warning clouds shadowing our faces, our mouths dipping into frowns. We were way beyond words, and, with a tear dripping down my cheek, there was only one thing I could say:

"I know ... there's something really unfair about this, right?"

Dawn nodded, glum.

We continued on in silence. At that moment, all hope of living a long life was gone. Looking at my beautiful, adoring wife and hearing her soft, sweet voice made that reality all the more unbearable.

I'm dying, and I know it.

"Dawn," I said, my gaze adrift in the open road before me, my tone dull. I could feel her turn to me. "Tell the kids about me."

"What do you mean?"

"You know, make sure one day you tell them all about me. I want them to know who I was, what I did, how much I loved them."

I then turned to her. She smiled thin-lipped and reached over and gently stroked my face.

Shortly after we got home, I hobbled upstairs into my office, closed the door, and called Evan. With my sensitivity to my own mortality increasing by the second, I cried as I broke the news.

"Come on, brother, don't give up," he pleaded.

After talking for a while, particularly about my business affairs and how I would no longer be coming into the office, I hung up the telephone, kept my gaze affixed to it, and stared blankly.

This can't be it, I thought. My life was just starting to get good. I'm madly in love with the most wonderful woman. I have two beautiful children who need me. And what about Mom?

I sat up, rested my elbows on the desk, and locked my hands together. I closed my eyes and started to pray. Were it not for my leg, I would have knelt. I hadn't prayed since I was twelve. I asked God for help ... for peace ... for healing.

At this point, I needed a miracle.

The Final Chapter

Every day was a struggle.

I lay there in the tranquility of our suburban home, unfurled from the fetal position which had become as comforting and familiar to me as a bird in its nest, my head resting on a cool, thin pillow dampened with drool. I was cloaked in my favorite nightwear—a faded cotton T-shirt and flannel pajama bottoms. Dawn slept peacefully beside me. The children were safely tucked in and, through the baby monitors, they soothed me with a symphony of sweet little breaths. Looking out the bay windows, I was entertained by the sights and sounds of nighttime creatures courting each other; fireflies flashed like a Fourth of July spectacle, crickets serenaded in a blissful chorus. They are hopeless romantics, returning each night in search of compatible mates.

My circumstances inspired me to consider how I would want to be remembered, and I then realized that it's rare that a guy gets to write his own obituary. Think about it—you have to know (or at least believe) the end is near, yet still have the faculties to compose an exhaustive biography.

So I gave it a shot and, as I reflected, a montage of memories flashed through my mind.

For the first twenty-five years or so, I flew below the radar screen as if in secret flight. The sole product of a humble home, my childhood was uneventful: no abuse, no drugs or alcohol, and no problems to speak of (well, except for that one time ... or maybe two or three now that I think about it, but nothing more than innocuous, boy-next-door-sews-his-oats-type stuff). I enjoyed sports—basketball especially—but truly excelled at music. I played the piano, and, though I trained with classical, my passion was jazz. I had the opportunity to experience performing for audiences, and even shared the stage with a legend.

I chose law as my profession and, at a young age, became a partner of one of the nation's elite Wall Street law firms. I derived great satisfaction in representing the interests of many gifted musicians, and was fortunate to be able to start an exciting new firm bearing my name. I owned a posh condominium overlooking Central Park and money was no longer a worry, the fruits of my assiduous labor.

But these days, none of that meant much to me, and not just because success had come at a hefty price. I lived for my family and the home that we had built together.

They were my legacy.

Though I had not abandoned all hope of living a long life, if ultimately that was where it would end, I can honestly say that, all things considered, I was exactly where I wanted to be.

I knew there were people who would miss me.

They would cry when I was gone. And not just in the immediate aftermath, but over the years, when they wished I could have been around for this and that or thought about how I would have loved to have been there ... what it would have meant to me.

As for those not as close, overall, I believed that they would remember me as a good, caring person. *That was sweet—it was something that Nick O'Reilly would have done,* they'd think.

Someone they could count on ... a go-to guy ... a good friend.

Someone they were happy to have known.

And it is on this note, one far more beautiful than Mozart or Beethoven ever played, that I choose to end the story of my journey. After all, it is my life, and, though factually it remains incomplete, emotionally it is as fulfilled and rewarded as I believe it will ever be. And if I learned anything during this journey—and indeed, I learned quite a bit—at the very least, it is that this is the way life should be lived. To be able to stop at any moment and say, I am proud of and very much at peace with who I am. To be able to look back without shame or regret for having made choices that, on their face, may be deemed mistakes or errors in judgment, because ultimately, they led you to the right place.

So, when it is all said and done, my life will not be defined by merely a collection of professional or artistic achievements. It is a story of love, family, and friendship—one far too deep and meaningful to squeeze onto the last page of a newspaper, no matter how fine the print.

Upon that realization, a sense of peace came over me, and I drifted into sleep.

The following morning, I woke up alone. With my face nearly buried in the pillow, only one eye was available and through it I read the clock, which told me that it was almost noon. Feeling guilty about sleeping in, I hastily pushed myself up into a sitting position. Moments later, Dawn entered, greeted me with a kiss, and snuggled.

We sat quietly and held each other until the doorbell rang. Jordan was home from soccer practice, and, as soon as Dawn opened the door, he immediately darted upstairs to see me. His team had had a scrimmage with another team, and he couldn't wait to share the outcome. Dawn followed Jordan into the bedroom and joined us on the bed.

"Hey, champ," I said with a smile. I extended my arms out for Jordan to hop up and join me.

"Daddy, guess what?"

"What's up, buddy?"

"I scored two goals today!"

"Wow, two goals? That's great," I said, giving him a high-five. "Did you guys win?"

Jordan nodded, and I asked for the score. "Three to one!"

"All right—your team won because of you! You scored the two big goals!"

Then I had to look away. *God, this pain is excruciating,* I thought, gritting my teeth. I forged a big, loving smile, determined to not let Jordan see me suffer. I masked my inner turmoil with a feigned sense of calm.

"Listen, buddy, I want to let you know that the thing inside Daddy is trying to grow again."

"It is?" he asked, wide-eyed. I nodded.

"I can't believe it either, but it's true. I have to take a lot of medicine to try and make it go away. The doctors are helping me, and we're trying very hard, okay?"

"But you said you're not leaving, right Daddy?"

A tear found its way to my eye. I didn't know how to respond.

"Are you going to be okay, Daddy?"

"I hope so, champ—I really hope so," I said, rubbing his head. Dawn leaned in.

"Honey, our family will always stay together. We'll always look out for one another because that's what loving families like ours do."

"That's right," I added.

"Okay," he said, pacified for the time being. "Mommy, can I go play with Nicole?"

"I think she's sleeping, but we can take a peek if you want. Would you like that?" Jordan smiled and nodded.

"Hey, why don't we all go look together," I suggested.

Jordan hopped out of bed and scooted out of the bedroom and down the hall to Nicole's room. We followed Jordan there and found him dragging a step stool across the floor so he could see over the side of the crib and peer down at his baby sister. We stood behind him with our arms around each other, the three of us watching as she awoke from her nap. She opened her beautiful emerald green eyes—her mother's eyes—and smiled at us.

Then Dawn and I turned and smiled at each other, kissed, and looked down at Jordan and Nicole. I shifted my gaze back to Dawn and smiled with an air of calm.

"I think it's time to schedule those appointments," I said. Dawn mirrored my smile and nodded with hope as Jordan made sweet baby talk with Nicole.

Then I took a good look at my family, as if for the last time.

"I love you all."

(A Rainy Day)

Dear Dawn,

Hopefully upon receipt of this card, you have accepted my proposal to spend the rest of our lives together.

In order to capture the essence of my deepest feelings, I waited until shortly before I arrived here this evening to pen this. Ironically, though, I feel like I've been gathering these thoughts since long before—years, perhaps.

It is my hope ... my dream ... that, despite your persistent pleas year after year for my permission, you will ultimately open this card on our twenty-fifth anniversary and that you will read it with me at your side and in the warm company of our children—Jordan and, God willing, many others—who have returned home to celebrate the milestone with us after venturing off to begin fruitful and productive lives of their own. I wonder, even at this early stage in our relationship, what and how many we will bear. Will Jordan have brothers or sisters? I hope they are legion, but, more importantly, that they are healthy and happy. And though the former is most often beyond one's control, with you as their mother, the latter will be a foregone conclusion.

Since I was a boy, my greatest passion has always been the piano. Though I believe I trained myself to play at a fairly respectable level, I am by no means a natural. I spent many years practicing and, along the way, learned that it takes the perfect combination of notes to make beautiful harmony. With you, I've finally struck all of the right keys and I believe that, together, we have made a masterpiece. I pray that the music will never end.

Because of you, I have much to look forward to in my life.
I look forward to finally seeing the world.
I look forward to just being myself without having anything

to prove—to being completely understood, through and through.

I look forward to the things that we will only share with each other, like warm hugs and long kisses for no specific reason.

I look forward to the perennial gleam and sparkle of emotion in our eyes when we greet each other.

I look forward to our grandchildren bouncing from my knees to yours.

I look forward to beginning and ending each day with "I love you."

Dawn, thank you for giving my life meaning.

I only hope that I can give you as much peace and happiness as you have given me.

My cup runneth over.

With great love and affection,
Nick

Acknowledgments

I'd like to thank my talented editor, Susan Schwartz, whose passion for this project, brilliant suggestions, and belief in me made *The Life O'Reilly* a better novel and made me a better writer.

I'd like to thank Jocelyn Kelley of Kelley & Hall Book Publicity, for her wisdom and great enthusiasm.

I am very fortunate to have so many great friends. During the course of this journey, you have been there for me in so many ways; some of you read early drafts (I'm sorry!) and each one of you asked time and time again how the book was coming along. Make no mistake about it—your interest, encouragement, and support helped me get to the finish line and I cannot possibly thank you enough. Extra thanks to the following people for going out on a limb to help get this project off the ground: Peter Alkalay, Mitchell Behr, Michael Carroll, Samantha Cohen, Sharon Fredman, Adina Kahn, Jason Katz, Stu Miller, Meredith Paley, and Jerry Scharoff.

I am also very fortunate to have such a loving and supportive family. Thank you to my grandparents, Esther and Hyman Lefkowitz and Harold and Edith Cohen, who are always with me. Thanks to my cousins, Ilene and Gary Fogelman, and my Aunt Jackie Matises, for all of their love and always being so supportive. Thanks to my brothers-and-sisters-in-law, Samantha Cohen, Pramila and Jason Krumholtz, and Jaimee and Brian Cowen, for their constant support and enthusiasm.

I would like to thank my mother-and-father-in-law, Barbara and Barry Krumholtz, who have treated me like a son since the day we came into each other's lives. Thank you for all of your love and support, for encouraging me to follow my dreams, and for your unwavering and genuine belief in me. You are a big part of this incredible journey.

I would like to thank my brother, Jonathan. Over the years we have shared so much and ultimately found in each other unending support and a lifelong friend. Thank you for being a great little brother, for all of the special moments and memories, and for being so supportive of this and everything else.

Extra special thanks to the best role models I could ever ask for—my parents, Marlene and Richard Cohen. Thank you for raising me to never give up, for instilling in me a very solid work ethic, and for teaching that nothing great comes without sacrifice. Thank you for your boundless love and devotion and for always being there, in good times and in bad. Mom and Dad, you are exceptional people and a big part of who I am and everything that I have achieved. It is impossible for me to pay tribute to you for all that you have done and continue to do, but I want you to know that I am eternally grateful and feel very blessed to have you as parents.

To my wonderful daughters, Reese and Drew, who made life so much more beautiful and fulfilling on the days that they were born. Though I am passionate about a lot of things, nothing makes me happier than being your daddy. You are beautiful inside and out and I already know that you have all the tools to grow up and become great people. I hope that this book will serve as a reminder that if you never lose sight of your dreams and always believe in yourselves, anything is possible.

Finally, this would not have been possible without the love, enthusiasm, and support of my wife and best friend, Dayna. Dayna, you are an amazing person. I would not be where I am today, and I certainly would not have been able to pull this off, without you. This project wasn't all about me—it was *our* dream to see this happen and, without question, the strength of our marriage and our love for each other got the job done. There is no way for me to thank you enough or to express how much you mean to me, but I want you to know that having you in my life makes me feel like the luckiest man in the world.

Breinigsville, PA USA
01 December 2009
228464BV00001B/32/P